M. D. TAYLOR
222 PANORAMIC WAY
BERKELEY, CA 94704

NOV 29 1983

CP = 5ω

THE
OLD MAN
IN THE CORNER

THE
OLD MAN
IN THE CORNER

Twelve Mysteries

The
Baroness Orczy

With an Introduction by E.F. Bleiler

Dover Publications, Inc.
New York

This Dover edition, first published in 1980, is a new selection of Old Man in the Corner stories, originally published in *Royal Magazine,* 1901–05. A new Introduction has been written by E. F. Bleiler especially for the present edition.

Book design by Carol Belanger Grafton

International Standard Book Number: 0-486-23972-1
Library of Congress Catalog Card Number: 79-55295

Manufactured in the United States of America
Dover Publications, Inc.
180 Varick Street
New York, N.Y. 10014

INTRODUCTION

It was all because of the steam-powered mill on the River Tarna in Hungary. If Baron Felix Orczy had not been an enthusiast of scientific farming, he would have let his peasants continue on in their Bronze-Age ways, cutting the grain with little sickles, threshing it with flails on a clay floor and grinding the grist with ox power.

But the Baron was a modernist and, despite peasant protests, spent a fortune on mechanical reapers and the steam mill, which were intended to revolutionize farming in this rich, agricultural area. At dusk, July 22, 1868, however, while the Orczys were entertaining guests in the gigantic manor with the huge Doric pillars, a glow was seen in the sky. At first it was thought to be sunset, but then the disaster was recognized. The peasants had burned down the mill and had also fired the Baron's wheat fields, which were ready to be reaped.

The results were threefold: financial problems for the Baron, who had much land but little cash; disillusionment with farming and abandonment of the wide estates; and, eventually, *The Scarlet Pimpernel* and the Old Man in the Corner.

Baroness Emma Orczy (1865–1947) was born into the landed aristocracy of Hungary. Her family owned large estates and her parents were cultured and artistic. Her father, indeed, was a gifted amateur composer; in later years one of his operas was performed in London (to excellent reviews) under Colonel Mapleson. As a result of the peasant uprising, however, the Orczys decided to leave the wheat country, and live as urbanites, educating their children to their future places among the Austro-Hungarian nobility. For a time the family stayed in Budapest, where Baron Felix took on the position of Superintendant of the Royal Theaters. Then, deciding that their children needed more polish, the Orczys moved to Brussels, then Paris and finally London.

Emma (or Emmuska, as she preferred to be called), according to the family plan, was to become a musician. But it soon became obvious that music was not for her. In Paris, Franz Liszt, a family friend, told her sadly, after listening to her play one of his pieces, "Non, ce n'est pas cela." What Rubinstein and Richter, who were also family friends said, the Baroness did not reveal, but possibly they were less polite than Liszt.

After the Orczys moved to London, it was decided that Emma

should become an artist. She was enrolled in an art school, and while it was discovered that "Non, ce n'est pas cela" also held for her painting, she met her future husband and collaborator, Montagu Barstow.

For several years the Barstows lived in London. Montagu did illustrations for books and periodicals and Emma assisted him. Indeed, Emma's first book, done anonymously, was a collection of fanciful animal illustrations for children, published by Raphael Tuck. Their life was uneventful, apart from the social whirl of London aristocracy, for the Baron's antecedents permitted them entry to the highest circles. On the opposite pole of experience, the Barstows, not too long after they were married, used to wander about the less savory parts of London. On one occasion (as the Baroness relates it) they were present when one of Jack the Ripper's victims was found.

If the Baroness was no musician and only a second-rate painter, she was to discover that she had another gift to a very high degree. This was story-telling. Despite the fact that she had never spoken a word of English until she was fifteen years old, she soon became one of the most widely read authors in the language.

The circumstances of her entry into fiction are known. When she and Barstow were living in rooms in London, in fairly straitened circumstances, she became aware that the landlady's daughter was perpetually sending little stories to the newspapers and periodicals. At first the Barstows laughed, but when the girl received a check for five guineas, the Baroness took serious thought. As her reasoning went, "If an inexperienced London girl, with only a fraction of my education, can make money this easily, why cannot I—who am at home in four languages, have travelled, and have associated with the great of Europe—do even better?"

She was right, of course. She mailed two stories to the offices of Pearson's, where her husband had a business connection, and to her surprise received an invitation to lunch with the editor, and a commission. In a very short time, around 1899–1900, such stories as "Juliette, A Tale of the Terror," "The Trappist's Vow," and "The Revenge of Ur-Tasen" began to appear in the sister periodicals, *Pearson's Magazine* and *The Royal Magazine.* She received £10 for each story, which was considerably less than the £45 which Doyle had received for the first Sherlock Holmes short stories in *The Strand* some eight or nine years earlier. About this same time her first novel, *The Emperor's Candlesticks,* appeared.

By most persons except detective-story enthusiasts Baroness Orczy is now remembered for the adventures of the Scarlet Pimpernel; seemingly an effete young English snob, but really a daredevil, the Scarlet Pimpernel rescues French aristocrats from the Revolution and brings them to a haven of safety in England. What with the Baroness's own history, it is easy to see why such a theme interested her.

As is often the case with books that later become best-sellers and almost folk-symbols, *The Scarlet Pimpernel* was rejected by one publisher after another. The best that the Baroness could achieve was a commitment from a second-line publisher that if she had her novel staged—since she had also prepared a dramatic version—it would publish her book. *The Scarlet Pimpernel* was staged in 1905 and after a slow start it became a hit, playing for four years. The book version was equally successful and remains in print to this day. The fortunes of the Barstows were made.

The Baroness continued writing until shortly before her death. The most successful of her works, financially speaking, were the books about Sir Percy Blakeney, the Scarlet Pimpernel. These were published in periodicals and multi-edition books, and translated into many languages. The original book was also made into a movie starring Leslie Howard, whom the Baroness did not consider especially well cast for the role.

The Barstows lived in England until World War I, but in 1916 they bought a small estate in Monte Carlo, where they spent the remainder of their lives, apart from yearly trips to England and elsewhere. During World War II they were trapped in first the Italian and later the German occupation of Monaco. Since the Baroness's sympathies were pro-British and anti-Austrian and Barstow was British, life was very difficult for them. Barstow died in 1943 and the Baroness in 1947.

Baroness Orczy's literary output was quite large, including, besides books, many periodical stories that have not been collected. Although she wrote in other fields, her forte was the historical romance and the detective short story. According to her memoirs, *Links in the Chain of Life,* her favorite work was *By the Gods Beloved* (American title, *The Gates of Kamt*), a novel about a colony of Ancient Egyptians surviving in the wastes of Africa. She had no illusions about her stature as a novelist, but considered herself a writer who made history vivid and attractive to the reader. She is remembered as an extraordinarily pleasant, shy woman, who felt and thought with the exuberance we usually associate with Hungarians.

II

Typologically the stories about the Old Man in the Corner are very important. They are the first significant stories about an armchair detective—one who resolves crimes simply from reports and by logic. They also present the ultimate development of the solution-denouement. Whereas explanations at the end of the story had been a standard feature of the detective story since Godwin and Charles Brockden Brown, the Baroness seems to have been the first to discard the story completely, and restrict herself to the ending, giving story details by flashback-quotation. As can be seen, this is a literary tour-de-force that requires considerably more skill than a chronological narrative in the conventional manner. According to the Baroness, her first step, at the advice of Barstow, was to create a detective in no respect like Sherlock Holmes and then to create cases around him. The result is before us.

The first Old Man in the Corner story appeared in *The Royal Magazine* for May 1901. Entitled "The Fenchurch Street Mystery," it was followed by five others in succeeding months. In the last of these stories, "The Mysterious Death in Percy Street," the Old Man, identity revealed, was given a comeuppance and forced into "retirement" by Polly Burton, but the series was so successful that a second series was commissioned and appeared in 1902, also in *The Royal Magazine.* This second series, which consisted of seven stories, devoted each case to a major city. At the time the story appeared, Pearson's publicity staff would plaster the city in question with posters announcing the story. A third group of stories appeared in 1904, and a final group, now markedly inferior to the earlier stories, in 1924 and 1925. Altogether there are 38 stories that describe the disentanglements accomplished by Bill Owen, the Old Man in the Corner, as he plays with his piece of string.

By an oddity of publishing history the third series of stories was the first to appear in book form, under the title *The Case of Miss Elliott* (1905). It was not until 1909 that the first two series appeared in book form, under the now famous title of *The Old Man in the Corner* (American title, *The Man in the Corner*). The final series was entitled *Unravelled Knots* (1925).

The Baroness also chronicled the adventures of two other detectives in *Lady Molly of Scotland Yard* (1910) and *Skin o' My Tooth* (1928). The first, narrated by a female Watson, describes the deductions of a lady detective associated with Scotland Yard; the second is concerned with the cases of Patrick Mulligan, an Irish lawyer-detective.

On the whole the Baroness, undoubtedly with Barstow's help, trod a safe path among the intricacies of British legal procedure, but there was a disaster in the second series of the Old Man in the Corner.

The Baroness knew Glasgow well enough, since she had spent some time there, and had no hesitation in writing "The Glasgow Mystery." But it turned out that more was involved than geography. She did not know Scottish law, and she made the mistake of referring to coroners, who do not exist in Scotland any more than does an accessory after the fact. *The Royal Magazine* received hundreds of indignant letters from north of the Tweed. *The Royal Magazine* sent them on to the Baroness for reply, together with its own letter of complaint. The Baroness was in despair, but Barstow provided advice that was effective but high-handed. "Throw away all the letters and berate your publisher for not having caught the error. You, as a Hungarian, cannot be expected to know the niceties of Scots law." It worked.

"The Glasgow Mystery," however, was suppressed. Reprinting it now is probably safe, for I cannot imagine that an American audience of today will worry much about Scottish coroners.

E. F. BLEILER

CONTENTS

THE
OLD MAN
IN THE CORNER

THE FENCHURCH STREET MYSTERY

DRAMATIS PERSONAE

THE MAN
who tells the story.
THE LADY JOURNALIST
who listens to it.
WILLIAM KERSHAW
(*the supposed victim*).
HIS WIFE.
FRANCIS SMETHURST
(*suspected murderer*).
KARL MÜLLER
(*friend of Kershaw*).

I

The man in the corner pushed aside his glass, and leant across the table.

"Mysteries!" he commented. "There is no such thing as a mystery in connection with any crime, provided intelligence is brought to bear upon its investigation."

Astonished I looked over the top of my newspaper at him. Had I been commenting audibly upon the article which was interesting me so much? I cannot say; certain it is that the man over there had spoken in direct answer to my thoughts.

His appearance, in any case, was sufficient to tickle my fancy. I don't think I had ever seen anyone so pale, so thin, with such funny light-coloured hair, brushed very smoothly across the top of a very obviously bald crown. I smiled indulgently at him. He looked so timid and nervous as he fidgeted incessantly with a piece of string; his long, lean, and trembling fingers tying and untying it into knots of wonderful and complicated proportions.

"And yet," I remarked kindly, but authoritatively, "this article, in an otherwise well-informed journal, will tell you that, even within the last year, no fewer than six crimes have completely baffled the police, and the perpetrators of them are still at large."

"Pardon me," he said gently, "I never for a moment ventured to suggest that there were no mysteries to the *police*; I merely remarked that there were none where intelligence was brought to bear upon the investigation of crime."

"Not even in the Fenchurch Street *mystery*, I suppose," I asked sarcastically.

"Least of all in the so-called Fenchurch Street *mystery*," he replied quietly.

Now, the Fenchurch Street mystery, as that extraordinary crime had popularly been called, had puzzled, I venture to say, the brains of every thinking man and woman for the last twelve months. The attitude of that timid man in the corner, therefore, was peculiarly exasperating, and I retorted with sarcasm destined to completely annihilate my self-complacent interlocutor.

"What a pity it is, in that case, that you do not offer your priceless services to our misguided though well-meaning police."

"Isn't it?" he replied with perfect good humour. "Well, you know for one thing, I doubt if they would accept them, and in the second place, my inclinations and my duty would—were I to become an active member of the detective force—nearly always be in direct conflict. As often as not my sympathies go to the criminal who is clever and astute enough to lead our entire police force by the nose.

"I don't know how much of the case you remember," he went on quietly. "It certainly, at first, began even to puzzle me. On the 12th of last December a woman, poorly dressed, but with an unmistakable air of having seen better days, gave information at Scotland Yard of the disappearance of her husband, William Kershaw, of no occupation, and apparently of no fixed abode. She was accompanied by a friend—a fat, oily-looking German, and between them they told a tale, which set the police immediately on the move.

"It appears that on the 10th of December, at about three o'clock in the afternoon, Karl Müller, the German, called on his friend, William Kershaw, for the purpose of collecting a small debt—some ten pounds or so—which the latter owed him. On arriving at the squalid lodging in Charlotte Street, Fitzroy Square, he found William Kershaw in a wild state of excitement, and his wife in tears. Müller attempted to state the object of his visit, but Kershaw, with wild gestures, waived him aside, and—in his own words—flabbergasted him by asking him point-blank for another loan of two pounds, which sum, he declared, would be the means of a speedy fortune for himself and the friend who would help him in his need.

"After a quarter of an hour spent in obscure hints, Kershaw, finding the cautious German obdurate, decided to let him into the secret plan, which, he averred, would place thousands into their hands."

Instinctively I had put down my paper; the mild stranger, with his nervous air and timid, watery eyes, had a peculiar way of telling his tale, which somehow fascinated me.

"I don't know," he resumed, "if you remember the story which the German told to the police, and which was corroborated in every detail by the wife or widow. Briefly it was this: Some thirty years previously, Kershaw, then twenty years of age, and a medical student at one of the London hospitals, had a chum named Barker, with whom he roomed, together with another.

"The latter, so it appears, brought home one evening a very considerable sum of money, which he had won on the turf, and the following morning he was found murdered in his bed. Kershaw, fortunately for himself, was able to prove a conclusive alibi; he had spent the night on duty at the hospital; as for Barker, he had disappeared, that is to say, as far as the police were concerned, but not as far as the watchful eyes of his friend Kershaw—at least, so the latter said. Barker very cleverly contrived to get away out of the country, and after sundry vicissitudes, finally settled down at Vladivostock, in Eastern Siberia, where, under the assumed name of Smethurst, he built up an enormous fortune, by trading in furs.

"Now mind you, every one knows Smethurst, the Siberian millionaire. Kershaw's story that he had once been called Barker, and had committed a murder thirty years ago was never proved, was it? I am merely telling you what Kershaw said to his friend the German and to his wife on that memorable afternoon of December the 10th.

"According to him, Smethurst had made one gigantic mistake in his clever career; he had on four occasions written to his late friend, William Kershaw. Two of these letters had no bearing on the case, since they were written more than twenty-five years ago, and Kershaw, moreover had lost them—so he said—long ago. According to him, however, the first of these letters was written when Smethurst, alias Barker, had spent all the money he had obtained from the crime, and found himself destitute in New York.

"Kershaw, then in fairly prosperous circumstances, sent him a £10 note for the sake of old times. The second, when the tables had turned, and Kershaw had begun to go downhill. Smethurst, as he then already called himself, sent his whilom friend £50. After that, as Müller gathered, Kershaw had made sundry demands on Smethurst's ever increasing purse, and had accompanied these demands by various threats, which, considering the distant country in which the millionaire lived, were worse than futile.

"But now the climax had come, and Kershaw after a final moment of hesitation, handed over to his German friend the two last letters purporting to have been written by Smethurst, and which, if you remember, played such an important part in the mysterious story of this extraordinary crime. I have a copy of both these letters, here," added the man in the corner as he took out a piece of paper from a very worn-out pocketbook, and, unfolding it very deliberately, he began to read:

SIR,

Your preposterous demands for money are wholly unwarrantable. I have already helped you quite as much as you deserve. However, for the sake of old times, and because you once helped me when I was in a terrible difficulty, I am willing to once more let you impose upon my good nature. A friend of mine here, a Russian merchant, to whom I have sold my business, starts in a few days for an extended tour to many European and Asiatic ports in his yacht, and has invited me to accompany him as far as England. Being tired of foreign parts, and desirous of seeing the old country once again after thirty years' absence, I have decided to accept his invitation. I don't know when we may actually be in Europe, but I promise you that as soon as we touch a suitable port I will write to you again, making an appointment for you to see me in London. But remember that if your demands are too preposterous I will not for a moment listen to them, and that I am the last man in the world to submit to persistent and unwarrantable blackmailing.

I am, sir,

Yours truly,

FRANCIS SMETHURST.

"The second letter was dated from Southampton," he went on with absolute calm, "and, curiously enough, was the only letter which Kershaw professed to have received from Smethurst, of which he had kept the envelope, and which was dated. It was quite brief," he added, referring once more to his piece of paper.

DEAR SIR,

Referring to my letter of a few weeks ago, I wish to inform you that the *Tsarskoe Selo* will touch at Tilbury on Tuesday next, the 10th. I shall land there, and immediately go up to London by the first train I can get. If you like you may meet me at Fenchurch Street Station, in the first-class waiting room in the late afternoon. Since I surmise that after thirty years' absence my face may not be familiar to you, I may as well tell you that you will recognise me by a heavy Astrakhan fur coat, which I shall wear, together with a cap of the same. You may then introduce yourself to me, and I will personally listen to what you may have to say.

Yours faithfully,

FRANCIS SMETHURST.

"It was this last letter which had caused William Kershaw's excitement and his wife's tears. In the German's own words, he was walking up and down the room like a wild beast, gesticulating wildly, and muttering sundry exclamations. Mrs. Kershaw, however, was full of apprehension. She mistrusted the man from foreign parts—who, according to her husband's story, had already one crime upon his conscience—who might, she feared, risk another, in order to be rid of a dangerous enemy. Woman-like, she thought the scheme a dishonourable one, for the law, she knew, is severe on the blackmailer.

"The assignation might be a cunning trap, in any case it was a curious one; why, she argued, did not Smethurst elect to see Kershaw at his hotel the following day. A thousand whys and wherefores made her anxious, but the fat German had been won over by Kershaw's visions of untold gold, held tantalisingly before his eyes. He had lent the necesssary £2, with which his friend intended to tidy himself up a bit before he went to meet his friend the millionaire. Half an hour afterwards Kershaw had left his lodgings, and that was the last the unfortunate woman saw of her husband, or Müller, the German, of his friend.

"Anxiously his wife waited that night, but he did not return, the next day she seems to have spent in making purposeless and futile inquiries about the neighbourhood of Fenchurch Street, and on the 12th she went to Scotland Yard, gave what particulars she knew, and placed in the hands of the police the two letters written by Smethurst."

II

The man in the corner had finished his glass of milk. His watery blue eyes looked across with evident satisfaction at my obvious eagerness and excitement.

"It was only on the 31st," he resumed after a while, "that a body, decomposed past all recognition, was found by two lightermen in the bottom of a disused barge. She had been moored at one time at the foot of one of those dark flights of steps which lead down between tall warehouses to the river in the East End of London. I have a photograph of the place here," he added, selecting one out of his pocket, and placing it before me.

"The actual barge, you see, had already been removed when I took this snapshot, but you will realise what a perfect place this alley is for the purpose of one man cutting another's throat in comfort, and without fear of detection. The body, as I said, was decomposed beyond all recognition; it had probably been there eleven days, but sundry articles such as a silver ring and a tie pin were recognisable and were identified by Mrs. Kershaw as belonging to her husband.

"She, of course, was loud in denouncing Smethurst, and the police had no doubt a very strong case against him, for two days after the discovery of the body in the barge, the Siberian millionaire, as he was already popularly called by enterprising interviewers, was arrested in his luxurious suite of rooms at the Hotel Cecil.

"To confess the truth, at this point, I was not a little puzzled. Mrs. Kershaw's story, and Smethurst's letters had both found their way into the papers, and following my usual method—mind you, I am only an amateur, I try to reason out a case for the love of the thing—I sought about for a motive for the crime, which the police declared Smethurst had committed. To effectually get rid of a dangerous blackmailer was the generally accepted theory. Well! did it ever strike you how paltry that motive really was?"

I had to confess, however, that it had never struck me in that light.

"Surely a man who had succeeded in building up an immense fortune by his own individual efforts was not the sort of fool to believe that he had anything to fear from a man like Kershaw. He must have *known* that Kershaw held no damning proofs against him—not enough to hang him anyway. Have you ever seen Smethurst?" he added, as he once more fumbled in his pocketbook.

I replied that I had seen Smethurst's picture in the illustrated papers at the time; then he added, placing a small photograph before me:

"What strikes you most about the face?"

"Well, I think its strange, astonished expression, due to the total absence of eyebrows, and the funny foreign cut of the hair."

"So close that it almost looks as if it had been shaved. Exactly. That is what struck me most when I elbowed my way into the Court that morning and first caught sight of the millionaire in the dock. He was a tall, soldierly-looking man, upright in stature, his face very bronzed and tanned. He wore neither moustache nor beard, his hair was cropped quite close to his head like a Frenchman's; but, of course, what was so very remarkable about him was that total absence of eyebrows and even eyelashes, which gave the face such a peculiar appearance— as you say, a perpetually astonished look.

"He seemed, however, wonderfully calm; he had been accommodated with a chair in the dock—being a millionaire—and chatted pleasantly with his lawyer, Sir Arthur Inglewood, in the intervals between the calling of the several witnesses for the prosecution; whilst during the examination of these witnesses he sat quite placidly, with his head shaded by his hand.

"Müller and Mrs. Kershaw repeated the story, which they had already told to the police. I think you said that you were not curious enough to go to the Court that day, and hear the case, so perhaps you have no recollection of Mrs. Kershaw. No? Ah, well! Here is a snapshot I managed to get of her once. That is her. Exactly as she stood in the box—over-dressed—in elaborate crape, with a bonnet which once had contained pink roses, and to which a remnant of pink petals still clung obtrusively amidst the deep black.

"She would not look at the prisoner, and turned her head resolutely towards the magistrate. I fancy she had been fond of that vagabond husband of hers: an enormous wedding ring encircled her finger, and that, too, was swathed in black. She firmly believed that Kershaw's murderer sat there in the dock, and she literally flaunted her grief before him.

"I was indescribably sorry for her. As for Müller, he was just fat, oily, pompous, conscious of his own importance as a witness; his fat fingers, covered with brass rings, gripped the two incriminating letters, which he had identified. They were his passports, as it were, to a delightful land of importance and notoriety. Sir Arthur Inglewood, I think, disappointed him, by stating that he had no questions to ask of him. Müller had been brimful of answers, ready with the most perfect indictment, the most elaborate accusations against the bloated millionaire who had decoyed his dear friend Kershaw, and murdered him in Heaven knows what an out-of-the-way corner of the East End.

"After this, however, the excitement grew apace. Müller had been dismissed, and had retired from the Court altogether, leading away Mrs. Kershaw, who had completely broken down.

"Constable D 21 was giving evidence as to the arrest, in the meanwhile. The prisoner, he said, had seemed completely taken by surprise, not understanding the cause or history of the accusation against him; however, when put in full possession of the facts, and realising, no doubt, the absolute futility of any resistance, he had quietly enough followed the constable into the cab. No one at the fashionable and crowded Hotel Cecil had even suspected that anything unusual had occurred.

"Then a gigantic sigh of expectancy came from everyone of the spectators. The 'fun' was about to begin. James Buckland, a porter at Fenchurch Street railway station, had just sworn to tell all the truth, etc. After all it did not amount to much. He said that at six o'clock in the afternoon of December the 10th, in the midst of one of the densest fogs he ever remembers, the 5:05 from Tilbury steamed into the station, being just about an hour late. He was on the arrival platform and was hailed by a passenger in a first-class carriage. He could see very little of him beyond an enormous black fur coat and a travelling cap of fur also.

"The passenger had a quantity of luggage, all marked F.S., and he directed James Buckland to place it all upon a four-wheel cab, with the exception of a small handbag, which he carried himself. Having seen that all his luggage was safely bestowed, the stranger in the fur coat paid the porter, and telling the cabman to wait until he returned, he walked away in the direction of the waiting rooms, still carrying his small handbag.

"'I stayed for a bit,' added James Buckland, 'talking to the driver about the fog and that, then I went about my business, seein' that the local from Southend 'ad been signalled.'

"The prosecution insisted most strongly upon the hour when the stranger in the fur coat, having seen to his luggage, walked away towards the waiting rooms. The porter was emphatic. 'It was not a minute later than 6:15,' he averred.

"Sir Arthur Inglewood still had no questions to ask, and the driver of the cab was called.

"He corroborated the evidence of James Buckland as to the hour when the gentleman in the fur coat had engaged him, and having filled his cab in and out with luggage, had told him to wait. And cabby did wait. He waited in the dense fog—until he was tired, until he seriously thought of depositing all the luggage in the lost property office and of looking out for another fare—waited until at last, at a quarter before nine, whom should he see walking hurriedly towards his cab but the gentleman in the fur coat and cap who got in quickly and told the driver to take him at once to the Hotel Cecil. This, cabby declared, had occurred at a quarter before nine. Still Sir Arthur Inglewood made no comment, and Mr. Francis Smethurst, in the crowded, stuffy court, had calmly dropped to sleep.

"The next witness, Constable Thomas Taylor, had noticed a shabbily-dressed individual, with shaggy hair and beard, loafing about the station and waiting rooms in the afternoon of December the 10th. He seemed to be watching the arrival platform of the Tilbury and Southend trains.

"Two separate and independent witnesses, cleverly unearthed by the police, had seen this same shabbily-dressed individual stroll into the first-class waiting room at about 6:15 on Wednesday, December the 10th, and go straight up to a gentleman in a heavy fur coat and cap, who had also just come into the room. The two talked together for a while; no one heard what they said, but presently they walked off together. No one seemed to know in which direction.

"Francis Smethurst was rousing himself from his apathy; he whispered to his lawyer, who nodded with a bland smile of encouragement. The employees of the Hotel Cecil gave evidence as to the arrival of Mr. Smethurst at about 9:30 P.M. on Wednesday, December the 10th, in a cab, with a quantity of luggage; and this closed the case for the prosecution.

"Everybody in that Court already *saw* Smethurst mounting the gallows. It was uninterested curiosity which caused the elegant audience to wait and hear what Sir Arthur Inglewood had to say. He, of course, is the most fashionable man in the law at the present moment. His lolling attitudes, his drawling speech, are quite the rage, and imitated by the gilded youth of society.

"Even at this moment, when the Siberian millionaire's neck literally and metaphorically hung in the balance, an expectant titter went round the fair spectators, as Sir Arthur stretched out his long loose limbs and lounged across the table. He waited to make his effect—Sir Arthur is a born actor—and there is no doubt that he made it, when in his slowest, most drawly tones he said quietly:

"'With regard to this alleged murder of one William Kershaw, on Wednesday, December the 10th, between 6:15 and 8:45 P.M., your Honour, I now propose to call two witnesses, who saw this same William Kershaw alive on Tuesday afternoon, December the 16th, that is to say, six days after the supposed murder.'

"It was as if a bombshell had exploded in the Court. Even his Honour was aghast, and I am sure the lady next to me only recovered from the shock of the surprise in order to wonder whether she need put off her dinner party after all.

"As for me," added the man in the corner, with that strange mixture of nervousness and self-complacency which I have never seen equalled, "well, you see, *I* had made up my mind long ago as to where the hitch lay in this particular case, and I was not so surprised as some of the others.

"Perhaps you remember the wonderful development of the case, which so completely mystified the police—and in fact everybody except myself. Torriani and a waiter at his hotel in the Commercial Road both deposed that at about 3:30 P.M. on December the 10th a shabbily dressed individual lolled into the coffee-room and ordered some tea. He was pleasant enough and talkative, told the waiter that his name was William Kershaw, that very soon all London would be talking about him, as he was about, through an unexpected stroke of good fortune, to become a very rich man, and so on, and so on, nonsense without end.

"When he had finished his tea, he lolled out again, but no sooner had he disappeared down a turning of the road, than the waiter discovered an old umbrella, left behind accidentally by the shabby, talkative individual. As is the custom in his highly-respectable restaurant, Signor Torriani put the umbrella carefully away in his office, on the chance of his customer calling to claim it when he had discovered his loss. And sure enough nearly a week later, on Tuesday, the 16th, at about 1 P.M. the same shabbily-dressed individual called and asked for his umbrella. He had some lunch, and chatted once again to the waiter.

Signor Torriani and the waiter gave a description of William Kershaw which coincided exactly with that given by Mrs. Kershaw of her husband.

"Oddly enough he seemed to be a very absentminded sort of person, for on this second occasion, no sooner had he left than the waiter found a pocketbook in the coffee-room, underneath the table. It contained sundry letters and bills, all addressed to William Kershaw. This pocketbook was produced, and Karl Müller, who had returned to the Court, easily identified it as having belonged to his dear and lamented friend 'Villiam.'

"This was the first blow to the case against the accused. It was a pretty stiff one, you will admit. Already it had begun to collapse like a house of cards. Still, there was the assignation, and the undisputed meeting between Smethurst and Kershaw, and those two and a half hours of a foggy evening to satisfactorily account for."

The man in the corner made a long pause, keeping me on tenterhooks. He had fidgeted with his bit of string till there was not an inch of it free from the most complicated and elaborate knots.

"I assure you," he resumed at last, "that at that very moment the whole mystery was, to me, as clear as daylight. I only marvelled how his Honour could waste his time and mine by putting what he thought were searching questions to the accused relating to his past. Francis Smethurst, who had quite shaken off his somnolence, spoke with a curious nasal twang, and with an almost imperceptible soupçon of foreign accent. He calmly denied Kershaw's version of his past; declared that he had never been called Barker, and had certainly never been mixed up in any murder case thirty years ago.

"'But you knew this man Kershaw,' persisted his Honour, 'since you wrote to him?'

"'Pardon me, your Honour,' said the accused quietly, 'I have never, to my knowledge, seen this man Kershaw, and I can swear that I never wrote to him.'

"'Never wrote to him?' retorted his Honour warningly. 'That is a strange assertion to make, when I have two of your letters to him in my hands at the present moment.'

"'I never wrote those letters, your Honour,' persisted the accused quietly, 'they are not in my handwriting.'

"'Which we can easily prove,' came in Sir Arthur Inglewood's drawly tones, as he handed up a packet to his Honour, 'here are a number of letters written by my client since he has landed in this country, and some of which were written under my very eyes.'

"As Sir Arthur Inglewood had said, this could be easily proved, and the prisoner, at his Honour's request, scribbled a few lines, together with his signature, several times upon a sheet of notepaper. It was easy to read upon the magistrate's astounded countenance, that there was not the slightest similarity in the two handwritings.

"A fresh mystery had cropped up. Who then had made the assignation with William Kershaw, at Fenchurch Street railway station? The prisoner gave a fairly satisfactory account of the employment of his time, since his landing in England.

"'I came over on the *Tsarskoe Selo,*' he said, 'a yacht belonging to a friend of mine. When we arrived at the mouth of the Thames there was such a dense fog that it was twenty-four hours before it was thought safe for me to land. My friend, who is a Russian, would not land at all; he was regularly frightened at this land of fogs. He was going on to Madeira immediately.

"'I actually landed on Tuesday, the 10th, and took a train at once for town. I did see to my luggage and a cab, as the porter and driver told your Honour: then I tried to find my way to a refreshment room, where I could get a glass of wine. I drifted into the waiting room, and there I was accosted by a shabbily-dressed individual, who began telling me a piteous tale. Who he was I do not know. He *said* he was an old soldier who had served his country faithfully, and then been left to starve. He begged of me to accompany him to his lodgings, where I could see his wife and starving children, and verify the truth and piteousness of his tale.

"'Well, your Honour,' added the prisoner with noble frankness, 'it was my first day in the old country. I had come back after thirty years, with my pockets full of gold, and this was the first sad tale I had heard; but I am a business man, and did not want to be exactly 'done' in the eye. I followed my man through the fog, out into the streets. He walked silently by my side for a time. I had not a notion where I was.

"'Suddenly I turned to him with some question, and realised in a moment that my gentleman had given me the slip. Finding, probably, that I would not part with my money till I *had* seen the starving wife and children, he left me to my fate, and went in search of more willing bait.

"'The place where I found myself was dismal and deserted. I could see no trace of cab or omnibus. I retraced my steps and tried to find my way back to the station, only to find myself in worse and more deserted neighborhoods. I became hopelessly lost and fogged. I don't wonder that two and a half hours elapsed while I thus wandered on in the dark and deserted streets; my sole astonishment is that I ever found the station at all that night, or rather close to it a policeman, who showed me the way.'

"'But how do you account for Kershaw knowing all your move-

ments?' still persisted his Honour, 'and his knowing the exact date of
your arrival in England? How do you account for these two letters, in
fact?'

"'I cannot account for it or them, your Honour,' replied the prisoner
quietly. 'I have proved to you, have I not, that I never wrote these letters, and that the man—er—Kershaw is his name?—was not murdered
by me?'

"'Can you tell me of anyone here or abroad who might have heard of
your movements, and of the date of your arrival?'

"'My late employees at Vladivostock, of course, knew of my depar-
ture, but none of them could have written these letters, since none of
them know a word of English.'

"'Then you can throw no light upon these mysterious letters? You
cannot help the police in any way towards the clearing up of this
strange affair?'

"'The affair is as mysterious to me as to your Honour, and to the
police of this country.'

"Francis Smethurst was discharged, of course; there was no sem-
blance of evidence against him sufficient to commit him for trial. The
two overwhelming points of his defence which had completely routed
the prosecution were, firstly, the proof that he had never written the
letters making the assignation, and secondly, the fact that the man
supposed to have been murdered on the 10th was seen to be alive and
well on the 16th. But then, who in the world was the mysterious individual who had apprised Kershaw of the movements of Smethurst, the
millionaire?"

III

The man in the corner cocked his funny thin head on one side and
looked at me; then he took up his beloved bit of string, and deliberately untied every knot he had made in it. When it was quite
smooth, he laid it out upon the table.

"I will take you, if you like, point by point, along the line of reasoning which I followed myself, and which will inevitably lead you, as it
led me, to the only possible solution of the mystery.

"First take this point," he said with nervous restlessness, once more
taking up his bit of string, and forming with each point raised a series
of knots which would have shamed a navigating instructor, "obviously,
it was *impossible* for Kershaw not to have been acquainted with
Smethurst, since he was fully apprised of the latter's arrival in England by two letters. Now it was clear to me from the first that *no one*
could have written those two letters except Smethurst. You will argue

that those letters were proved not to have been written by the man in the dock. Exactly. Remember, Kershaw was a careless man; he had lost both envelopes. To him they were insignificant. Now it was never *disproved* that those letters were written by Smethurst."

"But——" I suggested.

"Wait a minute," he interrupted, while knot number two appeared upon the scene, "it was proved that six days after the murder, William Kershaw was alive, and visiting the Torriani Hotel, where already he was known, and where he conveniently left a pocketbook behind, so that there should be no mistake as to his identity, but it was never questioned where Mr. Francis Smethurst, the millionaire, happened to spend that very same afternoon."

"Surely, you don't mean——?" I gasped.

"One moment, please," he added triumphantly. "How did it come about that the landlord of the Torriani Hotel was brought into court at all; how did Sir Arthur Inglewood, or rather his client, know that William Kershaw had on those two memorable occasions visited the hotel and that its landlord could bring such convincing evidence forward that would for ever exonerate the millionaire from the imputation of murder?"

"Surely," I argued, "the usual means, the police——"

"The police had kept the whole affair very dark, until the arrest at the Hotel Cecil. They did not put into the papers the usual: 'If any one happens to know of the whereabouts etc. etc.' Had the landlord of that hotel heard of the disappearance of Kershaw through the usual channels, he would have put himself in communication with the police. Sir Arthur Inglewood produced him. How did Sir Arthur Inglewood come on his track?"

"Surely, you don't mean——?"

"Point number four," he resumed imperturbably, "Mrs. Kershaw was never requested to produce a specimen of her husband's handwriting. Why? Because the police, clever as you say they are, never started on the right tack. They believed William Kershaw to have been murdered; they looked for William Kershaw.

"On December the 31st, what was presumed to be the body of William Kershaw was found by two lightermen; I have shown you a photograph of the place where it was found. Dark and deserted it is in all conscience, is it not? Just the place where a bully and a coward would decoy an unsuspecting stranger, murder him first, then rob him of his valuables, his papers, his very identity, and leave him there to rot. The body was found in a disused barge which had been moored some time against the wall, at the foot of these steps. It was in the last stages of decomposition, and, of course, could not be identified; but the police would have it, that it was the body of William Kershaw.

"It never entered their heads that it was the body of *Francis Smethurst, and that William Kershaw was his murderer.*

"Ah! it was cleverly, artistically conceived! Kershaw is a genius. Think of it all! His disguise! Kershaw had a shaggy beard, hair, and moustache. He shaved up to his very eyebrows! No wonder that even his wife did not recognise him across the Court; and remember she never saw much of his face while he stood in the dock. Kershaw was shabby, slouchy, he stooped.

"Smethurst, the millionaire, might have served in the Prussian army. Then that lovely trait about going to revisit the Torriani Hotel. Just a few days' grace, in order to purchase moustache and beard and wig, exactly similar to what he had himself shaved off. Making up to look like himself! Splendid! The leaving the pocketbook behind! He! He! He! Kershaw was not murdered! Of course not. He called at the Torriani Hotel six days after the murder, whilst Mr. Smethurst, the millionaire, hobnobbed in the park with duchesses! Hang such a man! Fie!"

He fumbled for his hat. With nervous, trembling fingers he held it deferentially in his hand, whilst he rose from the table. I watched him as he strode up to the desk, and paid twopence for his glass of milk and his bun. Soon he disappeared through the shop, whilst I still found myself hopelessly bewildered, with a number of snapshot photographs before me, still staring at a long piece of string, smothered from end to end in a series of knots, as bewildering, as irritating, as puzzling as the man who had lately sat in the corner.

THE MYSTERIOUS DEATH ON THE UNDERGROUND RAILWAY

DRAMATIS PERSONAE

THE MAN
who explains each mystery to
THE LADY JOURNALIST
whilst at lunch at an A.B.C.
MR. HAZELDENE
(*shipping agent*).
MRS. HAZELDENE
(*his wife, found dead on the Underground Railway*).
FRANK ERRINGTON
(*suspected of her murder*).
MR. ANDREW CAMPBELL   MR. JAMES VERNER
(*witnesses before the Magistrates at Bow Street*).

I

"Will you be good enough to give me a description of the man who sat next to you just now, while you were having your cup of coffee and scone?" said the man in the corner to me that day.

He had been sitting in his accustomed place when I came into the A.B.C. shop, but had made no remark all the time that I was partaking of my modest luncheon. I was just in the act of thinking how rude he was not to have said "Good morning," when his abrupt remark caused me to look up.

"Do you know at all if he was tall or short, dark or fair?" he insisted, seemingly not the least disconcerted by my somewhat rude survey of his eccentric personality, "Can you tell me at all what he was like?"

"Of course I can," I rejoined impatiently, "but I don't see that my description of one of the customers of an A.B.C. shop can have the slightest importance."

He was silent for a minute, while his nervous fingers fumbled about in his capacious pockets in search of the inevitable piece of string. When he had found this necessary "adjunct to thought," he viewed me again through his half-closed lids, and added maliciously:

"But supposing it were of paramount importance that you should give an accurate description of a man who sat next to you for half-an-hour today, how would you proceed?"

"I should say that he was of medium height——"

"Five foot eight, nine, or ten?" he interrupted quietly.

"How can one tell to an inch or two?" I rejoined crossly. "He was between colours."

"What's that?" he inquired blandly.

"Neither fair nor dark—his nose——"

"Well, what was his nose like? Will you sketch it?"

"I am not an artist. His nose was fairly straight—his eyes——"

"Were neither dark nor light—his hair had the same striking peculiarity—he was neither short nor tall—his nose was neither aquiline nor snub——" he recapitulated sarcastically.

"No," I retorted; "he was just ordinary-looking."

"Would you know him again—say tomorrow, and among a number of other men who were 'neither tall nor short, dark nor fair, aquiline nor snub-nosed,' etc?"

"I don't know—I might—he was certainly not striking enough to be specially remembered."

"Exactly," he said, while he leant forward excitedly, for all the world like a jack-in-the-box let loose. "Precisely; and you are a novelist—call yourself one, at least—and it should be part of your business to notice and describe people. I don't mean only the wonderful personage with the clear Saxon features, the fine blue eyes, the noble brow and classic face, but the ordinary person—the person who represents ninety out of every hundred of his own kind—the average Englishman, say, of the middle classes, who is neither very tall nor very short, who wears a moustache which is neither fair nor dark, but which masks his mouth, and a top hat which hides the shape of his head and brow, a man, in fact, who dresses like hundreds of his fellow creatures, moves like them, speaks like them, has no peculiarity.

"Try to describe *him,* to recognise him, say a week hence, among his other eighty-nine doubles; worse still, to swear his life away, if he happened to be implicated in some crime, wherein *your* recognition of him would place the halter round his neck.

"Try that, I say, and having utterly failed you will more readily understand how one of the greatest scoundrels unhung is still at large, and why the mystery on the Underground Railway was never cleared up.

"I think it was the only time in my life that I was seriously tempted to give the police the benefit of my own views upon the matter. You see, though I admire the brute for his cleverness, I did not see that his being unpunished could possibly benefit anyone.

"The Central London Railway had just been opened a few days, and the old Underground was being deserted for the time being for the sake of the novelty of the other line. Anyway, when that particular train steamed into Aldgate at about 4 P.M. on June 18th last, the first-class carriages were all but empty.

"The guard marched up and down the platform looking into all the carriages to see if anyone had left a halfpenny evening paper behind for him, and opening the door of one of the first class compartments, he noticed a lady sitting in the further corner, with her head turned away towards the window evidently oblivious of the fact that on this line, Aldgate is the terminal station.

"'Where are you for, lady?' he said.

"The lady did not move, and the guard stepped into the carriage, thinking that perhaps the lady was asleep. He touched her arm lightly and looked into her face. In his own poetic language he was 'struck all of a 'eap.' In the glassy eyes, the ashen colour of the cheeks, the rigidity of the head, there was the unmistakable look of death.

"Hastily the guard, having carefully locked the carriage door, summoned a couple of porters, and sent one of them off to the police station, and the other in search of the stationmaster.

"Fortunately at this time of day the up platform is not very crowded, all the traffic tending westward in the afternoon. It was only when an inspector and two police constables, accompanied by a detective in plain clothes and a medical officer, appeared upon the scene, and stood round a first-class railway compartment, that a few idlers realised that something unusual had occurred, and crowded round, eager and curious.

"Thus it was that the later editions of the evening papers, under the sensational heading, 'Mysterious Suicide on the Underground Railway,' had already an account of the extraordinary event. The medical officer had very soon come to the decision that the guard had not been mistaken, and that life was indeed extinct.

"The lady was young, and must have been very pretty, before the look of fright and horror had so terribly distorted her features. She was very elegantly dressed, and the more frivolous papers were able to give their feminine readers a detailed account of the unfortunate woman's gown, her shoes, hat, and gloves.

"It appears that one of the latter, the one on the right hand, was partly off, leaving the thumb and wrist bare. That hand held a small satchel, which the police opened, with a view to the possible identification of the deceased, but which was found to contain only a little loose silver, some smelling salts, and a small empty bottle which was handed over to the medical officer for purposes of analysis.

"It was the presence of that small bottle which had caused the report to circulate freely that the mysterious case on the Underground Railway was one of suicide. Certain it was that neither about the lady's person, nor in the appearance of the railway carriage, was there the slightest sign of struggle or even of resistance. Only the look in the poor woman's eyes spoke of sudden terror, of the rapid vision of an unexpected and violent death, which probably only lasted an infinitesimal fraction of a second, but which had left its indelible mark upon the face, otherwise so placid and so still."

II

"The body of the deceased was conveyed to the mortuary. So far, of course, not a soul had been able to identify her, or to throw the slightest light upon the mystery which hung around her death.

"Against that, quite a crowd of idlers—genuinely interested or not—obtained admission to view the body, on the pretext of having lost or mislaid a relative or a friend. At about 8:30 P.M. a young man, very well dressed, drove up to the station in a hansom, and sent in his card to the superintendent. It was Mr. Hazeldene, shipping agent, of 11, Crown Lane, E.C., and No. 19, Addison Row, Kensington.

"The young man looked in a pitiable state of mental distress; his hand clutched nervously a copy of the *St. James's Gazette,* which contained the fatal news. He said very little to the superintendent except that a person who was very dear to him had not returned home that evening.

"He had not felt really anxious until half-an-hour ago, when suddenly he thought of looking at his paper. The description of the deceased lady, though vague, had terribly alarmed him. He had jumped into a hansom, and now begged permission to view the body, in order that his worst fears might be allayed.

"You know what followed, of course," continued the man in the corner, "the grief of the young man was truly pitiable. In the woman lying there in a public mortuary before him, Mr. Hazeldene had recognised his wife.

"I am waxing melodramatic," said the man in the corner who looked up at me with a mild and gentle smile, while his nervous fingers vainly endeavoured to add another knot on the scrappy bit of string with which he was continually playing, "and I fear that your story will savour this time of the penny novelette, but you must admit, and no doubt you remember, that it was an intensely pathetic and truly dramatic moment.

"The unfortunate young husband of the deceased lady was not much worried with questions that night. As a matter of fact he was not in a fit condition to make any coherent statement. It was at the coroner's inquest on the following day, that certain facts came to light, which for the time being seemed to clear up the mystery surrounding Mrs. Hazeldene's death, only to plunge that same mystery, later on, into denser gloom than before.

"The first witness at the inquest was, of course, Mr. Hazeldene himself. I think everyone's sympathy went out to the young man, as he stood before the coroner and tried to throw what light he could upon the mystery. He was well dressed as he had been the day before, but he looked terribly ill and worried, and no doubt the fact that he had not shaved gave his face a careworn and neglected air.

"It appears that he and the deceased had been married some six years or so, and that they had always been happy in their married life. They had no children. Mrs. Hazeldene seemed to enjoy the best of health till lately, when she had had a slight attack of influenza, in which Dr. Arthur Jones had attended her. The doctor was present at this moment and would no doubt explain to the coroner and the jury whether he thought that Mrs. Hazeldene had the slightest tendency to heart disease, which might have had a sudden and fatal ending.

"The coroner was, of course, very considerate to the bereaved husband. He tried by circumlocution to get at the point he wanted, namely, Mrs. Hazeldene's mental condition lately. Mr. Hazeldene seemed loth to talk about this. No doubt he had been warned as ,o the existence of the small bottle found in his wife's satchel.

"'It certainly did seem to me at times,' he at last reluctantly admitted, 'that my wife did not seem quite herself. She used to be very gay and bright, and lately, I often saw her in the evening sitting, as if brooding over some matters, which evidently she did not care to communicate to me.'

"Still the coroner insisted, and suggested the small bottle.

"'I know, I know,' replied the young man with a short, heavy sigh. 'You mean—the question of suicide—I cannot understand it at all—it seems so sudden and so terrible—she certainly had seemed listless and troubled lately—but only at times—and yesterday morning, when I went to business, she appeared quite herself again, and I suggested that we should go to the opera in the evening. She was delighted, I know, and told me she would do some shopping, and pay a few calls in the afternoon.'

"'Do you know at all where she intended to go when she got into the Underground Railway?'

"'Well, not with certainty. You see she may have meant to get out at Baker Street, and go down to Bond Street to do her shopping. Then again, she sometimes goes to a shop in St. Paul's Churchyard, in which case, she would take a ticket to Aldersgate Street; but I cannot say.'

"'Now, Mr. Hazeldene,' said the coroner at last very kindly, 'will you try to tell me if there was anything in Mrs. Hazeldene's life which you know of, and which might in some measure explain the cause of the distressed state of mind, which you yourself had noticed? Did there exist any financial difficulty which might have preyed upon Mrs. Hazeldene's mind; was there any friend—to whose intercourse with Mrs. Hazeldene—you—er—at any time took exception to. In fact,' added the coroner, as if thankful that he had got over an unpleasant moment, 'can you give me the slightest indication which would tend to confirm the suspicion that the unfortunate lady, in a moment of mental anxiety or derangement, may have wished to take her own life.'

"There was silence in the court for a few moments. Mr. Hazeldene seemed to everyone there present to be labouring under some terrible moral doubt. He looked very pale and wretched, and twice attempted to speak, before he at last said in scarcely audible tones.

"'No; there were no financial difficulties of any sort. My wife had an independent fortune of her own—she had no extravagant tastes——'

"'Nor any friend you at any time objected to?' insisted the coroner.

"'Nor any friend, I—at any time objected to,' stammered the unfortunate young man, evidently speaking with an effort.

"I was present at the inquest," resumed the man in the corner, after he had drunk a glass of milk, and ordered another, "and I can assure you that the most obtuse person there plainly realized that Mr. Hazeldene was telling a lie. It was pretty plain to the meanest intelligence that the unfortunate lady had not fallen into a state of morbid dejection for nothing, and that perhaps there existed a third person who could throw more light on her strange and sudden death than the unhappy, bereaved young widower.

"That the death was more mysterious even than it had at first appeared, became very soon apparent. You read the case at the time, no doubt, and must remember the excitement in the public mind caused by the evidence of the two doctors. Dr. Arthur Jones, the lady's usual medical man, who had not attended her in a last very slight illness, but who had seen her in a professional capacity fairly recently, declared most emphatically that Mrs. Hazeldene suffered from no organic complaint which could possibly have been the cause of sudden death. Moreover, he had assisted Mr. Andrew Thorton, the district medical officer, in making a postmortem examination, and together they had come to the conclusion that death was due to the action of prussic acid, which had caused instantaneous failure of the heart, but how the drug had been administered neither he nor his colleague were at present able to state.

"'Do I understand, then, Dr. Jones, that the deceased died, poisoned with prussic acid?'

"'Such is my opinion,' replied the doctor.

"'Did the bottle found in her satchel contain prussic acid?'

"'It had contained some at one time, certainly.'

"'In your opinion, then, the lady caused her own death by taking a dose of that drug?'

"'Pardon me, I never suggested such a thing; the lady died poisoned by the drug, but how the drug was administered we cannot say. By injection of some sort, certainly. The drug certainly was not swallowed; there was not a vestige of it in the stomach.

"'Yes,' added the doctor in reply to another question from the coroner, 'death had probably followed the injection in this case almost immediately; say within a couple of minutes, or perhaps three. It was quite possible, that the body would not have more than one quick and sudden convulsion, perhaps not that; death in such cases is absolutely sudden and crushing.'

"I don't think that at the time anyone in the room realised how important the doctor's statement was, a statement which, by the way, was confirmed in all its details by the district medical officer, who had conducted the postmortem. Mrs. Hazeldene had died suddenly from an injection of prussic acid, administered no one knew how or when. She had been travelling in a first-class railway carriage, in a busy time of the day. That young and elegant woman must have had singular nerve and coolness to go through the process of a self-inflicted injection of a deadly poison in the presence of perhaps two or three other persons.

"Mind you, when I say that no one there realised the importance of the doctor's statement at that moment, I am wrong; there were three persons, who fully understood at once the gravity of the situation, and the astounding development which the case was beginning to assume.

"Of course, I should have put myself out of the question," added my strange interlocutor, with that inimitable self-conceit peculiar to himself. "I guessed then and there in a moment where the police were going wrong, and where they would go on going wrong until the mysterious death on the Underground Railway had sunk into oblivion, together with the other cases which they mismanage from time to time.

"I said there were three persons who understood the gravity of the two doctors' statements—the other two were, firstly, the detective who had originally examined the railway carriage, a young man of energy and plenty of misguided intelligence, the other was Mr. Hazeldene.

"At this point the interesting element of the whole story was first introduced into the proceedings, and this was done through the humble channel of Emma Funnel, Mrs. Hazeldene's maid, who, as far as was known then, was the last person who had seen the unfortunate lady alive and had spoken to her.

"'Mrs. Hazeldene lunched at home,' explained Emma, who was shy, and spoke almost in a whisper, 'she seemed well and cheerful. She went out at about half-past three, and told me she was going to

Spence's in St. Paul's Churchyard, to try on her new tailor-made gown. Mrs. Hazeldene had meant to go there in the morning, but was prevented as Mr. Errington called.'

"'Mr. Errington?' asked the coroner casually. 'Who is Mr. Errington?'

"But this, Emma found difficult to explain. 'Mr. Errington was— Mr. Errington, that's all.'

"'Mr. Errington was a friend of the family. He lived in a flat in the Albert Mansions. He very often came to Addison Crescent, and generally stayed late.'

"Pressed still further with questions, Emma at last stated that latterly Mrs. Hazeldene had been to the theatre several times with Mr. Errington, and that on those nights the master looked very gloomy, and was very cross.

"Recalled, the young widower was strangely reticent. He gave forth his answers very grudgingly, and the coroner was evidently absolutely satisfied with himself at the marvellous way in which, after a quarter of an hour of firm, yet very kind questionings, he had elicited from the witness what information he wanted.

"Mr. Errington was a friend of his wife. He was a gentleman of means, and seemed to have a great deal of time at his command. He himself did not particularly care about Mr. Errington, but he certainly had never made any observations to his wife on the subject.

"'But who is Mr. Errington?' repeated the coroner once more. 'What does he do? What is his business or profession?'

"'He has no business or profession.'

"'What is his occupation, then?'

"'He has no special occupation. He has ample private means. But he has a great and very absorbing hobby.'

"'What is that?'

"'He spends all his time in chemical experiments, and is, I believe, as an amateur, a very distinguished toxicologist.'"

III

"Did you ever see Mr. Errington, the gentleman so closely connected with the mysterious death on the Underground Railway?" asked the man in the corner as he placed one or two of his little snapshot photos before me. "There he is, to the very life. Fairly good-looking, a pleasant face enough, but ordinary, absolutely ordinary.

"It was this absence of any peculiarity which very nearly, but not quite, placed the halter round Mr. Errington's neck. But I am going too fast, and you will lose the thread.

"The public, of course, never heard how it actually came about that Mr. Errington, the wealthy bachelor of Albert Mansions, of the Grosvenor, and other young dandies' clubs, one fine day found himself before the magistrates at Bow Street charged with being concerned in the death of Mary Beatrice Hazeldene, late of No. 19, Addison Row.

"I can assure you both press and public were literally flabbergasted. You see Mr. Errington was a well-known and very popular member of a certain smart section of London society. He was a constant visitor at the opera, the racecourse, the Park, and the Carlton, he had a great many friends, and there was consequently quite a large attendance at the police court that morning.

"What had transpired was this:

"After the very scrappy bits of evidence which came to light at the inquest, two gentlemen bethought themselves that perhaps they had some duty to perform towards the State and the public generally. Accordingly, they had come forward in order to offer to throw what light they could upon the mysterious affair on the Underground Railway.

"The police naturally felt that their information, such as it was, came rather late in the day, but as it proved of paramount importance, and the two gentlemen, moreover, were of undoubtedly good position in the world, they were thankful for what they could get, and acted accordingly; they accordingly brought Mr. Errington up before the Magistrate on a charge of murder.

"The accused looked pale and worried when I first caught sight of him in the Court that day, which was not to be wondered at, considering the terrible position in which he found himself.

"He had been arrested at Marseilles, where he was preparing to start for Colombo.

"I don't think he realised how terrible his position really was, until later in the proceedings when all the evidence relating to the arrest had been heard, and Emma Funnel had repeated her statement as to Mr. Errington's call at 19, Addison Row in the morning, and Mrs. Hazeldene starting off for St. Paul's Churchyard at 3:30 in the afternoon.

"Mr. Hazeldene had nothing to add to the statements he had made at the coroner's inquest. He had last seen his wife alive on the morning of the fatal day. She had seemed very well and cheerful. I think everyone present understood that he was trying to say as little as possible that could in any way couple his deceased wife's name with that of the accused.

"And yet, from the servant's evidence, it undoubtedly leaked out that Mrs. Hazeldene, who was young, pretty, and evidently fond of admiration, had once or twice annoyed her husband by somewhat open, yet perfectly innocent, flirtations with Mr. Errington.

"I think everyone was most agreeably impressed by the widower's moderate and dignified attitude. You will see his photo there, among this bundle. That is just how he appeared in court. In deep black, of course, but without any sign of ostentation in his mourning. He had allowed his beard to grow lately, and wore it closely cut in a point. After his evidence, the sensation of the day occurred. A tall dark-haired man with the word "City" written metaphorically all over him, had kissed the book, and was waiting to tell the truth, and nothing but the truth.

"He gave his name as Andrew Campbell, head of the firm of Campbell & Co., brokers, of Throgmorton Street.

"In the afternoon of June 18th Mr. Campbell, travelling on the Underground Railway, had noticed a very pretty woman in the same carriage as himself. She had asked him if she was in the right train for Aldersgate. Mr. Campbell replied in the affirmative, and then buried himself in the Stock Exchange quotations of his evening paper. At Gower Street, a gentleman in a tweed suit and bowler hat got into the carriage, and took a seat opposite the lady.

"She seemed very much astonished at seeing him, but Mr. Andrew Campbell did not recollect the exact words she said.

"The two talked to one another a good deal, and certainly the lady appeared animated and cheerful. Witness took no notice of them; he was very much engrossed in some calculations, and finally got out at Farringdon Street. He noticed that the man in the tweed suit also got out close behind him, having shaken hands with the lady, and said in a pleasant way: '*Au revoir!* Don't be late tonight.' Mr. Campbell did not hear the lady's reply, and soon lost sight of the man in the crowd.

"Everyone was on tenterhooks, and eagerly waiting for the palpitating moment when witness would describe and identify the man who last had seen and spoken to the unfortunate woman, within five minutes probably of her strange and unaccountable death. Personally, I knew what was coming before the Scotch stockbroker spoke. I could have jotted down the graphic and lifelike description he would give of a probable murderer. It would have fitted equally well the man who sat and had luncheon at this table just now; it would certainly have described five out of every ten young Englishmen you know.

"The individual was of medium height, he wore a moustache which was not very fair nor yet very dark, his hair was between colours. He wore a bowler hat, and a tweed suit, and—and—that was all—Mr. Campbell might perhaps know him again, but then again, he might not—he was not paying much attention—the gentleman was sitting on the same side of the carriage as himself—and he had his hat on all the time. He himself was busy with his newspaper—yes—he might know him but he really could not say——

"Mr. Andrew Campbell's evidence was not worth very much, you will say. No. It was not in itself, and would not have justified any arrest were it not for the additional statements made by Mr. James Verner, manager of Messrs. Rodney & Co., colour printers.

"Mr. Verner is a personal friend of Mr. Andrew Campbell, and it appears that at Farringdon Street, where he was waiting for his train, he saw Mr. Campbell get out of a first-class railway carriage. Mr. Verner spoke to him for a second, and then, just as the train was moving off, he stepped into the same compartment which had just been vacated by the stockbroker, and the man in the tweed suit. He vaguely recollects a lady sitting in the opposite corner to his own with her face turned away from him, apparently asleep, but he paid no special attention to her. He was like nearly all business men when they are travelling—engrossed in his paper. Presently a special quotation interested him; he wished to make a note of it, took out a pencil from his waistcoat pocket, and seeing a clean piece of paste-board on the floor, he picked it up, and scribbled on it the memoranda he wished to keep. He then slipped the card into his pocketbook.

"'It was only two or three days later,' added Mr. Verner in the midst of breathless silence, 'that I had occasion to refer to these same notes again. In the meanwhile the papers had been full of the mysterious death on the Underground Railway, and the names of those connected with it were pretty familiar to me. It was, therefore, with much astonishment that on looking at the pasteboard which I had casually picked up in the railway carriage I saw the name on it "Frank Errington."'"

"There was no doubt that the sensation in Court was almost unprecedented. Never since the days of the Fenchurch Street mystery, and the trial of Smethurst had I seen so much excitement. Mind you, I was not excited—I knew by now every detail of that crime as if I had committed it myself. In fact, I could not have done it better, although I have been a student of crime for many years now. Many people there—his friends, mostly—believed that Errington was doomed. I think he thought so too, for I could see that his face was terribly white, and he now and then passed his tongue over his lips, as if they were parched.

"You see he was in the awful dilemma—a perfectly natural one, by the way—of being absolutely incapable of *proving* an alibi. The crime—if crime there was—had been committed three weeks ago. A man about town like Mr. Frank Errington might remember that he spent certain hours of a special afternoon at his club, or in the Park, but it is very doubtful in nine cases out of ten if he can find a friend who could positively swear as to having seen him there. No! no! Mr. Errington was in a tight corner and he knew it. You see, there were—

besides the evidence—two or three circumstances which did not improve matters for him. His hobby in the direction of toxicology, to begin with. The police had found in his room every description of poisonous substances, including prussic acid.

"Then, again, that journey to Marseilles, the start for Colombo, was, though perfectly innocent, a very unfortunate one. Mr. Errington had gone on an aimless voyage, but the public thought that he had fled terrified at his own crime. Sir Arthur Inglewood, however, here again displayed his marvellous skill on behalf of his client by the masterly way in which he literally turned all the witnesses for the Crown inside out.

"Having first got Mr. Andrew Campbell to state positively that in the accused he certainly did *not* recognise the man in the tweed suit, the eminent lawyer, after twenty minutes' cross-examination, had so completely upset the stockbroker's equanimity that it is very likely he would not have recognised his own office boy.

"But through all his flurry and all his annoyance Mr. Andrew Campbell remained very sure of one thing; namely, that the lady was alive and cheerful, and talking pleasantly with the man in the tweed suit up to the moment when the latter, having shaken hands with her, left her with a pleasant '*Au revoir!* Don't be late tonight.' He had heard neither scream nor struggle, and in his opinion, if the individual in the tweed suit had administered a dose of poison to his companion, it must have been with her own knowledge and free will; and the lady in the train most emphatically neither looked nor spoke like a woman prepared for a sudden and violent death.

"Mr. James Verner, against that, swore equally positively that he had stood in full view of the carriage door, from the moment that Mr. Campbell got out until he himself stepped into the compartment, that there was no one else in that carriage between Farringdon Street and Aldgate, and that the lady, to the best of his belief, had made no movement during the whole of that journey.

IV

"No; Frank Errington was *not* committed for trial on the capital charge," said the man in the corner with one of his sardonic smiles, "thanks to the cleverness of Sir Arthur Inglewood, his lawyer. He absolutely denied his identity with the man in the tweed suit, and swore he had not seen Mrs. Hazeldene since eleven o'clock in the morning of that fatal day. There was no *proof* that he had; moreover, according to Mr. Campbell's opinion, the man in the tweed suit was in all probability not the murderer. Common sense would not admit that a woman could have a deadly poison injected into her without her knowledge, while chatting pleasantly to her murderer.

"Mr. Errington lives abroad now. He is about to marry. I don't think any of his real friends for a moment believed that he committed the dastardly crime. The police think they know better. They do know this much, that it could not have been a case of suicide, that if the man who undoubtedly travelled with Mrs. Hazeldene on that fatal afternoon had no crime upon his conscience he would long ago have come forward and thrown what light he could upon the mystery.

"As to who that man was, the police in their blindness have not the faintest doubt. Under the unshakable belief that Errington is guilty they have spent the last few months in unceasing labour to try and find further and strong proofs of his guilt. But they won't find them, because there are none. There are no positive proofs against the actual murderer, for he was one of those clever blackguards who think of everything, forsee every eventuality, who know human nature well, and can foretell exactly what evidence will be brought against them, and act accordingly.

"This blackguard from the first kept the figure, the personality, of Frank Errington before his mind. Frank Errington was the dust which the scoundrel threw metaphorically in the eyes of the police, and you must admit that he succeeded in blinding them—to the extent even of making them entirely forget the one simple little sentence, overheard by Mr. Andrew Campbell, and which was, of course, the clue to the whole thing—the only slip the cunning rogue made—'*Au revoir!* Don't be late tonight.' Mrs. Hazeldene was going that night to the opera with her husband——

"You are astonished?" he added with a shrug of the shoulders, "you do not see the tragedy yet, as I have seen it before me all along. The frivolous young wife, the flirtation with the friend?—all a blind, all pretence. I took the trouble which the police should have taken immediately, of finding out something about the finances of the Hazeldene *ménage*. Money is in nine cases out of ten the keynote to a crime. I found that the will of Mary Beatrice Hazeldene had been proved by the husband, her sole executor, the estate being sworn at £15,000. I found out, moreover, that Mr. Edward Sholto Hazeldene was a poor shipper's clerk when he married the daughter of a wealthy builder in Kensington—and then I made note of the fact that the disconsolate widower had allowed his beard to grow since the death of his wife.

"There's no doubt that he was a clever rogue," added the strange creature leaning excitedly over the table, and peering into my face. "Do you know how that deadly poison was injected into the poor woman's system? By the simplest of all means, one known to every scoundrel in Southern Europe. A ring—yes! a ring, which has a tiny hollow needle capable of holding a sufficient quantity of prussic acid to have killed two persons instead of one. The man in the tweed suit shook hands with his fair companion—probably she hardly felt the prick, not sufficiently in any case to make her utter a scream. And, mind you, the scoundrel had every facility, through his friendship with Mr. Errington, of procuring what poison he required, not to mention his friend's visiting card. We cannot gauge how many months ago he began to try and copy Frank Errington in his style of dress, the cut of his moustache, his general appearance, making the change probably so gradual, that no one in his own *entourage* would notice it. He selected for his model a man his own height and build, with the same coloured hair."

"But there was the terrible risk of being identified by his fellow-traveller in the Underground," I suggested.

"Yes, there certainly was that risk; he chose to take it, and he was wise. He reckoned that several days would in any case elapse before that person, who, by the way, was a business man absorbed in his newspaper, would actually see him again. The great secret of successful crime is to study human nature," added the man in the corner, as he began looking for his hat and coat. "Edward Hazeldene knew it well."

"But the ring?" I said.

"He may have bought that when he was on his honeymoon," he suggested with a grim chuckle, "the tragedy was not planned in a week; it may have taken years to mature. But you will own that there goes a frightful scoundrel unhung. I have left you his photograph as he was a year ago, and as he is now. You will see he has shaved his beard again, but also his moustache. I fancy he is a friend now of Mr. Andrew Campbell."

He left me wondering. I don't know what I did believe; his whole story sounded so farfetched and strange. Was he really giving me the results of continued thought, or was he experimenting as to exactly how far the credulity of a lady novelist could go?

THE MYSTERIOUS DEATH IN PERCY STREET

DRAMATIS PERSONAE

THE MAN
in the corner seat of the A.B.C. shop who
explains the mystery to the
LADY JOURNALIST
who narrates the story.
MRS. OWEN
(caretaker, found dead in Percy Street).
ARTHUR GREENHILL
(suspected of Mrs. Owen's murder).
CHARLES PITT
(artist).

I

That day I went to the A.B.C. shop with a fixed purpose, that of making the man in the corner give me his views of Mrs. Owen's mysterious death in Percy Street.

It certainly had always interested and puzzled me. I had had countless arguments with relations and friends as to the three great possible solutions of the puzzle—"Accident, Suicide, Murder?"

"Undoubtedly neither accident nor suicide," he said drily.

I was not aware that I had spoken. What an uncanny habit that creature had of reading my thoughts!

"You incline to the idea, then, that Mrs. Owen was murdered. Do you know by whom?"

He laughed, and drew forth the piece of string he always fidgetted with when unravelling some mystery.

"You would like to know who murdered that old woman?" he asked at last.

"I would like to hear your views on the subject." I replied.

"I have no views," he said drily. "No one can know who murdered the woman, since no one ever saw the person who did it. No one can give the faintest description of the mysterious man who alone could have committed that clever deed, and the police are playing a game of blind man's buff."

"But you must have formed some theory of your own," I persisted.

It annoyed me that the funny creature was obstinate about this point, and I tried to nettle his vanity.

"I suppose that as a matter of fact your original remark that 'there are no such things as mysteries' does not apply universally. There is a mystery—that of the death in Percy Street, and you, like the police, are unable to fathom it."

He pulled up his eyebrows and looked at me for a minute or two.

"Confess that that murder was one of the cleverest bits of work, accomplished outside Russian diplomacy," he said with a nervous laugh, "I must say that were I the judge, called upon to pronounce sentence of death on the man who conceived that murder, I could not bring myself to do it. I would politely request the gentleman to enter our Foreign Office—we have need of such men. The whole *mise-en-scène* was truly artistic, worthy of its *milieu*—Rubens Studios in Percy Street, Tottenham Court Road.

"Have you ever noticed them? They are only studios by name, and are merely a set of rooms in a corner house, with the windows slightly enlarged, and the rents charged accordingly in consideration of that additional five inches of smoky daylight, filtering through dusty windows. On the ground floor there is the order office of some stained glass works, with a workshop in the rear, and on the first-floor landing, a small room allotted to the caretaker, with gas, coal, and fifteen shillings a week, for which princely income, she is deputed to keep tidy and clean the general aspect of the house.

"Mrs. Owen, who was the caretaker in January, 1898, was a quiet, respectable woman, who eked out her scanty wages by sundry—mostly very meagre—tips doled out to her by impecunious artists in exchange for promiscuous domestic services in and about the respective studios.

"But if Mrs. Owen's earnings were not large, they were very regular, and she had no fastidious tastes. She and her cockatoo lived on her wages; and all the tips added up, and never spent, year after year, went to swell a very comfortable little account at interest in the Bambridge Bank. This little account had mounted up to a very tidy sum, and the thrifty widow—or old maid—no one ever knew which she was—was generally referred to by the young artists of the Rubens Studios as a 'lady of means'—but this is a digression.

"No one slept on the premises except Mrs. Owen and her cockatoo. The rule was that one by one as the tenants left their rooms in the evening, they took their respective keys to the caretaker's room. She would then in the early morning, tidy and dust the studios, and the office downstairs, lay the fire and carry up coals.

"The foreman of the glassworks was the first to arrive in the morning. He had a latchkey, and let himself in, after which it was the custom of the house that he should leave the street door open for the benefit of the other tenants and their visitors.

"Usually, when he came at about nine o'clock, he found Mrs. Owen busy about the house doing her work, and he had often a brief chat with her about the weather, but on this particular morning of February 2nd he neither saw nor heard her. However, as the shop had been tidied and the fire laid, he surmised that Mrs. Owen had finished her work earlier than usual, and thought no more about it. One by one the tenants of the Studios turned up, and the day sped on without anyone's attention being drawn noticeably to the fact the caretaker had not appeared upon the scene.

"It had been a bitterly cold night, and the day was even worse; a cutting northeasterly gale was blowing, there had been a great deal of snow during the night which lay quite thick on the ground, and at five o'clock in the afternoon when the last glimmer of the pale winter daylight had disappeared, the confraternity of the brush put palette and easel aside and prepared to go home. The first to leave was Mr. Charles Pitt; he locked up his studio and as usual took his key into the caretaker's room.

"He had just opened the door when an icy blast literally struck him in the face, both the windows were wide open, and the snow and sleet were beating thickly into the room, forming already a white carpet upon the floor.

"The room was in semiobscurity, and at first Mr. Pitt saw nothing, but instinctively realising that something was wrong, he lit a match, and saw before him the spectacle of that awful and mysterious tragedy which has ever since puzzled both police and public. On the floor, already half covered by the drifting snow, lay the body of Mrs. Owen face downwards, in a nightgown, with feet and ankles bare, and these and her hands were of a deep purple colour; whilst in a corner of the room huddled up with the cold, the body of the cockatoo lay stark and stiff."

II

"At first there was only talk of a terrible accident, the result of some inexplicable carelessness which perhaps the evidence at the inquest would help to elucidate.

"Medical assistance came too late, the unfortunate woman was indeed dead, frozen to death, inside her own room. Further examination, showed that she had received a severe blow at the back of the head, which must have stunned her and caused her to fall, helpless, beside the open window. Temperature at five degrees below zero had done the rest. Detective Inspector Howell discovered close to the window a wrought-iron gas bracket, the height of which corresponded exactly with the bruise at the back of Mrs. Owen's head.

"Hardly had a couple of days elapsed when public curiosity was whetted by a few startling headlines, such as the halfpenny evening papers alone know how to concoct.

"'The mysterious death in Percy Street,' 'Is it Suicide or Murder?' 'Thrilling details—Strange developments.' 'Sensational Arrest.'

"What had happened was simply this:

"At the inquest a few certainly very curious facts connected with Mrs. Owen's life had come to light, and this had led to the apprehension of a young man of very respectable parentage on a charge of being concerned in the tragic death of the unfortunate caretaker.

"To begin with, it happened that her life, which in an ordinary way should have been very monotonous and regular, seemed at any rate latterly to have been more than usually chequered and excited. Every witness who had known her in the past concurred in the statement that since October last a great change had come over the worthy and honest woman.

"I happen to have a photo of Mrs. Owen as she was before this great change occurred in her quiet and unevenful life, and which led as far as the poor soul was concerned to such disastrous results.

"Here she is to the life," added the funny creature, placing the photo before me—"as respectable, as stodgy, as uninteresting as it is well possible for a member of your charming sex to be; not a face you will admit to induce any youngster to temptation or to lead him to commit a crime.

"Nevertheless one day, all the tenants of the Rubens Studios were surprised and shocked to see Mrs. Owen, quiet respectable Mrs. Owen, sallying forth at six o'clock in the afternoon, attired in an extravagant bonnet and a cloak trimmed with imitation astrakhan which—slightly open in front—displayed a gold locket and chain of astonishing proportions.

"Many were the comments, the hints, the bits of sarcasm levelled at the worthy woman by the frivolous confraternity of the brush.

"The plot thickened when from that day forth a complete change came over the worthy caretaker of the Rubens Studios. While she appeared day after day before the astonished gaze of the tenants and the scandalised looks of the neighbours, attired in new and extravagant dresses, her work was hopelessly neglected, and she was always 'out' when wanted.

"There was, of course, much talk and comment in various parts of the Rubens Studios on the subject of Mrs. Owen's 'dissipations.' The tenants began to put two and two together, and after a very little while the general concensus of opinion became firmly established that the honest caretaker's demoralisation coincided week for week, almost day for day, with young Greenhill's establishment in No. 8 Studio.

"Everyone had remarked that he stayed much later in the evening than anyone else, and yet no one presumed that he stayed for the purposes of work. Suspicions soon rose to certainty when Mrs. Owen and Arthur Greenhill were seen by one of the glass workmen dining together at Gambia's Restaurant in Tottenham Court Road.

"The workman, who was having a cup of tea at the counter, noticed particularly that when the bill was paid, the money came out of Mrs. Owen's purse. The dinner had been sumptuous—veal cutlets, a cut from the joint, dessert, coffee and liqueurs. Finally the pair left the restaurant apparently very gay, young Greenhill smoking a choice cigar.

"Irregularities such as these were bound sooner or later to come to the ears and eyes of Mr. Allman, the landlord of the Rubens Studios; and a month after the New Year, without further warning, he gave her a week's notice to quit his house.

"'Mrs. Owen did not seem the least bit upset when I gave her notice,' Mr. Allman declared in his evidence; 'on the contrary, she told me that she had ample means, and had only worked latterly for the sake of something to do. She added that she had plenty of friends who would look after her, for she had a nice little pile to leave to anyone who would know how "to get the right side of her."'

"Nevertheless, in spite of this cheerful interview, Miss Bedford, the tenant of No. 6 Studio, had stated that when she took her key to the caretaker's room at 6:30 that afternoon, she found Mrs. Owen in tears. The caretaker refused to be comforted, nor would she speak of her trouble to Miss Bedford.

"Twenty-four hours later she was found dead.

"The jury returned an open verdict, and Detective Inspector Jones was charged by the police to make some inquiries about young Mr. Greenhill, whose intimacy with the unfortunate woman, had been universally commented upon.

"The detective however, pushed his investigations as far as the Bambridge Bank. There he discovered that after her interview with Mr. Allman, Mrs. Owen had withdrawn what money she had on deposit, some £800, the result of twenty-five years' saving and thrift.

"The immediate result of Detective Inspector Jone's labours was that Mr. Arthur Greenhill, Lithographer, was brought before the magistrate at Bow Street on the charge of being concerned in the death of Mrs. Owen, caretaker of the Rubens Studios, Percy Street.

"Now that Magisterial inquiry is one of the few interesting ones which I had the misfortune to miss," continued the man in the corner, with a nervous shake of the shoulders. "But you know as well as I do, how the attitude of the young prisoner impressed the magistrate and police so unfavourably, that with every new witness brought forward, his position became more and more unfortunate.

"Yet he was a good-looking, rather coarsely built young fellow, with one of those awful Cockney accents which literally make one jump. But he looked painfully nervous, stammered at every word spoken, and repeatedly gave answers entirely at random.

"His father acted as lawyer for him, a rough-looking elderly man, who had the appearance of a common country attorney, rather than of a London solicitor.

"The police had built up a fairly strong case against the lithographer. Medical evidence revealed nothing new: Mrs. Owen had died from exposure, the blow at the back of the head not being sufficiently serious to cause anything but temporary disablement. When the medical officer had been called in, death had intervened for some time; it was quite impossible to say how long, whether one hour or five or twelve.

"The appearance and state of the room, when the unfortunate woman was found by Mr. Charles Pitt, were again gone over in minute detail. Mrs. Owen's clothes, which she had worn during the day, were folded neatly on a chair. The key of her cupboard was in the pocket of her dress. The door had been slightly ajar, but both the windows were wide open; one of them, which had the sash-line broken, had been fastened up most scientifically with a piece of rope.

"Mrs. Owen had obviously undressed preparatory to going to bed, and the magistrate very naturally soon made the remark, how untenable the theory of an accident must be. No one in their five senses would undress, with a temperature at below zero, and the windows wide open.

"The cashier of the Bambridge related the caretaker's visit at the bank.

"'It was then about one o'clock,' he stated, 'Mrs. Owen called and presented a cheque to self for £827, the amount of her balance. She seemed exceedingly happy and cheerful, and talked about needing plenty of cash, as she was going abroad to join her nephew, for whom she would in future keep house. I warned her about being sufficiently careful with so large a sum, and parting from it injudiciously, as women of her class are very apt to do. She laughingly declared that not only was she careful of it in the present, but meant to be so for the far-off future, for she intended to go that very day to a lawyer's office and to make a will.'

"The cashier's evidence was certainly startling in the extreme, since in the widow's room no trace of any kind was found of any money; against that, two of the notes handed over by the bank to Mrs. Owen on that day were cashed by young Greenhill on the very morning of her mysterious death. One was handed in by him to the West End Clothier's Company, in payment for a suit of clothes, and the other he changed at the Post Office in Oxford Street.

"After that all the evidence had of necessity to be gone through again on the subject of young Greenhill's intimacy with Mrs. Owen. He listened to it all with an air of the most painful nervousness, his cheeks were positively green, his lips seemed dry and parched, for he repeatedly passed his tongue over them, and when Constable E 18 deposed that at 2 A.M. on the morning of February 2nd he had seen the accused and spoken to him at the corner of Percy Street and Tottenham Court Road, young Greenhill all but fainted.

"The contention of the police was that the caretaker had been murdered and robbed during that night, before she went to bed, that young Greenhill had done the murder, seeing that he was the only person known to have been intimate with the woman, and that it was moreover proved unquestionably that he was in the immediate neighborhood of the Rubens Studios at an extraordinarily late hour of the night.

"His own account of himself, and of that same night, could certainly not be called very satisfactory. Mrs. Owen was a relative of his late mother's he declared. He himself was a lithographer by trade, with a good deal of time and leisure on his hands. He certainly had employed some of that time in taking the old woman to various places of amusement. He had on more than one occasion suggested that she should give up menial work, and come and live with him, but, unfortunately, she was a great deal imposed upon by her nephew, a man of the name of Owen, who exploited the good-natured woman in every possible way, and who had on more than one occasion made severe attacks upon her savings at the Bambridge Bank.

"Severely cross-examined by the prosecuting counsel about this supposed relative of Mrs. Owen, Greenhill admitted that he did not know him, had in fact never seen him. He knew that his name was Owen and that was all. His chief occupation consisted in sponging on the kindhearted old woman, but he only went to see her in the evenings, when he presumably knew that she would be alone, and invariably after all the tenants of the Rubens Studios had left for the day.

"I don't know whether at this point, it strikes you at all, as it did both magistrate and counsel, that there was a direct contradiction in this statement, and that made by the cashier of the Bambridge, on the subject of his last conversation with Mrs. Owen. 'I am going abroad to join my nephew, for whom I am going to keep house,' was what the unfortunate woman had said.

"Now Greenhill, in spite of his nervousness and at times contradictory answers, strictly adhered to his point, that there was a nephew in London, who came frequently to see his Aunt.

"Anyway, the sayings of the murdered woman could not be taken as evidence in law. Mr. Greenhill senior put the objection, adding: 'There may have been two nephews,' which the magistrate and the prosecution were bound to admit.

"With regard to the night immediately preceding Mrs. Owen's death, Greenhill stated that he had been with her to the theatre, had seen her home, and had had some supper with her in her room. Before he left her, at 2 A.M., she had of her own accord made him a present of £10, saying: 'I am a sort of Aunt to you, Arthur, and if you don't have it, Bill is sure to get it.'

"She had seemed rather worried in the early part of the evening, but later on she cheered up.

"'Did she speak at all about this nephew of hers or about her money affairs?' asked the magistrate.

"Again the young man hesitated, but said, 'No! she did not mention either Owen or her money affairs.'

"If I remember rightly," added the man in the corner, "for recollect, I was not present, the case was here adjourned. But the magistrate would not grant bail. Greenhill was removed looking more dead than alive—though everyone remarked that Mr. Greenhill senior looked determined and not the least worried. In the course of his examination on behalf of his son, of the medical officer and one or two other witnesses, he had very ably tried to confuse them, on the subject of the hour, at which Mrs. Owen was last known to be alive.

"He made a very great point of the fact that the usual morning's work was done throughout the house, when the inmates arrived. Was it conceivable, he argued, that a woman would do that kind of work overnight, especially as she was going to the theatre, and therefore would wish to dress in her smarter clothes? It certainly was a very nice point levelled against the prosecution, who promptly retorted: Just as conceivable as that a woman in those circumstances of life, should, having done her work, undress beside an open window at nine o'clock in the morning with the snow beating into the room.

"Now it seems that Mr. Greenhill senior could produce any amount of witnesses who could help to prove a conclusive alibi on behalf of his son, if only sometime subsequent to that fatal 2 A.M. the murdered woman had been seen alive by some chance passerby.

"However, he was an able man, and an earnest one, and I fancy the magistrate felt some sympathy for his strenuous endeavours on his son's behalf. He granted a week's adjournment which seemed to satisfy Mr. Greenhill completely.

"In the meanwhile the papers had talked and almost exhausted the subject of the mystery in Percy Street. There had been, as you no doubt know from personal experience, innumerable arguments on the puzzling alternatives:

"Accident?

"Suicide?

"Murder?

"The court was crowded when the case against young Greenhill was resumed. It needed no great penetration to remark at once, that the prisoner looked more hopeful, and his father quite elated.

"Again a great deal of minor evidence was taken, and then came the turn of the defence. Mr. Greenhill called Mrs. Hall, confectioner, of Percy Street, opposite the Rubens Studios. She deposed that at 8 o'clock in the morning of February 23rd, while she was tidying her shop window, she saw the caretaker of the Studios opposite, as usual, on her knees, her head and body wrapped in a shawl, cleaning her front steps. Her husband also saw Mrs. Owen, and Mrs. Hall remarked to her husband how thankful she was that her own shop had tiled steps, which did not need scrubbing on so cold a morning.

"Mr. Hall, confectioner, of the same address, corroborated this statement, and Mr. Greenhill, with absolute triumph, produced a third witness, Mrs. Martin, of Percy Street, who from her window on the second floor, had at 7:30 A.M. seen the caretaker shaking mats outside her front door. The description this witness gave of Mrs. Owen's getup, with the shawl round her head coincided point by point with that given by Mr. and Mrs. Hall.

"After that Mr. Greenhill's task became an easy one; his son was at home having his breakfast at 8 o'clock that morning, not only himself but his servants would testify to that.

"The weather had been so bitter that the whole of that day Arthur had not stirred from his own fireside. Mrs. Owen was murdered after 8 A.M. on the day, since she was seen alive by three people at that hour, therefore his son could not have murdered Mrs. Owen. The police must find the criminal elsewhere, or else bow to the opinion originally expressed by the public that Mrs. Owen had met with a terrible untoward accident, or that perhaps she may have wilfully sought her own death in that extraordinary and tragic fashion.

"Before young Greenhill was finally discharged, one or two witnesses were again examined, chief among these being the foreman of the glassworks. He had turned up at the Rubens Studios at 9 o'clock and been in business all day. He averred positively that he did not specially notice any suspicious-looking individual crossing the hall that day. 'But,' he remarked with a smile, 'I don't sit and watch everyone who goes up and down stairs. I am too busy for that. The street door is always left open; anyone can walk in, up or down, who knows the way.'

"That there was a mystery in connection with Mrs. Owen's death—of that the police have remained perfectly convinced; whether young Greenhill held the key of that mystery or not, they have never found out to this day.

"I could enlighten them as to the cause of the young lithographer's anxiety at the magisterial inquiry, but, I assure you, I do not care to do the work of the police for them. Why should I? Greenhill will never suffer from unjust suspicions. He, and his father alone—besides myself—know in what a terribly tight corner he all but found himself.

"The young man did not reach home till nearly *five* o'clock that morning. His last train had gone; he had to walk, lost his way, and wandered about Hampstead for hours. Think what his position would have been if the worthy confectioners of Percy Street had not seen Mrs. Owen 'wrapped up in a shawl, on her knees, doing the front steps.' Moreover, Mr. Greenhill, senior, is a solicitor, who has a small office in John Street, Bedford Row.

"The afternoon before her death, Mrs. Owen had been to that office and had there made a will by which she left all her savings to young Arthur Greenhill, lithographer. Had that will been in other than paternal hands, it would have been proved, in the natural course of such things, and one other link would have been added to the chain, which nearly dragged Arthur Greenhill to the gallows—'the link of a very strong motive.'

"Can you wonder that the young man turned livid, until such time as it was proved beyond a doubt that the murdered woman was alive hours after he had reached the safe shelter of his home?"

III

"I saw you smile, when I used the word 'Murdered,'" continued the man in the corner, growing quite excited, now that he was approaching the *dénouement* of his story. "I know that the public, after the magistrate had discharged Arthur Greenhill, were quite satisfied to think that the mystery in Percy Street was a case of accident—or suicide."

"No," I replied, "there could be no question of suicide, for two very distinct reasons."

He looked at me with some degree of astonishment. I supposed he was amazed at my venturing to form an opinion of my own.

"And may I ask what, in your opinion, these reasons are?" he asked very sarcastically.

"To begin with, the question of money," I said—"has any more of it been traced so far?"

"Not another £5 note," he said with a chuckle, "they were all cashed in Paris, during the Exhibition, and you have no conception, how easy a thing that is to do at any or the hotels or smaller *Agents de Change.*"

"That nephew was a clever blackguard," I commented.

"You believe then, in the existence of that nephew?"

"Why should I doubt it? Someone must have existed, who was sufficiently familiar with the house to go about in it in the middle of the day, without attracting anyone's attention."

"In the middle of the day?" he said with a chuckle.

"Any time after 8:30 in the morning. "

"So you too, believe in the 'caretaker, wrapped up in a shawl,' cleaning her front steps?" he queried.

"But——"

"It never struck you, in spite of the training your intercourse with me must have given you, that the person who carefully did all the work in the Rubens Studios, laid the fires and carried up the coals, merely did it in order to gain time; in order that the bitter frost might really and effectually do its work, and Mrs. Owen be not missed until she was truly dead."

"But —— " I suggested again.

"It never struck you that one of the greatest secrets of successful crime is to lead the police astray with regard to the time when the crime was committed. That was, if you remember, the great point in the Regent's Park murder.

"In this case the 'nephew' since we admit his existence, would—even if he were ever found, which is doubtful—be able to prove as good an alibi as young Greenhill."

"But I don't understand——"

"How the murder was committed?" he said eagerly! "Surely you can see it all for yourself, since you admit the 'nephew'—a scamp perhaps—who sponges on the good-natured woman. He terrorises and threatens her, so much so that she fancies her money is no longer safe even in the Bambridge Bank. Women of that class are apt at times to mistrust the Bank of England. Anyway she withdraws her money. Who knows what she meant to do with it, the immediate future?

"In any case, after her death she wishes to secure it to a young man whom she likes, and who has known how to win her good graces. That afternoon, the nephew begs, intreats for more money, they have a row; the poor woman is in tears, and is only temporarily consoled by a pleasant visit at the theatre.

"At 2 o'clock in the morning young Greenhill parts from her. Two minutes later the nephew knocks at the door. He comes with a plausible tale of having missed his last train, and asks for a 'shakedown' somewhere in the house. The good-natured woman suggests a sofa in one the studios, and then quietly prepares to go to bed. The rest is very simple and elementary. The nephew sneaks into his Aunt's room, finds her standing in her nightgown; terrified, she staggers, knocks her head against the gas bracket, and falls on the floor stunned, while the nephew seeks for her keys and takes possession of the £800. You will admit that the subsequent *mise-en-scène* is worthy of a genius.

"No struggle, not the usual hideous accessories round a crime. Only the open windows, the bitter northeasterly gale, and the heavily falling snow—two silent accomplices, as silent as the dead."

"After that, the murderer with perfect presence of mind, busies himself in the house, doing the work which will insure that Mrs. Owen shall not be missed at any rate for some time. He dusts and tidies, he even slips on his Aunt's skirt and bodice, wraps his head in a shawl, and boldly allows those neighbours who are astir to see what they believe to be Mrs. Owen. Then he goes back to her room, resumes his normal appearance, and quietly leaves the house."

"He may have been seen."

"He *was* seen by two or three people, but no one thought anything of seeing a man leave the house at that hour. It was very cold, the snow was falling thickly, and as he wore a muffler round the lower part of his face, those who saw him would not undertake to know him again."

"That man was never seen or heard of again?" I asked.

"He has disappeared off the face of the earth. The police are searching for him, and perhaps some day they will find him—then society will be rid of one of the most ingenious men of the age."

IV

He had paused, absorbed in meditation. I also was silent. Some memory too vague as yet to take a definite form, was persistently haunting me—one thought was hammering away in my brain, and playing havoc with my nerves. That thought was the inexplicable feeling with me, that there was something in connection with that hideous crime which I ought to recollect, something which—if I could only remember what it was—would give me the clue to the tragic mystery, and for once insure my triumph over this self-conceited and sarcastic scarecrow in the corner.

He was watching me through his great bone-rimmed spectacles, and I could see the knuckles of his bony hands, just above the top of the table fidgeting, fidgeting, fidgeting, till I wondered if there existed another set of fingers in the world who could undo the knots his lean ones made in that tiresome piece of string.

Then suddenly—*à propos* of nothing, *I remembered*—the whole thing stood before me, short and clear like a vivid flash of lightning: Mrs. Owen lying dead in the snow, beside her own open window; one of them with a broken sash-line, tied up most scientifically with a piece of string. I remember the talk there had been at the time about this improvised sash-line.

That was after young Greenhill had been discharged, and the question of suicide had been voted an impossibility.

I remember that in the illustrated papers photographs appeared of this wonderfully knotted piece of string, so contrived that the weight of the frame could but tighten the knots, and thus keep the window open. I remembered that people deduced many things from that improvised sash-line, chief among these deductions being that the murderer was a sailor—so wonderful, so complicated, so numerous were the knots which secured that window frame.

But I knew better—in my mind's eye I saw those fingers rendered doubly nervous by the fearful cerebral excitement, grasping at first mechanically, even thoughtlessly, a bit of twine with which to secure the window; then the ruling habit strongest through all, I could see it; the lean and ingenious fingers fidgeting, fidgeting with that piece of string, tying knot after knot, more wonderful, more complicated, than any I had yet witnessed.

"If I were you," I said, without daring to look into that corner where he sat, "I would break myself of the habit of perpetually making knots in a piece of string."

He did not reply, and at last I ventured to look up—the corner was empty, and through the glass door beyond the desk where he had just deposited his few coppers, I saw the tails of his tweed coat, his extraordinary hat, his meagre, shrivelled-up personality, fast disappearing down the street.

I have never set eyes on the man in the corner from that day to this.

THE DUBLIN MYSTERY

DRAMATIS PERSONAE

THE MAN IN THE CORNER
of the A.B.C. shop who tells the story to
THE LADY JOURNALIST.
PERCIVAL BROOKS.
MURRAY BROOKS
(*his younger brother*).
HENRY ORANMORE, K.C.   WALTER HIBBERT
(*barristers*).
JOHN O'NEIL
(*butler to the Brooks*).

I

"I always thought that the history of that forged will was about as interesting as any I had read," said the man in the corner that day. He had been silent for some time, and was meditatively sorting and looking through a packet of small photographs in his pocketbook. I guessed that some of these would presently be placed before me for my inspection, and I had not long to wait.

"That is old Brooks," he said, pointing to one of the photographs, "Millionaire Brooks as he was called, and these are his two sons, Percival and Murray. It was a curious case, wasn't it? Personally I don't wonder that the police were completely at sea. If a member of that highly estimable force happened to be as clever as the clever author of that forged will, we should have very few undetected crimes in this country."

"That is why I always try to persuade you to give our poor ignorant police the benefit of your great insight and wisdom." I said.

"I know," he said blandly, "you have been most kind in that way, but I am only an amateur. Crime interests me only when it resembles a clever game of chess, with many intricate moves which all tend to one solution, the checkmating of the antagonist—the detective force of the country. Now confess that, in the Dublin mystery, the clever police there were absolutely checkmated."

"Absolutely."

"Just as the public was. There were actually two crimes there which have completely baffled detection. The murder of Patrick Wethered the lawyer, and the forged will of Millionaire Brooks. There are not many millionaires in Ireland; no wonder old Brooks was a notability in his way, since his business—bacon-curing, I believe it is—is said to be worth over £2,000,000 of solid money.

"His younger son Murray was a refined, highly-educated man, and was moreover the apple of his father's eye, as he was the spoilt darling of Dublin society; good-looking, a splendid dancer, and a perfect rider, he was the acknowledged 'catch' of the matrimonial market of Ireland, and many a very aristocratic house was opened hospitably to the favourite son of the millionaire.

"Of course Percival Brooks, the eldest son, would inherit the bulk of the old man's property and also probably the larger share in the business; he, too, was good-looking, more so than his brother, he too, rode, danced, and talked well, but it was many years ago that mammas with marriageable daughters had given up all hopes of Percival Brooks as a probable son-in-law. That young man's infatuation for Maisie Fortescue, a lady of undoubted charm but very doubtful antecedents, who had astonished the London and Dublin music halls with her extravagant dances—was too well known and too old-established to encourage any hopes in other quarters.

"Whether Percival Brooks would ever marry Maisie Fortescue was thought to be very doubtful. Old Brooks had the full disposal of all his wealth, and it would have fared ill with Percival if he introduced an undesirable wife into the magnificent Fitzwilliam Place establishment.

"That is how matters stood," continued the man in the corner, "when Dublin society one morning learnt with deep regret and dismay that old Brooks had died very suddenly at his residence after only a few hours' illness. At first it was generally understood that he had had an apoplectic stroke; anyway, he had been at business hale and hearty as ever the day before his death, which occurred late on the evening of December 1st.

"It was the morning papers of December 2nd which told the sad news to the readers, and it was those selfsame papers which on that eventful morning contained another, even more startling piece of news, which proved the prelude to a series of sensations, such as tranquil, placid Dublin had not experienced for many years. This was, that on that very afternoon which saw the death of Dublin's greatest millionaire, Mr. Patrick Wethered, his solicitor, was murdered in Phoenix Park at five o'clock in the afternoon, while actually walking to his own house from his visit to his client in Fitzwilliam Place.

"Patrick Wethered was as well known as the proverbial town pump;

his mysterious and tragic death filled all Dublin with dismay. The lawyer, who was a man sixty years of age, had been struck on the back of his head by a heavy stick, garrotted, and subsequently robbed, for neither money, watch, or pocketbook were found upon his person, whilst the police soon gathered from Patrick Wethered's household that he had left home at two o'clock that afternoon, carrying both watch and pocketbook, and undoubtedly money as well.

"An inquest was held, and a verdict of wilful murder was found against some person or persons unknown.

"But Dublin had not exhausted its stock of sensations yet. Millionaire Brooks had been buried with due pomp and magnificence and his will had been proved (his business and personality being estimated at £2,500,000), by Percival Gordon Brooks, his eldest son and sole executor. The younger son, Murray, who had devoted the best years of his life to being a friend and companion to his father, while Percival ran after ballet dancers and music-hall stars—Murray who had avowedly been the apple of his fathers eye in consequence—was left with a miserly pittance of £300 a year, and no share whatever in the gigantic business of Brooks & Sons, bacon curers of Dublin.

"Something had evidently happened within the precincts of the Brooks' town mansion, which the public and Dublin society tried in vain to fathom. Elderly mammas and blushing *débutantes* were already thinking of the best means whereby next season they might more easily show the cold shoulder to young Murray Brooks, who had so suddenly become a hopeless 'detrimental' in the marriage market, when all these sensations terminated in one gigantic, overwhelming bit of scandal, which for the next three months furnished food for gossip in every drawing room in Dublin.

"Mr. Murray Brooks, namely, had entered a claim for probate of a will made by his father in 1891, declaring that the later will made the very day of his father's death and proved by his brother as sole executor was null and void, that will being a forgery."

II

"The facts that transpired in connection with this extraordinary case were sufficiently mysterious to puzzle everybody. As I told you before, all Mr. Brooks' friends never quite grasped the idea that the old man should so completely have cut off his favourite son with the proverbial shilling.

"You see Percival had always been a thorn in the old man's flesh. Horse racing, gambling, theatres, and music halls were, in the old pork-butcher's eyes, so many deadly sins which his son committed every day of his life, and all the Fitzwilliam Place household could testify to the many and bitter quarrels which had arisen between father and son over the latter's gambling or racing debts. Many people asserted that Brooks would sooner have left his money to charitable institutions than seen it squandered upon the brightest stars that adorned the music-hall stage.

"The case came up for hearing early in the spring. In the meanwhile Percival Brooks had given up his racecourse associates, settled down in the Fitzwilliam Place mansion and conducted his father's business, without a manager, but with all the energy and forethought which he had previously devoted to more unworthy causes.

"Murray had elected not to stay on in the old house; no doubt associations were of too painful and recent a nature; he was boarding with the family of a Mr. Wilson Hibbert, who was the late Patrick Wethered's, the murdered lawyer's, partner. They were quiet, homely people, who lived in a very pokey little house in Kilkenny Street, and poor Murray must, in spite of his grief, have felt very bitterly the change from his luxurious quarters in his father's mansion to his present tiny room and homely meals.

"Percival Brooks, who was now drawing an income of over a hundred thousand a year was very severely criticised for adhering so strictly to the letter of his father's will, and only paying his brother that paltry £300 a year, which was very literally but the crumbs off his own magnificent dinner table.

"The issue of that contested will case was therefore awaited with eager interest. In the meanwhile the police, who had at first seemed fairly loquacious on the subject of the murder of Mr. Patrick Wethered, suddenly became strangely reticent and by their very reticence aroused a certain amount of uneasiness in the public mind, until one day the *Irish Times* published the following extraordinary, enigmatic paragraph.

"'We hear on authority, which cannot be questioned, that certain extraordinary developments are expected in connection with the brutal murder of our distinguished townsman Mr. Wethered; the police, in fact, are vainly trying to keep it a secret that they hold a clue which is as important as it is sensational, and that they only await the impending issue of a well-known litigation in the probate court to effect an arrest.'

"The Dublin public flocked to the court to hear the arguments in the great will case. I myself journeyed down to Dublin. As soon as I succeeded in fighting my way to the densely crowded court, I took stock of the various actors in the drama, which I as a spectator was prepared to enjoy. There were Percival Brooks and Murray his brother, the two litigants, both good-looking and well dressed and both striving, by keeping up a running conversation with their lawyer, to appear unconcerned and confident of the issue. With Percival Brooks was Henry Oranmore, the eminent Irish K.C., whilst Walter Hibbert, a rising young barrister, the son of Wilson Hibbert, appeared for Murray.

"The will of which the latter claimed probate was one dated 1891, and had been made by Mr. Brooks during a severe illness which threatened to end his days. This will had been deposited in the hands of Messrs. Wethered & Hibbert, solicitors to the deceased, and by it Mr. Brooks left his personalty equally divided between his two sons, but had left his business entirely to his youngest son, with a charge of £2000 a year upon it, payable to Percival. You see that Murray Brooks therefore had a very deep interest in that second will being found null and void.

"Old Mr. Hibbert had very ably instructed his son, and Walter Hibbert's opening speech was exceedingly clever. He would show, he said, on behalf of his client, that the will dated December 1st, 1900 could never have been made by the late Mr. Brooks as it was absolutely contrary to his avowed intentions, and that if the late Mr. Brooks did on the day in question make any fresh will at all, it certainly was *not* the one proved by Mr. Percival Brooks, for that was absolutely a forgery from beginning to end. Mr. Walter Hibbert proposed to call several witnesses in support of both these points.

"On the other hand, Mr. Henry Oranmore, K.C., very ably and courteously replied that he too had several witnesses to prove that Mr. Brooks certainly did make a will on the day in question, and that whatever his intentions may have been in the past, he must have modified them on the day of his death, for the will proved by Mr. Percival Brooks was found after his death under his pillow, duly signed and witnessed and in every way legal.

"Then the battle began in sober earnest. It chiefly centred round the prosaic figure of John O'Neill, the butler at Fitzwilliam Place, who had been in Mr. Brooks' family for thirty years.

"'I was clearing away my breakfast things,' said John, 'when I heard the master's voice in the study close by. Oh my, he was that angry! I could hear the words "disgrace," and "villain," and "liar," and "ballet dancer," and one or two other ugly words as applied to some female lady, which I would not like to repeat. At first I did not take much notice, as I was quite used to hearing my poor dear master having words with Mr. Percival. So I went downstairs carrying my breakfast things; but I had just started cleaning my silver when the study bell goes ringing violently, and I hear Mr. Percival's voice shouting in the hall: "John! quick! Send for Dr. Mulligan at once. Your master is not well! Send one of the men, and you come up and help me get Mr. Brooks to bed."

"'I sent one of the grooms for the doctor,' continued John, who seemed still affected at the recollection of his poor master, to whom he had evidently been very much attached, 'and I went up to see Mr. Brooks. I found him lying on the study floor, his head supported in Mr. Percival's arms. "My father has fallen in a faint," said the young master; "help me to get him up to his room before Dr. Mulligan comes."

"'Mr. Percival looked very white and upset, which was only natural; and when we had got my poor master to bed, I asked if I should not go and break the news to Mr. Murray, who had gone to business an hour ago. However, before Mr. Percival had time to give me an order, the doctor came. I thought I had seen death plainly writ in my master's face, and when I showed the doctor out an hour later, and he told me that he would be back directly, I knew that the end was near.

"'Mr. Brooks rang for me a minute or two later. He told me to send at once for Mr. Wethered, or else for Mr. Hibbert, if Mr. Wethered could not come. "I haven't many hours to live, John," he says to me— "my heart is broke, the doctor says my heart is broke. A man shouldn't marry and have children, John, for they will sooner or later break his heart." I was so upset I couldn't speak; but I sent round at once for Mr. Wethered, who came himself just about three o'clock that afternoon.

"'After he had been with my master about an hour, I was called in, and Mr. Wethered said to me that Mr. Brooks wished me and one other of us servants to witness that he had signed a paper which was on a table by his bedside. I called Pat Mooney, the head footman, and before us both Mr. Brooks put his name at the bottom of that paper. Then Mr. Wethered give me the pen and told me to write my name as a witness, and that Pat Mooney was to do the same. After that we were both told that we could go.'

"He was present on the following day when the undertakers, who had come to lay his master out, found a paper underneath his pillow. John O'Neill, who recognised the paper as the one to which he had appended his signature the day before, took it to Mr. Percival, and gave it into his hands.

"In answer to Mr. Walter Hibbert, John asserted positively that he took the paper from the undertaker's hand and went straight with it to Mr. Percival's room.

"'He was alone,' said John, 'I gave him the paper. He just glanced at it, and I thought he looked rather astonished, but he said nothing, and I at once left the room.'

"'When you say that you recognised the paper as the one which you had seen your master sign the day before, how did you actually recognise that it was the same paper?' asked Mr. Hibbert amidst breathless interest on the part of the spectators. I narrowly observed the witness's face.

"'It looked exactly the same paper to me, sir,' replied John somewhat vaguely.

"'Did you look at the contents, then?'

"'No, sir; certainly not.'

"'Had you done so the day before?'

"'No, sir, only at my master's signature.'

"'Then you only thought by the *outside* look of the paper that it was the same.'

"'It looked the same thing, sir,' persisted John obstinately.

"You see," continued the man in the corner, leaning eagerly forward across the narrow marble table, "the contention of Murray Brooks' adviser was that Mr. Brooks, having made a will and hidden it—for some reason or other under his pillow—that will had fallen, through the means related by John O'Neill, into the hands of Mr. Percival Brooks, who had destroyed it and substituted a forged one in its place, which adjudged the whole of Mr. Brooks' millions to himself. It was a terrible and very daring accusation directed against a gentlemen who, in spite of his many wild oats sowed in early youth, was a prominent and important figure in Irish high-life.

"All those present were aghast at what they heard, and the whispered comments I could hear around me showed me that public opinion at least did not uphold Mr. Murray Brooks' daring accusation against his brother.

"But John O'Neill had not finished his evidence, and Mr. Walter Hibbert had a bit of sensation still up his sleeve. He had, namely, produced a paper, the will proved by Mr. Percival Brooks, and had asked John O'Neill if once again he recognised the paper.

"'Certainly, sir,' said John unhesitatingly, 'that is the one the undertaker found under my poor dead master's pillow, and which I took to Mr. Percival's room immediately.'

"Then the paper was unfolded and placed before the witness.

"'Now, Mr. O'Neill, will you tell me if that is your signature?'

"John looked at it for a moment; then he said: 'Excuse me, sir,' and produced a pair of spectacles which he carefully adjusted before he again examined the paper. Then he thoughtfully shook his head.

"'It don't look much like my writing, sir,' he said at last. 'That is to say,' he added, by way of elucidating the matter, 'it does look like my writing, but then I don't think it is.'

"There was at that moment a look in Mr. Percival Brooks' face,"

continued the man in the corner quietly, "which then and there gave
me the whole history of that quarrel, that illness of Mr. Brooks, of the
will, aye! and of the murder of Patrick Wethered too.

"All I wondered at was how every one of those learned counsel on
both sides did not get the clue just the same as I did, but went on argu-
ing, speechifying, cross-examining for nearly a week, until they arrived
at the one conclusion which was inevitable from the very first, namely,
that the will *was* a forgery—a gross, clumsy, idiotic forgery, since both
John O'Neill and Pat Mooney, the two witnesses, absolutely repudiated the signatures as their own. The only successful bit of calligraphy the forger had done was the signature of old Mr. Brooks.

"It was a very curious fact, and one which had undoubtedly aided
the forger in accomplishing his work quickly, that Mr. Wethered the
lawyer having, no doubt, realised that Mr. Brooks had not many moments in life to spare, had not drawn up the usual engrossed, magnificent document dear to the lawyer heart, but had used for his
client's will one of those regular printed forms which can be purchased
at any stationer's.

"Mr. Percival Brooks, of course, flatly denied the serious allegation
brought against him. He admitted that the butler had brought him the
document the morning after his father's death, and that he certainly,
on glancing at it, had been very much astonished to see that that document was his father's will. Against that he declared that its contents
did not astonish him in the slightest degree, that he himself knew of
the testator's intentions, but that he certainly thought his father had
intrusted the will to the care of Mr. Wethered, who did all his business
for him.

"'I only very cursorily glanced at the signature,' he concluded,
speaking in a perfectly calm, clear voice, 'you must understand that
the thought of forgery was very far from my mind, and that my
father's signature is exceedingly well imitated, if, indeed, it is not his
own, which I am not at all prepared to believe. As for the two witnesses' signatures, I don't think I had ever seen them before. I took the
document to Messrs. Barkston & Maud, who had often done business
for me before, and they assured me that the will was in perfect form
and order.'

"Asked why he had not intrusted the will to his father's solicitors, he
replied:

"'For the very simple reason, that exactly half an hour before the
will was placed in my hands, I had read that Mr. Patrick Wethered
had been murdered the night before. Mr. Hibbert, the junior partner,
was not personally known to me.'

"After that, for form's sake, a good deal of expert evidence was

heard on the subject of the dead man's signature. But that was quite
unanimous, and merely went to corroborate what had already been established beyond a doubt, namely, that the will dated December 1st,
1900 was a forgery, and probate of the will dated 1891 was therefore
granted to Mr. Murray Brooks, the sole executor mentioned therein."

III

"Two days later the police applied for a warrant for the arrest of Mr.
Percival Brooks on a charge of forgery.

"The Crown prosecuted, and Mr. Brooks had again the support of
Mr. Oranmore, the eminent K.C. Perfectly calm, like a man conscious
of his own innocence and unable to grasp the idea that justice does
sometimes miscarry, Mr. Brooks, the son of the millionaire, himself
still the possessor of a very large fortune, under the former will, stood
up in the dock on that memorable day in May, 1902, which still no
doubt lives in the memory of his many friends.

"All the evidence with regard to Mr. Brooks' last moments and the
forged will was gone through over again. That will, it was the contention of the Crown, had been forged so entirely in favour of the accused,
cutting out everyone else, that obviously no one but the beneficiary
under that false will would have had any motive in forging it.

"Very pale, and with a frown between his deep set handsome Irish
eyes, Percival Brooks listened to this large volume of evidence piled up
against him by the Crown.

"At times he held brief consultations with Mr. Oranmore, who
seemed as cool as a cucumber. Have you ever seen Oranmore in court?
He is a character worthy of Dickens. His pronounced brogue, his fat,
podgy clean-shaven face, his not always immaculately clean large
hands, have often delighted the caricaturist. As it very soon transpired
during that memorable magisterial inquiry he relied for a verdict in
favour of his client upon two main points, and he had concentrated all
his skill upon making these two points as telling as he possibly could.

"The first point was the question of time. John O'Neill, cross-
examined by Oranmore, stated without hesitation that he had given the
will to Mr. Percival at eleven o'clock in the morning. And now the
eminent K.C. brought forward and placed in the witness box the very
lawyers into whose hands the accused had then immediately placed the
will. Now Mr. Barkston, a very well-known solicitor of King Street,
declared positively that Mr. Percival Brooks was in his office at a
quarter before twelve; two of his clerks testified to the same time
exactly, and it was *impossible,* contended Mr. Oranmore, that within
three-quarters of an hour Mr. Brooks could have gone to a stationer's,

bought a will form, copied Mr. Wethered's writing, his father's signature, and that of John O'Neill and Pat Mooney.

"Such a thing might have been planned, arranged, practised, and ultimately after a great deal of trouble, successfully carried out, but human intelligence could not grasp the other as a possibility.

"Still the judge wavered. The eminent K.C. had shaken but not shattered his belief in the prisoner's guilt. But there was one point more, and this Oranmore, with the skill of a dramatist, had reserved for the fall of the curtain.

"He noted every sign in the judge's face, he guessed that his client was not yet absolutely safe, then only did he produce his last two witnesses.

"One of them was Mary Sullivan, one of the housemaids in the Fitzwilliam Mansion. She had been sent up by the cook at a quarter past four o'clock on the afternoon of December 1st with some hot water, which the nurse had ordered for the master's room. Just as she was about to knock at the door, Mr. Wethered was coming out of the room. Mary stopped with the tray in her hand, and at the door Mr. Wethered turned and said quite loud; 'Now, don't fret, don't be anxious; do try and be calm. Your will is safe in my pocket, nothing can change it, or alter one word of it but yourself.'

"It was of course a very ticklish point in law whether the housemaid's evidence could be accepted. You see she was quoting the words of a man since dead, spoken to another man also dead. There is no doubt that had there been very strong evidence on the other side against Percival Brooks, Mary Sullivan's would have counted for nothing, but as I told you before the judge's belief in the prisoner's guilt was already very seriously shaken, and now the final blow aimed at it by Mr. Oranmore shattered his last lingering doubts.

"Dr. Mulligan, namely, had been placed by Mr. Oranmore into the witness-box. He was a medical man of unimpeachable authority, in fact absolutely at the head of his profession in Dublin. What he said practically corroborated Mary Sullivan's testimony. He had gone in to see Mr. Brooks at half-past four, and understood from him that his lawyer had just left him.

"Mr. Brooks certainly, though terribly weak, was calm and more composed. He was dying from a sudden heart attack, and Dr. Mulligan foresaw the almost immediate end. But he was still conscious and managed to murmur feebly, 'I feel much easier in my mind now, doctor—I have made my will—Wethered has been—he's got it in his pocket—it is safe there—safe from that——' but the words died on his lips, and after that he spoke but little. He saw his two sons before he died, but hardly knew them or even looked at them."

IV

"You see," concluded the man in the corner, "you see that the prosecution was bound to collapse. Oranmore did not give it a leg to stand upon. The will was forged, it is true, forged in the favour of Percival Brooks and of no one else, forged for him and for his benefit. Whether he knew and connived at the forgery, was never proved or, as far as I know, even hinted, but it was impossible to go against all the evidence, which pointed that, as far as the act itself was concerned, he at least was most innocent. You see Dr. Mulligan's evidence was not to be shaken. Mary Sullivan's was equally strong.

"There were two witnesses swearing positively that old Brooks' will was in Mr. Wethered's keeping when that gentleman left Fitzwilliam Mansion at a quarter-past-four. At five o'clock in the afternoon, the lawyer was found dead in Phoenix Park. Between a quarter-past-four and eight o'clock in the evening Percival Brooks never left the house—that was subsequently proved by Oranmore beyond a doubt. Since the will found under old Brooks' pillow was a forged will, where then was the will he did make, and which Wethered carried away with him in his pocket?"

"Stolen, of course," I said, "by those who murdered and robbed him; it may have been of no value to them, but they naturally would destroy it, lest it might prove a clue against them."

"Then you think it was mere coincidence?" he asked excitedly.

"What?"

"That Wethered was murdered and robbed at the very moment that he carried the will in his pocket, whilst another was being forged in its place?"

"It certainly would be very curious, if it *were* a coincidence," I said musingly.

"Very," he repeated with biting sarcasm, whilst nervously his bony fingers played with the inevitable bit of string. "Very curious indeed. Just think of the whole thing. There was the old man with all his wealth, and two sons, one to whom he is devoted, and the other with whom he does nothing but quarrel. One day there is another of these quarrels, but more violent, more terrible than any that have previously occurred, with the result that the father, heartbroken by it all, has an attack of the heart—practically dies of a broken heart. After that he alters his will, and subsequently a will is proved which turns out to be a forgery.

"Now everybody, police, press, and public alike, at once jump to the conclusion that, as Percival Brooks benefits by that forged will, Percival Brooks must be the forger."

"Seek for him whom the crime benefits, is your own axiom," I argued.

"I beg your pardon?"

"Percival Brooks benefited to the tune of £2,000,000."

"I beg your pardon. He did nothing of the sort. He was left with less than half the share that his younger brother inherited."

"Now, yes; but that was a former will and——"

"And that forged will was so clumsily executed, the signature so carelessly imitated, that the forgery was bound to come to light. Did *that* never strike you?"

"Yes, but——"

"There is no but," he interrupted. "It was all as clear as daylight to me, from the very first. The quarrel with the old man, which broke his heart was not with his eldest son, with whom he was used to quarrelling, but with the second son whom he idolised, in whom he believed. Don't you remember how John O'Neill heard the words 'liar' and 'deceit'? Percival Brooks had never deceived his father. His sins were all on the surface. Murray had led a quiet life, had pandered to his father, and fawned upon him, until, like most hypocrites, he at last got found out. Who knows what ugly gambling debt or debt of honour, suddenly revealed to old Brooks, was the cause of that last and deadly quarrel?

"You remember that it was Percival who remained beside his father and carried him up to his room. Where was Murray throughout that long and painful day, when his father lay dying—he, the idolised son, the apple of the old man's eye? You never hear his name mentioned as being present there all that day. But he knew that he had offended his father mortally, and that his father meant to cut him off with a shilling. He knew that Mr. Wethered had been sent for, that Wethered left the house soon after four o'clock.

"And here the cleverness of the man comes in. Having lain in wait for Wethered and knocked him on the back of the head with a stick, he could not very well make that will disappear altogether. There remained the faint chance of some other witnesses knowing that Mr. Brooks had made a fresh will, Mr. Wethered's partner, his clerk, or one of the confidential servants in the house. Therefore *a* will must be discovered after the old man's death.

"Now Murray Brooks was not an expert forger, it takes years of training to become that. A forged will executed by himself would be sure to be found out—yes, that's it, sure to be found out. The forgery will be palpable—let it be palpable, and then it will be found out, branded as such, and the original will of 1891, so favourable to the young blackguard's interests will be held as valid. Was it devilry or merely additional caution which prompted Murray to pen that forged will so glaringly in Percival's favour? It is impossible to say.

"Anyhow, it was the cleverest touch in that marvellously-devised crime. To plan that evil deed was great, to execute it was easy enough. He had several hours' leisure in which to do it. Then at night it was simplicity itself to slip the document under the dead man's pillow. Sacrilege causes no shudder to such natures as Murray Brooks. The rest of the drama you know already——"

"But Percival Brooks?"

"The jury returned a verdict of 'Not guilty.' There was no evidence against him."

"But the money? Surely the scoundrel does not have the enjoyment of it still?"

"No; he enjoyed it for a time, but he died about three months ago, and forgot to take the precaution of making a will, so his brother Percival has got the business after all. If you ever go to Dublin I should order some of Brooks' bacon if I were you. It is very good."

THE GLASGOW MYSTERY

DRAMATIS PERSONAE

THE MAN IN THE CORNER
who tells the story to
THE LADY JOURNALIST.
MRS. CARMICHAEL
(*the landlady who was murdered*).
MR. YARDLEY
(*a poet living in her house*).
MR. JAMES LUCAS
(*another of her boarders*).
UPTON
(*her manservant*).
EMMA
(*her cook*).

I

"It has often been declared," remarked the man in the corner, "that a murder—a successful murder, I mean—can never be committed single-handed in a busy city, and that on the other hand, once a murder *is* committed by more than one person, one of the accomplices is sure to betray the other, and that is the reason why comparatively so few crimes remain undetected. Now I must say I quite agree with this latter theory."

It was some few weeks after my first introduction to the man in the corner and the inevitable bit of string he always played with when unravelling his mysteries, and some time before he recounted to me his grim version of the tragedy in Percy street, which I have already retold.

Now I had made it a hard and fast rule whenever he made an assertion of that kind to disagree with it. This invariably irritated him; he became comically excited, produced his bit of string, and started off at rattling speed, after a few rude remarks directed at lady journalists in general and myself in particular, on one of his madly bewildering, true cock-and-bull stories.

"What about the Glasgow murder, then?" I remarked sceptically.

"Ah, the Glasgow murder," he repeated "Yes, what about the Glasgow murder? I see you are one of those people who, like the police, believe that Yardley was an accomplice to that murder, and you still continue to hope, as they do, that sooner or later he, and the other man, Upton, will meet, divide the spoils, and throw themselves into the expectant arms of the Glasgow police."

"Do you mean to tell me that you don't think Yardley had anything to do with that murder?"

"What does it matter what a humble amateur like myself thinks of that or any other case? Pshaw!" he added, breaking his bit of string between his bony fingers in his comical excitement. "Why, think a moment how simple is the whole thing! There was Mrs. Carmichael, the widow of a medical officer, young, good-looking, and fairly well-off, who for the sake of company, more than for actual profit-making, rents one of the fine houses in Woodbine Crescent with a view to taking in 'paying guests.' Her house is beautifully furnished—I told you she was fairly well-off. She has no difficulty in getting boarders.

"The house is soon full. At the time of which I am speaking she had ten or eleven 'guests'—mostly men out at business all day, also a married couple, an officer's widow with her daughter, and two journalists. At first she kept four female servants; then one day there was a complaint among the gentlemen boarders that their boots were insufficiently polished and their clothes very sketchily brushed. Chief among these complainants was Mr. Yardley, a young man who wrote verses for magazines, called himself a poet, and, in consequence, indulged in sundry eccentric habits which furnished food for gossip both in the kitchen and in the drawing-room over the coffee cups.

"As I said before, it was he who was loudest in his complaint on the subject of his boots; it was he, again, who, when Mrs. Carmichael expressed herself willing to do anything to please her boarders, recommended her a quiet, respectable man named Upton to come in for a couple of hours daily, clean boots, knives, windows, and what-nots, and make himself 'generally useful'—I believe that is the technical expression. Upton, it appears, had been known to Mr. Yardley for some time, had often run errands and delivered messages for him, and had even been intrusted with valuable poetical MSS. to be left at various editorial offices.

"It was in July of last year, was it not, that Glasgow—honest, stodgy, busy Glasgow—was thrilled to its very marrow by the recital in its evening papers of one of the most ghastly and most dastardly crimes?

"At two o'clock that afternoon, namely, Mrs. Carmichael, of Woodbine Crescent, was found murdered in her room. Her safe had been opened, and all its contents—which were presumed to include a good deal of jewellery and money—had vanished. The evening papers had also added that the murderer was known to the police, and that no doubt was entertained as to his speedy arrest.

"It appears that in the household at Woodbine Crescent it was the duty of Mary, one of the maids, to take up a cup of tea to Mrs. Carmichael every morning at seven o'clock. The girl was not supposed to go into the room, but merely to knock at the door, wait for a response from her mistress, and then leave the tray outside on the mat.

"Usually Mrs. Carmichael took the tray in immediately, and was down to breakfast with her boarders at half-past eight. But on that eventful morning Mary seems to have been in a hurry. She could not positively state afterwards whether she had heard her mistress's answer to her knock or not; against that, she was quite sure that she had taken up the tray at seven o'clock precisely.

"When everybody went down to breakfast a couple of hours or so later, it was noticed that Mrs. Carmichael had not taken in her tea tray as usual. A few anxious comments were made as to the genial hostess being unwell, and then the matter was dropped. The servants did not seem to have been really anxious about their mistress during the morning. Mary, who had been in the house two years, said that once before Mrs. Carmichael had stayed in bed with a bad headache until one o'clock.

"However, when the lunch hour came and went, Mrs. Tyrrell, one of the older lady boarders, became alarmed. She went up to her hostess's door and knocked at it loudly and repeatedly, but received no reply. The door, mind you, was locked or bolted, presumably, of course, from the inside. After consultation with her fellow boarders, Mrs. Tyrrell at last, feeling that something must be very wrong, took it upon herself to call in the police. Constable Rae came in; he too knocked and called, shook the door, and finally burst it open.

"It is not for me," continued the man in the corner, "to give you a description of that room as it appeared before the horrified eyes of the constable, the servants, and lady boarders; that lies more in your province than in mine.

"Suffice it to say that the unfortunate lady lay in her bed with her throat cut.

"No key or bolt was found on the inside of the door; the murderer, therefore, having accomplished his ghastly deed, must have locked his victim in, and probably taken the key away with him. Hardly had the terrible discovery been made than Emma the cook, half hysterical with fear and horror, rushed up to Constable Rae, and, clutching him wildly by the arm, whispered under her breath, 'Upton, Upton; he did it, I know . . . My poor mistress; he cut her throat with that fowl carver this morning. I saw it·in his hand . . . It is him, constable!'

"'Where is he?' asked the constable peremptorily. 'See that no one leaves the house. Who has seen this man?'

"But neither the constable, nor anyone else for that matter, was much surprised to find that on searching the house throughout, the man Upton had disappeared."

II

"At first, of course, the case seemed simplicity itself. No doubt existed, either in the public mind or that of the police, as to Upton being the author of the grim and horrible tragedy. The only difficulty, so far, was the fact that Upton had managed not only to get away on the day of the murder, but also had contrived to evade the rigorous search instituted throughout the city after him by the police—a search, I assure you, in which many an amateur detective readily joined.

"The inquest had been put off for a day or two in the hope that Upton might be found before it occurred. However, three days had now elapsed, and it could not be put off any longer. Little did the public expect the sensational developments which the case suddenly began to assume.

"The medical evidence revealed nothing new. On the contrary, it added its usual quota of vague indefiniteness which so often helps to puzzle the police. The medical officer had been called in by Constable Rae, directly after his discovery of the murder. That was about two o'clock in the afternoon. Death had occurred a good many hours before that time, stated Dr. Dawlish—possibly nine or ten hours; but it might also have been eleven or twelve hours previously.

"Then Emma the cook was called. Her evidence was, of course, most important, as she had noticed and talked to the man Upton the very morning of the crime. He came as usual to his work, about a quarter to seven, but the cook immediately noticed that he seemed very strange and excited.

"'What do you mean by strange?' asked the coroner.

"'Well, it was strange of him, sir, to start first thing in the morning cleaning knives when we had as many knives as we wanted clean for breakfast.'

"'Yes? He started cleaning knives, and then what did he do?'

"'Oh, he turned and turned that there knife machine so as I told him he would be turning all the edges. Then he suddenly took up the fowl carver and said to me; "This fowl carver is awful blunt—where's the steel?" I says to him: "In the sideboard, of course, in the dining room," and he goes off with the fowl carver in his hand, and that is the last I ever saw of that carver and of Upton himself.'

"'Have you known Upton long?' asked the coroner.

"'No, sir, he had only been in the house two days. Mr. Yardley gave him a character, and the mistress took him on, to clean boots and knives. His hours were half-past six to ten, but he used to turn up about a quarter to seven. He seemed obliging and willing, but not much up to his work, and didn't say much. But I hadn't seen him so funny except that morning when the poor missus was murdered.'

"'Is this the carver you speak of?' asked the coroner, directing a constable to show one he held in his hand to the witness.

"With renewed hysterical weeping Emma identified the carver as the one she had last seen in Upton's hand. It appears that Detective McMurdoch had found the knife, together with the key of Mrs. Carmichael's bedroom door, under the hall mat. Sensational, wasn't it?" laughed the man in the corner; "quite in the style of the penny novelette—sensational, but not very mysterious.

"Then Mrs. Tyrrell had to be examined, as it was she who had first been alarmed about Mrs. Carmichael, and who had taken it upon herself to call in the police. Whether through spite or merely accidentally Mrs. Tyrrell insisted in her evidence on the fact that it was Mr. Yardley who was indirectly responsible for the awful tragedy, since it was he who had introduced the man Upton into the house.

"The coroner felt more interested. He thought he would like to put a few questions to Mr. Yardley. Now Mr. Yardley when called up did not certainly look prepossessing; and from the first most persons present were prejudiced against him. He was, as I think I said before, that *rara avis,* a successful poet: he wrote dainty scraps for magazines and weekly journals.

"In appearance he was a short, sallow, thin man, with no body and long limbs, and carried his head so much to one side as to almost appear deformed. Here is a snapshot I got of him some time subsequently. He is no beauty, is he?

"Still his manner, his small shapely hands, and quiet voice undoubtedly proclaimed him a gentleman.

"It was very well known throughout the household that Mr. Yardley was very eccentric; being a poet he would enjoy the privilege with impunity. It appears that his most eccentric habit was to get up at unearthly hours in the morning—four o'clock sometimes—and wander about the streets of Glasgow.

"'I have written my best pieces,' he stated in response to the coroner's astonished remark upon this strange custom of his, 'leaning against a lamp post in Sauchiehall Street at five o'clock in the morning. I spend my afternoons in the various public libraries, reading. I have only boarded and lodged in this house for two or three months, but, as the servants will tell you, I leave it long before they are up in the morning. I am never in to breakfast or luncheon, but always in to dinner. I go to bed early, naturally, as I require several hours sleep.'

"Mr. Yardley was then very closely questioned as to his knowledge of the man Upton.

"'I first met the man,' replied Mr. Yardley, 'about a year ago. He was loafing in Buchanan Street, outside the *Herald* office, and spoke to me, telling me a most pitiable tale—namely, that he was an ex-compositor, had had to give up his work owing to failing eyesight, that he had striven for weeks and months to get some other kind of employment, spending in the meanwhile the hard-earned savings of many years' toil; that he had come to his last shilling two days ago, and had been reduced to begging, not for money, but for some kind of job—anything to earn a few honest coins.

"'Well, I somehow liked the look of the man; moreover, as I just happened to want to send a message to the other end of the city, I sent Upton. Since then I have seen him almost every day. He takes my manuscripts for me to the editorial offices, and runs various errands. I have recommended him to one or two of my friends, and they have always found him honest and sober. He has eked out a very meagre livelihood in this way, and when Mrs. Carmichael thought of having a man in the house to do odd jobs, I thought I should be doing a kind act by recommending Upton to her. Little did I dream then what terrible consequences such a kind act would bring in its trail. I can only account for the man's awful crime by thinking that perhaps his mind had become suddenly unhinged.'

"All this seemed plain and straightforward enough. Mr. Yardley spoke quietly, without the slightest nervousness or agitation. The coroner and jury both pressed him with questions on the subject of Upton, but his attitude remained equally self-possessed throughout. Perhaps he felt, after a somewhat severe cross-examination on the part of the coroner, who prided himself on his talent in that direction, that a certain amount of doubt might lurk in the minds of the jury and consequently the public. Be that as it may, he certainly begged that two or three of the servants might be recalled in order to enable them to state definitely that he was out of the house, as usual, when they came downstairs that morning.

"One of the housemaids, recalled, fully corroborated that statement. Mr. Yardley's room, she said, was on the ground floor, next to the dining-room. She went into it soon after half-past six, turned down the bed, and began tidying it up generally.

"There was only one other witness of any importance to examine. One other boarder—Mr. James Lucas, a young journalist, employed on the editorial staff of the *Glasgow Banner*.

"The reason why he had been called specially was because he was well known to be one of the privileged guests of the house, and had been more intimate with the deceased than any of her other boarders. This privilege, it appears, chiefly consisted in being admitted to coffee, and possibly whiskey and soda after dinner, in Mrs. Carmichael's special private sitting room. Moreover, there was a generally accepted theory among the other boarders that Mr. James Lucas entertained certain secret hopes with regard to his amiable hostess, and that, but for the fact that he was several years her junior, she might have encouraged these hopes.

"Now, Mr. James Lucas was the exact opposite of Mr. Yardley, the poet; tall, fair, athletic, his appearance would certainly prepossess everyone in his favour. He seemed very much upset, and recounted with much, evidently genuine, feeling, his last interview with the unfortunate lady—the evening before the murder.

"'I spent about an hour with Mrs. Carmichael in her sitting room,' he concluded, 'and parted from her about ten o'clock. I then went to my club, where I stayed pretty late, until closing time, in fact. After that I went for a stroll, and it was a quarter past two by my watch when I came in. I let myself in with my latchkey.

"'It was pitch-dark in the outer hall, and I was groping for my candle, when I heard the sound of a door opening and shutting on one of the floors above, and directly after someone coming down the stairs. As you have seen yourself, the outer hall is divided from the inner one by a glass door, which on this occasion stood open. In the inner hall there was a faint glimmer of light, which worked its way down from a skylight on one of the landings, and by this glimmer I saw Mr. Yardley descending the stairs, cross the hall, and go into his room. He did not see me, and I did not speak.'

"An extraordinary, almost breathless, hush had descended over all those assembled there. The coroner sat with his chin buried in his hand, his eyes resting searchingly on the witness who had just spoken. The jury had not uttered a sound. At last the coroner queried:

"'Is the jury to understand, Mr. Lucas, that you can swear positively that at a quarter-past two in the morning, or thereabouts, you saw Mr. Yardley come down the stairs from one of the floors above and go into his own room, which is on the ground floor?'

"'Positively.'

"That was enough. Mr. Lucas was dismissed and Mr. Yardley was recalled. As he once more stood before the coroner, his curious one-sided stoop, his sallowness, and length of limb seemed even more marked than before. Perhaps he was a shade or two paler, but certainly neither his hands nor his voice trembled in the slightest degree.

"Questioned by the coroner, he replied quietly:

"'Mr. Lucas was obviously mistaken. At the hour he names I was in bed and asleep.'

"There had been excitement and breathless interest when Mr. James

Lucas had made his statement, but that excitement and breathlessness was as nothing compared with the absolutely dumbfounded awe which fell over everyone there, as the sallow, half-deformed, little poet, gave the former witness so completely, so emphatically the lie.

"The coroner himself hardly knew how to keep up his professional dignity as he almost gasped the query:

"'Then is the jury to understand that you can swear positively that at a quarter-past two o'clock on that particular morning you were in bed and asleep?'

"'Positively.'

"It seemed as if Mr. Yardley had repeated purposely the other man's emphatic and laconic assertion. Certainly his voice was as steady, his eye as clear, his manner as calm as that of Mr. Lucas. The coroner and jury were silent, and Mr. Yardley turned to where young Lucas had retired in a further corner of the room. The eyes of the two met, almost like the swords of two duellists before the great attack; neither flinched. One or the other was telling a lie. A terrible lie since it might entail loss of honour, or life perhaps to the other, yet *neither* flinched. One was telling a lie, remember, and in everyone's mind there arose at once the great all absorbing queries 'Which?' and 'Wherefore!'"

III

I had been so absorbed in listening to the thrilling narrative of that highly dramatic inquest that I really had not noticed until then that the man in the corner was recounting it as if he had been present at it himself.

"That is because I heard it all from an eyewitness," he suddenly replied with that eerie knack he seemed to possess of reading my thoughts, "but it must have been very dramatic, and, above all, terribly puzzling. You see there were two men swearing against one another, both in good positions, both educated men; it was impossible for any jury to take either evidence as absolutely convincing, and it could not be proved that either of them lied. Mr. Lucas might have done so from misapprehension. There was just a possibility that he had had more whiskey at his club than was good for him. Mr. Yardley, on the other hand, if he lied, lied because he had something to hide, something to hide in that case which might have been terrible.

"Of course Dr. Dawlish was recalled, and with wonderful learning and wonderful precision he repeated his vague medical statements:

"'When I examined the body with my colleague. Dr. Swanton, death had evidently supervened several hours ago. Personally, I believe that it must have occurred certainly more like twelve hours ago than seven.'

"More than that he could not say. After all, medical science has its limits.

"Then Emma, the cook, was again called. There was an important point which, oddly enough, had been overlooked up to this moment. The question, namely, of the doormat under which the knife (which, by the way, was bloodstained) and also the key of Mrs. Carmichael's bedroom door was found. Emma, however, could make a very clear and very definite statement on that point. She had cleaned the hall and shaken the mat at half-past six that morning. At that hour the housemaid was making Mr. Yardley's bed; he had left the house already. There certainly was neither key nor knife under the mat then.

"The balance of evidence, which perhaps for one brief moment had inclined oh, ever so slightly, against Mr. Yardley, returned to its original heavy weight against the man Upton. Of course there was practically nothing to implicate Mr. Yardley seriously. The coroner made a resumé of the case before his jury worthy of a judge in the High Courts.

"He recapitulated all the evidence. It was very strong, undeniable, damning against Upton, and the jury could arrive but at one conclusion with regard to him. Then there was the medical evidence. That certainly favoured Upton a very little, if at all. Remember that both the medical gentlemen refused to make a positive statement as to the time; their evidence could not, therefore, be said to weigh either for or against anyone.

"There was then the strange and unaccountably conflicting evidence between two gentlemen of the house—Mr. Lucas and Mr. Yardley. That was a matter which for the present must rest between either of these gentlemen and their conscience. There was also the fact that the man Upton—the evident actual murderer—had been introduced into the house by Mr. Yardley. The jury knew best themselves if this fact should or should not weigh with them in their decision.

"That was the sum total of the evidence. The jury held but a very brief consultation. Their foreman pronounced their verdict of 'Wilful murder against Upton.' Not a word about Mr. Yardley. What could they have said? There was really no evidence against him—not enough, certainly, to taint his name for ever with so hideous a blight.

"In a case like that, remember, the jury are fully aware that the police would never for a moment lose sight of a man who had so narrowly escaped a warrant as Yardley had done. Relying on the certainty that very soon Upton would be arrested, it was not to be doubted for a moment but that he would betray his accomplice, if he had one. Criminals in such a plight nearly always do. In the meanwhile, every step of Yardley's would be dogged, unbeknown to himself, even if he attempted to leave the country. As for Upton——"

The man in the corner paused. He was eyeing me through his great bone-rimmed spectacles, watching with ironical delight my evident breathless interest in his narrative. I remembered that Glasgow murder so well. I remember the talks, the arguments, the quarrels that would arise in every household. Was Yardley an accomplice? Did he kill Mrs. Carmichael at two in the morning? Did he tell a lie? If so, why? Did Mr. James Lucas tell a lie? Many people, I remember, held this latter theory, more particularly as Mrs. Carmichael's will was proved some days later, and it was found that she had left all her money to him.

For a little while public opinion veered dead against him. Some people thought that if he were innocent he would refuse to touch a penny of her money; others, of a more practical turn of mind, did not see why he should not. He was a struggling young journalist; the lady had obviously been in love with him, and intended to marry him; she had a perfect right—as she had no children or any near relative—to leave her money to whom she chose, and it would indeed be hard on him, if, through the act of some miscreant, he should at one fell swoop be deprived both of wife and fortune.

Then, of course, there was Upton—Upton! Upton! whom the police could not find! who must be guilty, seeing that he so hid himself, who never would have acted the hideous comedy with the carver. Why should he have wilfully drawn attention to himself, and left, as it were, his visiting card on the scene of the murder?

Why? why? why?

"Ah, yes, why?" came as a funny, shrill echo from my eccentric *vis-à-vis*. "I see that in spite of my earnest endeavour to teach you to think out a case logically and clearly, you start off with a preconceived notion, which naturally leads you astry *because* it is preconceived, just like any blundering detective in these benighted islands."

"Preconceived?" I retorted indignantly. "There is no question of preconception. Whether Mr. Yardley knew of the contemplated murder or not, whether he was an accomplice or Mr. Lucas, there is one thing very clear—namely, that Upton was not innocent in the matter."

"What makes you say that?" he asked blandly.

"Obviously, because if he were innocent he would not have acted the hideous tragic comedy with the carver; he would not, above all, have absolutely damned himself by disappearing out of the house and out of sight at the very moment when the discovery of Mrs. Carmichael's murdered body had become imminent."

"It never struck you, I suppose," retorted the man in the corner with quiet sarcasm, "how *very* damning Upton's actions were on that particular morning?"

"Of course they were *very* damning. That is just my contention."

"And you have never then studied my methods of reasoning sufficiently to understand that when a criminal—a clever criminal, mind you—appears to be damning himself in the most brainless fashion, that is the time to guard against the clever pitfalls he is laying up for the police?"

"Exactly. That is why I, as well as many people connected with journalism, believe that Upton was acting a comedy in order to save his accomplice. The question only remains as to who the accomplice was."

"He must have been singularly unselfish and self-sacrificing, then."

"How do you mean?"

"According to your argument. Upton heaped up every conceivable circumstantial evidence against himself in order to shield his accomplice. Firstly he acts the part of strange, unnatural excitement, he loudly proclaims the fact that he leaves the kitchen with the fowl carver in his hand, thirdly he deposits that same bloodstained knife and the key of Mrs. Carmichael's room under the mat a few moments before he leaves the house. You must own that the man must have been singularly unselfish since, if he is ever caught, nothing would save him from the gallows, whilst, unless a great deal more evidence can be brought up, his accomplice could continue to go free."

"Yes, that might be," I said thoughtfully; "it was of course a part of the given plan. Many people held that Upton and Yardley were great friends—they might have been brothers, who knows?"

"Yes, who knows?" he repeated scornfully, as getting more and more excited his long thin fingers wound and unwound his bit of string, making curious complicated knots, and then undoing them feverishly.

"Do brothers usually so dote on each other, that they are content to swing for one another? And have you never wondered why the police never found Upton? How did he get away? Where is he? Has the earth swallowed him up?

"Surely a clumsy brute like that, who gives himself hopelessly away on the very day when he commits a murder, cannot have brains enough to hide altogether away from the police—a man who before a witness selects the weapon with which he means to kill his victim, and who then deliberately leaves it bloodstained there where it is sure to be found at once? Why imagine such a consummate fool evading the police, not a day, not a week, not a month, but nearly two years now, which means altogether? Why, such a fool as you, the public, and the police have branded him would have fallen into a trap within twenty-four hours of his attempt at evasion; whereas the man who planned and accomplished that murder was a genius before he became a blackguard."

"That's just what I said. He was doing it to shield his accomplice."

"His accomplice!" gasped the funny creature, with ever increasing excitement. "Yes, the accomplice he loved and cherished above all—his brother you say, perhaps. No, someone he would love ten thousand times more than any brother."

"Then you mean——"

"*Himself*, of course! Didn't you see it all along? Lord bless my soul! The young man—poet or blackguard, what you will—who comes into a boardinghouse, then realises that its mistress is wealthy. He studies the rules of the house, the habits of its mistress, finds out about her money, her safe, her jewels, and then makes his plans. Oh, they were magnificently laid! That man ought to have been a great diplomatist, a great general—he was only a great scoundrel.

"The sort of disguise he assumed is so easy to manage. Only remember one thing: When a fool wishes to sink his identity he does so *after* he has committed a crime and is wanted by the police; he is bound, therefore, for the best part of the remainder of his life, to keep up the disguise he has selected at all times, every hour, every minute of the day; to alter his voice, his walk, his manners. On the other hand, how does a clever man like Yardley proceed?

"He chooses his disguise and assumes it *before* the execution of his crime; it is then only a matter of a few days, and when all is over, the individual, the known criminal, disappears; and, mind you, he takes great care that the criminal shall be known. Now in this case Upton is introduced into the house; say he calls one evening on Mr. Yardley's recommendation; Mrs. Carmichael sees him in the hall for a few moments, arranges the question of work and wages, and after that he comes every morning, with a dirty face, towzled hair, false beard and moustache—the usual type of odd job man very much down in his luck—his work lies in the kitchen, no one sees him upstairs, whilst the cook and kitchen folk never see Mr. Yardley.

"After a little while something—carelessness perhap—might reveal the trick, but the deception is only carried on two days. Then the murder is accomplished and Upton disappears. In the meanwhile Mr. Yardley continues his eccentric habits. He goes out at unearthly hours; he is a poet; he is out of the house while Upton carries on the comedy with the carving knife. He knows that there never will be any evidence against him as Yardley; he has taken every care that all should be against Upton, all; hopeless, complete, absolute, damning!

"Then he leaves the police to hunt for Upton. He 'lies low' for a time, after a little while he will go abroad, I dare say he has done so already. A jeweller in Vienna, or perhaps St. Petersburg, will buy some loose stones of him, the stones he has picked out of Mrs. Carmichael's brooches and rings, the gold he will melt down and sell, the notes he can cash at any foreign watering place, without a single question being asked of him. English banknotes find a very ready market abroad, and 'no questions asked.'

"After that he will come back to his friends in Glasgow and write dainty bits of poetry for magazines; the only difference being that he will write them at more reasonable hours. And during all the time the police will hunt for Upton.

"It was clever, was it not? You have his photo? I gave it you just now. Clever looking, isn't he? As Upton he wore a beard and dyed his hair very black; it must have been a great trouble every morning, mustn't it?"

THE LIVERPOOL MYSTERY

DRAMATIS PERSONAE

THE MAN IN THE CORNER
who tells the story to
THE LADY JOURNALIST.
PRINCE SEMIONICZ.
HIS FRENCH SECRETARY.
MESSRS. WINSLOW & VASSALL
(jewellers in Liverpool).
SCHWARZ
(German assistant at Winslow & Vassall's).

I

"A title—a foreign title, I mean—is always very useful for purposes of swindles and frauds," remarked the man in the corner to me one day. "The cleverest robberies of modern times were perpetrated lately in Vienna by a man who dubbed himself Lord Seymour; whilst over here the same class of thief calls himself Count Something ending in 'o,' or Prince the other, ending in 'off.'"

"Fortunately for our hotel and lodging-house keepers over here," I replied, "they are beginning to be more alive to the ways of foreign swindlers, and look upon all titled gentry who speak broken English as possible swindlers or thieves."

"The result sometimes being exceedingly unpleasant to the real 'grands seigneurs' who honour this country at times with their visits," replied the man in the corner. "Now, take the case of Prince Semionicz, a man whose sixteen quarterings are duly recorded in Gotha, who carried enough luggage with him to pay for the use of every room in a hotel for at least a week, whose gold cigarette case with diamond and turquoise ornament was actually stolen without his taking the slightest trouble in trying to recover it; that same man was undoubtedly looked upon with suspicion by the manager of the Liverpool North-Western Hotel from the moment that his secretary—a dapper, somewhat vulgar little Frenchman—bespoke on behalf of his employer, with himself and a valet, the best suite of rooms the hotel contained.

"Obviously those suspicions were unfounded, for the little secretary, as soon as Prince Semionicz had arrived, deposited with the manager a pile of bank notes, also papers and bonds, the value of which would exceed tenfold the most outrageous bill that could possibly be placed before the noble visitor. Moreover, M. Albert Lambert explained that the Prince, who only meant to stay in Liverpool a few days, was on his way to Chicago, where he wished to visit Princess Anna Semionicz, his sister, who was married to Mr. Girwan, the great copper king and multimillionaire.

"Yet, as I told you before, in spite of all these undoubted securities, suspicion of the wealthy Russian Prince lurked in the minds of most Liverpudlians who came in business contact with him. He had been at the North-Western two days when he sent his secretary to Winslow and Vassall, the jewellers of Bold Street, with a request that they would kindly send a representative round to the hotel with some nice pieces of jewellery, diamonds and pearls chiefly, which he was desirous of taking as a present to his sister in Chicago.

"Mr. Winslow took the order from M. Albert with a pleasant bow. Then he went to his inner office and consulted with his partner, Mr. Vassall, as to the best course to adopt. Both the gentlemen were desirous of doing business, for business had been very slack lately: neither wished to refuse a possible customer, or to offend Mr. Pettitt, the manager of the North-Western, who had recommended them to the Prince. But that foreign title and the vulgar little French secretary stuck in the throats of the two pompous and worthy Liverpool jewellers, and together they agreed, firstly, that no credit should be given; and, secondly, that if a cheque or even a banker's draft were tendered, the jewels were not to be given up until that cheque or draft was cashed.

"Then came the question as to who should take the jewels to the hotel. It was altogether against business etiquette for the senior partners to do such errands themselves; moreover it was thought that it would be easier for a clerk to explain without giving undue offence that he could not take the responsibility of a cheque or draft without having cashed it previously to giving up the jewels.

"Then there was the question of the probable necessity of conferring in a foreign tongue. The head assistant, Charles Needham, who had been in the employ of Winslow and Vassall for over twelve years, was, in true British fashion, ignorant of any language save his own; it was therefore decided to dispatch Mr. Schwarz, a young German clerk lately arrived.

"Mr. Schwarz was Mr. Winslow's nephew and godson, a sister of that gentleman having married the head of the great German firm of Schwarz & Co., silversmiths, of Hamburg and Berlin.

"The young man had soon become a great favourite with his uncle, whose heir he would presumably be, as Mr. Winslow had no children.

"At first Mr. Vassall made some demur about sending Mr. Schwarz with so many valuable jewels alone in a city which he had not yet had the time to study thoroughly; but finally he allowed himself to be persuaded by his senior partner, and a fine selection of necklaces, pendants, bracelets, and rings, amounting in value to over £16,000, having been made, it was decided that Mr. Schwarz should go to the North-Western in a cab the next day at about three o'clock in the afternoon. This he accordingly did, the following day being a Thursday.

"Business went on in the shop as usual under the direction of the head assistant, until about five o'clock Mr. Winslow returned from his club, where he usually spent an hour over the papers every afternoon, and asked for his nephew. To his astonishment Mr. Needham informed him that Mr. Schwarz had not yet returned. This seemed a little strange, and Mr. Winslow, with a slightly anxious look in his face, went in to consult his junior partner. Mr. Vassall offered to go round to the hotel and interview Mr. Pettitt.

"'I was beginning to get anxious myself," he said, 'but did not quite like to say so. I have been in over half-an-hour, hoping every moment that you would come in, and that perhaps you could give me some reassuring news. I thought that perhaps you had met Mr. Schwarz, and were coming back together.'

"However Mr. Vassall walked round to the hotel and interviewed the hall porter. The latter perfectly well remembered Mr. Schwarz sending in his card to Prince Semionicz.

"'At what time was that?' asked Mr. Vassall.

"'About ten minutes past three, sir, when he came; it was about an hour later when he left.'

"'When he left?' gasped, more than said, Mr. Vassall.

"'Yes, sir. Mr. Schwarz left here about a quarter before four, sir.'

"'Are you quite sure?'

"'Quite sure. Mr. Pettitt was in the hall when he left, and he asked him something about business. Mr. Schwarz laughed and said, "not bad." I hope there's nothing wrong, sir,' added the man.

"'Oh—er—nothing—thank you. Can I see Mr. Pettitt?'

"'Certainly, sir.'

"Mr. Pettitt, the manager of the hotel, shared Mr. Vassall's anxiety immediately when he heard that the young German had not yet returned home.

"'I spoke to him a little before four o'clock. We had just switched on the electric light, which we always do these winter months at that hour. But I shouldn't worry myself, Mr. Vassall; the young man may have

seen to some business on his way home. You'll probably find him in
when you go back.'

"Apparently somewhat reassured, Mr. Vassall thanked Mr. Pettitt
and hurried back to the shop, only to find that Mr. Schwarz had not
returned, though it was now close on eight o'clock.

"Mr. Winslow looked so haggard and upset that it would have been
cruel to heap reproaches upon his other troubles or to utter so much as
the faintest suspicion that young Schwarz's permanent disappearance
with £16,000 in jewels and money was within the bounds of
probability.

"There was one chance left, but under the circumstances a very
slight one indeed. The Winslows' private house was up the Birkenhead
end of the town. Young Schwarz had been living with them ever since
his arrival in Liverpool, and he may have—either not feeling well or for
some other reason—gone straight home without calling at the shop. It
was unlikely as valuable jewellery was never kept at the private house,
but—it just might have happened.

"It would be useless," continued the man in the corner, "and decidedly uninteresting were I to relate to you Messrs. Winslow's and
Vassall's further anxieties with regard to the missing young man. Suffice it to say that on reaching his private house Mr. Winslow found
that his godson had neither returned nor sent any telegraphic message
of any kind.

"Not wishing to needlessly alarm his wife, Mr. Winslow made an attempt at eating his dinner, but directly after he hurried back to the
North-Western Hotel, and asked to see Prince Semionicz. The Prince
was at the theatre with his secretary, and probably would not be home
until nearly midnight.

"Mr. Winslow, then, not knowing what to think, nor yet what to fear,
and in spite of the horror he felt of giving publicity to his nephew's
disappearance, thought it his duty to go round to the police station and
interview the inspector. It is wonderful how news of that type travels in
a large city like Liverpool. Already the morning papers of the following
day were full of the latest sensation: 'Mysterious disappearance of a
well-known tradesman.'

"Mr. Winslow found a copy of the paper containing the sensational
announcement on his breakfast table. It lay side by side with a letter
addressed to him in his nephew's handwriting, which had been posted
in Liverpool.

II

"Mr. Winslow placed that letter, written to him by his nephew, into
the hands of the police. Its contents, therefore, quickly became public
property. The astounding statements made therein by Mr. Schwarz

created, in quiet, businesslike Liverpool, a sensation which has seldom
been equalled.

"It appears that the young fellow did call on Prince Semionicz at a
quarter past three on Wednesday, December 10th, with a bag full of
jewels, amounting in value to some £16,000. The prince duly admired,
and finally selected from among the ornaments, a necklace, pendant
and bracelet, the whole being priced by Mr. Schwarz, according to his
instructions, at £10,500. Prince Semionicz was most prompt and businesslike in his dealings.

"'You will require immediate payment for these, of course,' he said
in perfect English, 'and I know you businessmen prefer solid cash to
cheques, especially when dealing with foreigners. I always provide
myself with plenty of Bank of England notes in consequence,' he added
with a pleasant smile, 'as £10,500 in gold would perhaps be a little in-
convenient to carry. If you will kindly make out the receipt my
secretary, M. Lambert, will settle all business matters with you.'

"He thereupon took the jewels he had selected and locked them up
in his dressing case, the beautiful silver fittings of which Mr. Schwarz
just caught a short glimpse of. Then, having been accommodated with
paper and ink, the young jeweller made out the account and receipt
whilst M. Lambert, the secretary, counted out before him 105 crisp
Bank of England notes of £100 each. Then, with a final bow to his exceedingly urbane and eminently satisfactory customer, Mr. Schwarz
took his leave. In the hall he saw and spoke to Mr. Pettitt, and then he
went out into the street.

"He had just left the hotel and was about to cross towards St.
George's Hall when a gentleman, in a magnificent fur coat, stepped
quickly out of a cab which had been stationed near the kerb, and
touching him lightly upon the shoulder said with an unmistakable air
of authority, at the same time handing him a card:

"'That is my name. I must speak with you immediately.'

"Schwarz glanced at the card and by the light of the arc lamps above
his head read on it the name of 'Dimitri Slaviansky Burgreneff, De la
IIIe Section Police Imperial de S. M. le Czar.'

"Quickly the owner of the unpronounceable name and the significant
titles, pointed to the cab from which he had just alighted, and Schwarz,
whose every suspicion with regard to his princely customer bristled up
in one moment, clutched his bag and followed his imposing interlocutor; as soon as they were both comfortably seated in the cab the latter
began with courteous apology in broken but fluent English:

"'I must ask your pardon, sir, for thus trespassing upon your valuable time, and I certainly should not have done so but for the certainty
that our interests in a certain matter which I have in hand are
practically identical, in so far that we both should wish to outwit a
clever rogue.'

"Instinctively, and his mind full of terrible apprehension, Mr. Schwarz's hand wandered to his pocketbook filled to overflowing with the bank notes which he had so lately received from the Prince.

"'Ah, I see,' interposed the courteous Russian with a smile, 'he has played the confidence trick on you, with the usual addition of so many so-called bank notes.'

"'So-called,' gasped the unfortunate young man.

"'I don't think I often err in my estimate of my own countrymen,' continued M. Burgreneff; 'I have vast experience, you must remember. Therefore, I doubt if I am doing M.—er—what does he call himself?— Prince something—an injustice if I assert, even without handling those crisp bits of paper you have in your pocketbook, that no bank would exchange them for gold.'

"Remembering his uncle's suspicion and his own, Mr. Schwarz cursed himself for his blindness and folly in accepting notes so easily without for a moment imagining that they might be false. Now, with every one of those suspicions fully on the alert, he felt the bits of paper with nervous, anxious fingers, while the imperturbable Russian calmly struck a match.

"'See here,' he said, pointing to one of the notes, 'the shape of that "w" in the signature of the chief cashier. I am not an English police officer, but I could pick out that spurious "w" among a thousand genuine ones. You see, I have seen a good many.'

"Now, of course, poor young Schwarz had not seen very many Bank of England notes. He could not have told whether one 'w' in Mr. Bowen's signature is better than another, but, though he did not speak English nearly as fluently as his pompous interlocutor, he understood every word of the appalling statement the latter had just made.

"'Then that Prince,' he said, 'at the hotel?——'

"'Is no more Prince than you and I, my dear sir,' concluded the gentleman of His Imperial Majesty's police, calmly.

"'And the jewels? Mr. Winslow's jewels?'

"'With the jewels there may be a chance—oh! a mere chance. These forged bank notes, which you accepted so trustingly, may prove the means of recovering your property.'

"'How?'

"'The penalty of forging and circulating spurious bank notes is very heavy. You know that. The fear of seven years' penal servitude will act as a wonderful sedative upon the—er—Prince's joyful mood. He will give up the jewels to me all right enough, never you fear. He knows,' added the Russian officer grimly, 'that there are plenty of old scores to settle up, without the additional one of forged bank notes. Our interests, you see, are identical. May I rely on your cooperation?'

"'Oh, I will do as you wish,' said the delighted young German. 'Mr.

Winslow and Mr. Vassall, they trusted me, and I have been such a fool. I hope it is not too late.'

"'I think not,' said M. Burgreneff, his hand already on the door of the cab. 'Though I have been talking to you I have kept an eye on the hotel, and our friend the Prince has not yet gone out. We are accustomed, you know, to have eyes everywhere, we of the Russian secret police. I don't think that I will ask you to be present at the confrontation. Perhaps you will wait for me in the cab. There is a nasty fog outside, and you will be more private. Will your give me those beautiful bank notes? Thank you! Don't be anxious. I won't be long.'

"He lifted his hat, and slipped the notes into the inner pocket of his magnificent fur coat. As he did so, Mr. Schwarz caught sight of a rich uniform and a wide sash, which no doubt was destined to carry additional moral weight with the clever rogue upstairs.

"Then His Imperial Majesty's police officer stepped quickly out of the cab, and Mr. Schwarz was left alone.

III

"Yes, left severely alone," continued the man in the corner with a sarcastic chuckle. "So severely alone in fact that one quarter of an hour after another passed by and still the magnificent police officer in the gorgeous uniform did not return. Then, when it was too late, Schwarz cursed himself once again for the double-dyed idiot that he was. He had been only too ready to believe that Prince Semionicz was a liar and a rogue, and under these unjust suspicions he had fallen an all-too-easy prey to one of the most cunning rascals he had ever come across.

"An inquiry from the hall porter at the North-Western elicited the fact that no such personage as Mr. Schwarz described had entered the hotel. The young man asked to see Prince Semionicz, hoping against hope that all was not yet lost. The Prince received him most courteously; he was dictating some letters to his secretary, while the valet was in the next room preparing his master's evening clothes. Mr. Schwarz found it very difficult to explain what he actually did want.

"There stood the dressing case in which the Prince had locked up the jewels, and there the bag from which the secretary had taken the bank notes. After much hesitation on Schwarz's part and much impatience on that of the Prince, the young man blurted out the whole story of the so-called Russian police officer whose card he still held in his hand.

"The Prince, it appears, took the whole thing wonderfully good-naturedly; no doubt he thought the jeweller a hopeless fool. He showed him the jewels, the receipt he held, and also a large bundle of bank

notes similar to those Schwarz had with such culpable folly given up to
the clever rascal in the cab.

"'I pay all my bills with Bank of England notes, Mr. Schwarz. It
would have been wiser, perhaps, if you had spoken to the manager of
the hotel about me before you were so ready to believe any cock-and-
bull story about my supposed rogueries.'

"Finally he placed a small 16mo volume before the young jeweller,
and said with a pleasant smile:

"'If people in this country who are in a large way of business, and
are therefore likely to come in contact with people of foreign na-
tionality, were to study these little volumes before doing business with
any foreigner who claims a title, much disappointment and a great loss
would often be saved. Now in this case had you looked up page 797 of
this little volume of Gotha's Almanac you would have seen my name in
it and known from the first that the so-called Russian detective was a
liar.'

"There was nothing more to be said, and Mr. Schwarz left the hotel.
No doubt now that he had been hopelessly duped; he dared not go
home and half hoped by communicating with the police that they
might succeed in arresting the thief before he had time to leave Liverpool. He interviewed Detective-Inspector Watson, and was at once
confronted with the awful difficulty which would make the recovery of
the bank notes practically hopeless. He had never had the time or opportunity of jotting down the numbers of the notes.

"Mr. Winslow, though terribly wrathful against his nephew, did not
wish to keep him out of his home. As soon as he had received
Schwarz's letter, he traced him, with Inspector Watson's help, to his
lodgings in North Street, where the unfortunate young man meant to
remain hidden until the terrible storm had blown over, or perhaps
until the thief had been caught red-handed with the booty still in his
hands.

"This happy event, needless to say, never did occur, though the
police made every effort to trace the man who had decoyed Schwarz
into the cab. His appearance was such an uncommon one; it seemed
most unlikely that no one in Liverpool should have noticed him after
he left that cab. The wonderful fur coat, the long beard, all must have
been noticeable, even though it was past four o'clock on a somewhat
foggy December afternoon.

"But every investigation proved futile; no one answering Schwarz's
description of the man had been seen anywhere. The papers continued
to refer to the case as "The Liverpool Mystery." Scotland Yard sent
Mr. Fairburn down—the celebrated detective—at the request of the
Liverpool police, to help in the investigations, but nothing availed.

"Prince Semionicz with his suite left Liverpool, and he who had attempted to blacken his character, and had succeeded in robbing Messrs. Winslow and Vassall of £10,500, had completely disappeared."

IV

The man in the corner readjusted his collar and necktie, which, during the narrative of this interesting mystery, had worked its way up his long, crane-like neck under his large flappy ears. His costume of checked tweed of a peculiarly loud pattern had tickled the fancy of some of the waitresses who were standing gazing at him and giggling in one corner. This evidently made him nervous. He gazed up very meekly at me, looking for all the world like a bald-headed adjutant dressed for a holiday.

"Of course, at first all sorts of theories of the theft got about. One of the most popular, and at the same time most quickly exploded, being that young Schwarz had told a cock-and-bull story, and was the actual thief himself.

"However, as I said before that was very quickly exploded, as Mr. Schwarz, senior, a very wealthy merchant, never allowed his son's carelessness to be a serious loss to his kind employers. As soon as he thoroughly grasped all the circumstances of the extraordinary case, he drew a cheque for £10,500 and remitted it to Messrs. Winslow and Vassall. It was just, but it was also high-minded.

"All Liverpool knew of the generous action, as Mr. Winslow took care that it should; and any evil suspicion regarding young Mr. Schwarz vanished as quickly as it had come.

"Then, of course, there was the theory about the Prince and his suite, and to this day I fancy there are plenty of people in Liverpool, and also in London, who declare that the so-called Russian police officer was a confederate. No doubt that theory was very plausible, and Messrs. Winslow and Vassall spent a good deal of money in trying to prove a case against the Russian Prince.

"Very soon, however, that theory was also bound to collapse. Mr. Fairburn, whose reputation as an investigator of crime waxes in direct inverted ratio to his capacities, did hit upon the obvious course of interviewing the managers of the larger London and Liverpool *agents-de-change*. He soon found that Prince Semionicz had converted a great deal of Russian and French money into English bank notes since his arrival in this country a few days ago. More than £30,000 in good, solid honest money, was traced to the pockets of the gentleman with the sixteen quarterings. It seemed, therefore, more than improbable, that a man who was obviously fairly wealthy would risk imprisonment and hard labour, if not worse, for the sake of increasing his fortune by £10,000.

"However, the theory of the Prince's guilt has taken firm root in the dull minds of our police authorities. They have had every information with regard to Prince Semionicz's antecedents from Russia; his position, his wealth, have been placed above suspicion, and yet they suspect and go on suspecting him or his secretary. They have communicated with the police of every European capital; and while they still hope to obtain sufficient evidence against those they suspect, they calmly allow the guilty to enjoy the fruit of his clever roguery."

"The guilty?" I said. "Who do you think——?"

"Who do I think knew at that moment that young Schwarz had money in his possession?" he said excitedly, wriggling in his chair like a jack in the box. "Obviously someone was guilty of that theft who knew that Schwarz had gone to interview a rich Russian and would in all probability return with a large sum of money in his possession."

"Who, indeed, but the Prince and his secretary?" I argued. "But just now you said——"

"Just now I said that the police were determined to find the Prince and his secretary guilty; they did not look further than their own stumpy noses. Messrs. Winslow and Vassall spent money with a free hand in those investigations. Mr. Winslow, as the senior partner, stood to lose over £9000 by that robbery. Now with Mr. Vassall it was different.

"When I saw how the police went on blundering in this case I took the trouble to make certain inquiries, the whole thing interested me so much, and I learnt all that I wished to know. I found out, namely, that Mr. Vassall was very much a junior partner in the firm, that he only drew ten percent of the profits, having been promoted lately to a partnership from having been senior assistant.

"Now the police did not take the trouble to find that out."

"But you don't mean that——"

"I mean that in all cases where robbery affects more than one person the first thing to find out is whether it affects the second party equally with the first. I proved that to you, didn't I, over that robbery in Phillimore Terrace. There, as here, one of the two parties stood to lose very little in comparison with the other——."

"Even then——" I began.

"Wait a moment, for I found out something more. The moment I had ascertained that Mr. Vassall was not drawing more than about £500 a year from the business profits I tried to ascertain at what rate he lived and what were his chief vices. I found that he kept a fine house in

Albert Terrace. Now the rents of those houses are £250 a year. Therefore speculation, horseracing or some sort of gambling, must help to keep up that establishment. Speculation and most forms of gambling are synonymous with debt and ruin. It is only a question of time. Whether Mr. Vassall was in debt or not at the time that I cannot say, but this I do know that ever since that unfortunate loss to him of about £1000 he has kept his house in nicer style than before, and he now has a good banking account at the Lancashire and Liverpool bank, which he opened a year after his 'heavy loss.'"

"But it must have been very difficult——" I argued.

"What?" he said. "To have planned out the whole thing? For carrying it out was mere child's play. He had twenty-four hours in which to put his plan into execution. Why, what was there to do? Firstly, to go to a local printer in some out of the way part of the town and get him to print a few cards with the high-sounding name. That, of course, is done 'while you wait.' Beyond that there was the purchase of a good secondhand uniform, fur coat, and a beard and a wig from a costumier's.

"No, no, the execution was not difficult; it was the planning of it all, the daring that was so fine. Schwarz, of course, was a foreigner; he had only been in England a little over a fortnight. Vassall's broken English misled him; probably he did not know the junior partner very intimately. I have no doubt that but for his uncle's absurd British prejudice and suspicions against the Russian Prince, Schwarz would not have been so ready to believe in the latter's roguery. As I said, it would be a great boon if English tradesmen studied Gotha more; but it was clever, wasn't it? I couldn't have done it much better myself."

That last sentence was so characteristic. I wished I could render its supreme overwhelming self-conceit. Before I could think of some plausible argument against his theory he was gone, and I was trying vainly to find another solution to the Liverpool mystery.

THE CASE OF MISS ELLIOTT

DRAMATIS PERSONAE

THE OLD MAN IN THE CORNER
who relates the story to
THE LADY JOURNALIST.
MISS ELLIOTT
(*matron of the Convalescent Home*).
DR. KINNAIRD
(*president of the Convalescent Home*).
DR. STAPYLTON
(*hon. sec. and treasurer of the Convalescent Home*).
MARY DAWSON
(*nurse of the Convalescent Home*).
MR. JAMES ELLIOTT
(*brother of the matron*).
DR. EARNSHAW
(*a consultant of the Convalescent Home*).
CONSTABLE FISKE.

I

The man in the corner was watching me over the top of his great bone-rimmed spectacles.

"Well?" he asked after a little while.

"Well," I repeated with some acerbity. I had been wondering for the last ten minutes how many more knots he would manage to make in that same bit of string, before he actually started undoing them again.

"Do I fidget you?" he asked apologetically, whilst his long bony fingers buried themselves, string, knots, and all, into the capacious pockets of his magnificent tweed ulster.

"Yes, that is another awful tragedy," he said quietly after a while. "Lady doctors are having a pretty bad time of it just now."

This was only his usual habit of speaking in response to my thoughts. There was no doubt that at the present moment my mind was filled with that extraordinary mystery which was setting all Scotland Yard by the ears and had completely thrown into the shade the sad story of Miss Hickman's tragic fate.

The *Daily Telegraph* had printed two columns headed "Murder or Suicide?" on the subject of the mysterious death of Miss Elliott, matron of the Convalescent Home, in Suffolk Avenue—and I must confess that a more profound and bewildering mystery had never been set before our able detective department.

"It has puzzled them this time, and no mistake," said the man in the corner, with one of his most gruesome chuckles, "but I dare say the public is quite satisfied that there is no solution to be found, since the police have found none."

"Can you find one?" I retorted with withering sarcasm.

"Oh, my solution would only be sneered at," he replied. "It is far too simple—and yet how logical! There was Miss Elliott, a good-looking, youngish, ladylike woman, fully qualified in the medical profession and in charge of the Convalescent Home in Suffolk Avenue, which is a private institution largely patronised by the benevolent.

"For sometime, already, there had appeared vague comments and rumours in various papers, that the extensive charitable contributions did not all go towards the upkeep of the Home. But, as is usual in institutions of that sort, the public was not allowed to know anything very definite, and contributions continued to flow in, whilst the Honorary Treasurer of the great Convalescent Home kept up his beautiful house in Hamilton Terrace, in a style which would not have shamed a peer of the realm.

"That is how matters stood, when on November 2nd last the morning papers contained the brief announcement that at a quarter past midnight two workmen walking along Blomfield Road, Maida Vale, suddenly came across the body of a young lady, lying on her face, close to the wooden steps of the narrow footbridge which at this point crosses the canal.

"This part of Maida Vale is, as you know, very lonely at all times, but at night it is usually quite deserted. Blomfield Road, with its row of small houses and bits of front gardens, faces the canal, and beyond the footbridge is continued in a series of small riverside wharves, which is practically unknown ground to the average Londoner. The footbridge itself, with steps at right angles and high wooden parapet, would offer excellent shelter at all hours of the night for any nefarious deed.

"It was within its shadows that the men had found the body, and to their credit be it said, they behaved like good and dutiful citizens—one of them went off in search of the police, whilst the other remained beside the corpse.

"From papers and books found upon her person, it was soon ascertained that the deceased was Miss Elliott, the young matron of the Suffolk Avenue Convalescent Home; and as she was very popular in her profession and had a great many friends, the terrible tragedy caused a sensation, all the more acute as very quickly the rumour gained ground that the unfortunate young woman had taken her own life in a most gruesome and mysterious manner.

"Preliminary medical and police investigation had revealed the fact that Miss Elliott had died through a deep and scientifically administered gash in the throat, whilst the surgical knife with which the deadly wound was inflicted still lay tightly grasped in her clenched hand."

II

The man in the corner, ever conscious of any effect he produced upon my excited imagination, had paused for a while, giving me time, as it were, to coordinate in my mind the few simple facts he had put before me. I had no wish to make a remark, knowing of old that my one chance of getting the whole of his interesting argument was to offer neither comment nor contradiction.

"When a young, good-looking woman in the heyday of her success in an interesting profession," he began at last, "is alleged to have committed suicide, the outside public immediately want to know the reason why she did such a thing, and a kind of freemasonic, amateur detective work goes on, which generally brings a few important truths to light. Thus, in the case of Miss Elliott, certain facts had begun to leak out, even before the inquest, with its many sensational developments. Rumours concerning the internal administration, or rather maladministration of the Home began to take more definite form.

"That its finances had been in a very shaky condition for some time was known to all those who were interested in its welfare. What was not so universally known was that few hospitals had had more munificent donations and subscriptions showered upon them in recent years, and yet it was openly spoken of by all the nurses that Miss Elliott had on more than one occasion petitioned for actual necessities for the patients—necessities which were denied to her on the plea of necessary economy.

"The Convalescent Home was, as sometimes happens in institutions of this sort, under the control of a committee of benevolent and fashionable people who understood nothing about business, and less still about the management of a hospital. Dr. Kinnaird, president of the institution, was a young, eminently successful consultant; he had recently married the daughter of a peer, who had boundless ambitions for herself and her husband.

"Dr. Kinnaird, by adding the prestige of his name to the Home, no doubt felt that he had done enough for its welfare. Against that, Dr.

Stapylton, hon. sec. and treasurer of the Home, threw himself heart and soul into the work connected with it, and gave a great deal of his time to it. All subscriptions and donations went, of course, through his hands, the benevolent and fashionable committee being only too willing to shift all their financial responsibilities onto his willing shoulders. He was a very popular man in society—a bachelor with a magnificent house in Hamilton Terrace, where he entertained the more eminent and fashionable clique in his own profession.

"It was the evening papers, however, which contained the most sensational development of this tragic case. It appears that on the Saturday afternoon Mary Dawson, one of the nurses in the Home, was going to the house surgeon's office with a message from the head nurse, when her attention was suddenly arrested in one of the passages by the sound of loud voices proceeding from one of the rooms. She paused to listen for a moment and at once recognised the voices of Miss Elliott and of Dr. Stapylton, the honorary treasurer and chairman of the Committee.

"The subject of conversation was evidently that of the eternal question of finance. Miss Elliott spoke very indignantly and Nurse Dawson caught the words:

"'Surely you must agree with me that Dr. Kinnaird ought to be informed at once.'

"Dr. Stapylton's voice in reply seems to have been at first bitingly sarcastic, then threatening. Dawson heard nothing more after that and went on to deliver her message. On her way back she stopped in the passage again, and tried to listen. This time it seemed to her as if she could hear the sound of someone crying bitterly, and Dr. Stapylton's voice speaking very gently.

"'You may be right, Nellie,' he was saying. 'At any rate wait a few days, before telling Kinnaird. You know what he is—he'll make a frightful fuss and——'

"Whereupon Miss Elliott interrupted him.

"'It isn't fair on Dr. Kinnaird to keep him in ignorance any longer. Whoever the thief may be it is your duty or mine to expose him, and if necessary bring him to justice.'

"There was a good deal of discussion at the time, if you remember, as to whether Nurse Dawson had overheard and repeated this speech accurately: whether, in point of fact, Miss Elliott had used the words '*or* mine' or '*and* mine.' You see the neat little point, don't you?" continued the man in the corner. "The little word 'and' would imply that she considered herself at one with Dr. Stapylton in the matter, but 'or' would mean that she was resolved to act alone if he refused to join her in unmasking the thief.

"All these facts, as I remarked before, had leaked out, as such facts have a way of doing. No wonder, therefore, that on the day fixed for the inquest the coroner's court was filled to overflowing, both with the public—ever eager for new sensations—and with the many friends of the deceased lady, among whom young medical students of both sexes and nurses in uniform were most conspicuous.

"I was there early, and therefore had a good seat, from which I could comfortably watch the various actors in the drama about to be performed. People who seemed to be in the know pointed out various personages to one another, and it was a matter of note that, in spite of professional engagements, the members of the staff of the Convalescent Home were present in full force and stayed on almost the whole time. The personages who chiefly arrested my attention were, firstly, Dr. Kinnaird, a good-looking Irishman of about forty, and president of the institution; also Dr. Earnshaw, a rising young consultant, with boundless belief in himself written all over his pleasant, rubicund countenance.

"The expert medical evidence was once again thoroughly gone into. There was absolutely no doubt that Miss Elliott had died from having her throat cut with the surgical knife which was found grasped in her right hand. There were absolutely no signs of a personal struggle in the immediate vicinity of the body, and rigid examination proved that there was no other mark of violence upon the body; there was nothing, therefore, to prove that the poor girl had not committed suicide in a moment of mental aberration or of great personal grief.

"Of course, it was strange that she should have chosen this curious mode of taking her own life. She had access to all kinds of poisons, amongst which her medical knowledge could prompt her to choose the least painful and most efficacious ones. Therefore, to have walked out on a Sunday night to a wretched and unfrequented spot and there committed suicide in that grim fashion seemed almost the work of a madwoman. And yet the evidence of her family and friends all tended to prove that Miss Elliott was a peculiarly sane, large-minded, and happy individual.

"However, the suicide theory was at this stage of the proceedings taken as being absolutely established, and when Police-Constable Fiske came forward to give his evidence no one in the court was prepared for a statement which suddenly revealed this case to be as mysterious as it was tragic.

"Fiske's story was this: close upon midnight on that memorable Sunday night he was walking down Blomfield Road along the side of the canal and towards the footbridge, when he overtook a lady and gentleman who were walking in the same direction as himself. He turned to look at them, and noticed that the gentleman was in evening dress and wore a high hat, and that the lady was crying.

"Blomfield Road is at best very badly lighted, especially on the side next to the canal, where there are no lamps at all. Fiske, however, was prepared to swear positively that the lady was the deceased. As for the gentleman, he might know him again or he might not.

"Fiske then crossed the footbridge, and walked on towards the Harrow Road. As he did so, he heard St. Mary Magdalen's church clock chime the hour of midnight. It was a quarter of an hour after that, that the body of the unfortunate girl was found, and clasping in her hand the knife with which that awful deed had been done. By whom? Was it really by her own self? But if so, why did not that man in evening dress who had last seen her alive come forward and throw some light upon this fast thickening veil of mystery?

"It was Mr. James Elliott, brother of the deceased, however, who first mentioned a name then in open court, which has ever since in the minds of everyone been associated with Miss Elliott's tragic fate.

"He was speaking in answer to a question of the coroner's anent his sister's disposition and recent frame of mind.

"'She was always extremely cheerful,' he said, 'but recently had been peculiarly bright and happy. I understood from her that this was because she believed that a man for whom she had a great regard was also very much attached to her, and meant to ask her to be his wife.'

"'And do you know who this man was?' asked the coroner.

"'Oh, yes,' replied Mr. Elliott, 'it was Dr. Stapylton.'

"Everyone had expected that name, of course, for everyone remembered Nurse Dawson's story, yet when it came, there crept over all those present an indescribable feeling that something terrible was impending.

"'Is Dr. Stapylton here?'

"But Dr. Stapylton had sent an excuse. A professional case of the utmost urgency had kept him at a patient's bedside. But Dr. Kinnaird, the president of the institution, came forward.

"Questioned by the coroner, Dr. Kinnaird, however, who evidently had a great regard for his colleague, repudiated any idea that the funds of the institution had ever been tampered with by the treasurer.

"'The very suggestion of such a thing,' he said, 'was an outrage upon one of the most brilliant men in the profession.'

"He further added that, although he knew that Dr. Stapylton thought very highly of Miss Elliott, he did not think that there was any actual engagement, and most decidedly he (Dr. Kinnaird) had heard nothing of any disagreement between them.

"'Then did Dr. Stapylton never tell you that Miss Elliott had often chafed under the extraordinary economy practised in the richly-endowed Home?' asked the coroner again.

"'No,' replied Dr. Kinnaird.

"'Was not that rather strange reticence?'

"'Certainly not. I am only the honorary president of the institution—Stapylton has chief control of its finances.'

"'Ah!' remarked the coroner blandly.

"However, it was clearly no business of his at this moment to enter into the financial affairs of the Home. His duty at this point was to try and find out if Dr. Stapylton and the man in evening dress were one and the same person.

"The men who found the body testified to the hour: a quarter past midnight. As Fiske had seen the unfortunate girl alive a little before twelve, she must have been murdered or had committed suicide between midnight and a quarter past. But there was something more to come.

"How strange and dramatic it all was," continued the man in the corner, with a bland smile, altogether out of keeping with the poignancy of his narrative; "all these people in that crowded court trying to reconstruct the last chapter of that bright young matron's life and then—but I must not anticipate.

"One more witness was to be heard—one whom the police, with a totally unconscious sense of what is dramatic, had reserved for the last. This was Dr. Earnshaw, one of the staff of the Convalescent Home. His evidence was very short, but of deeply momentous import. He explained that he had consulting rooms in Weymouth Street, but resided in Westbourne Square. On Sunday, November 1st, he had been dining out in Maida Vale, and returning home a little before midnight saw a woman standing close by the steps of the footbridge in the Blomfield Road.

"'I had been coming down Formosa Street and had not specially taken notice of her, when just as I reached the corner of Blomfield Road she was joined by a man in evening dress and high hat. Then I crossed the road, and recognised both Miss Elliott and——'

"The young doctor paused, almost as if hesitating before the enormity of what he was about to say, whilst the excitement in court became almost painful.

"'And——?' urged the coroner.

"'And Dr. Stapylton,' said Dr. Earnshaw at last, almost under his breath.

"'You are quite sure?' asked the coroner.

"'Absolutely positive. I spoke to them both and they spoke to me.'

"'What did you say?'

"'Oh, the usual, "Hello, Stapylton!" to which he replied, "Hello!" I then said "Goodnight" to them both, and Miss Elliott also said "Goodnight." I saw her face more clearly then, and thought that she looked very tearful and unhappy, and Stapylton looked ill-tempered. I wondered why they had chosen that unhallowed spot for a midnight walk.'

"'And you say the hour was——?' asked the coroner.

"'Ten minutes to twelve. I looked at my watch as I crossed the foot-bridge, and had heard a quarter to twelve strike five minutes before.'

"Then it was that the coroner adjourned the inquest. Dr. Stapylton's attendance had become absolutely imperative. According to Dr. Earnshaw's testimony, he had been with deceased certainly a quarter of an hour before she met her terrible death. Fiske had seen them together ten minutes later; she was then crying bitterly. There was as yet no actual charge against the fashionable and rich doctor, but already the ghostly bird of suspicion had touched him with its ugly wing."

III

"As for the next day," continued the man in the corner after a slight pause, "I can assure you that there was not a square foot of standing room in the coroner's court for the adjourned inquest. It was timed for eleven A.M., and at six o'clock on that cold winter's morning the pavement outside the court was already crowded. As for me, I always manage to get a front seat, and I did on that occasion, too. I fancy that I was the first among the general public to note Dr. Stapylton, as he entered the room accompanied by his solicitor, and by Dr. Kinnaird, with whom he was chatting very cheerfully and pleasantly.

"Mind you, I am a great admirer of the medical profession, and I think a clever and successful doctor usually has a most delightful air about him—the consciousness of great and good work done with profit to himself—which is quite unique and quite admirable.

"Dr. Stapylton had that air even to a greater extent than his colleague, and from the affectionate way in which Dr. Kinnaird finally shook him by the hand, it was quite clear that the respected chief of the Convalescent Home, at any rate, refused to harbour any suspicion of the integrity of its treasurer.

"Well, I must not weary you by dwelling on the unimportant details of this momentous inquest. Constable Fiske, who was asked to identify the gentleman in evening dress whom he had seen with the deceased at a few minutes before twelve, failed to recognise Dr. Stapylton very positively: pressed very closely, he finally refused to swear either way. Against that, Dr. Earnshaw repeated, clearly and categorically, looking his colleague straight in the face the while, the damnatory evidence he had given the day before.

"I saw Dr. Stapylton, I spoke to him, and he spoke to me,' he repeated most emphatically.

"Everyone in that court was watching Dr. Stapylton's face, which wore an air of supreme nonchalance, even of contempt, but certainly neither of guilt nor fear.

"Of course, by that time *I* had fully made up my mind as to where the hitch lay. in this extraordinary mystery; but no one else had, and everyone held their breath as Dr. Stapylton quietly stepped into the box, and after a few preliminary questions the coroner asked him very abruptly:

"'You were in the company of the deceased a few minutes before she died, Dr. Stapylton?'

"'Pardon me,' replied the latter quietly, 'I last saw Miss Elliott alive on Saturday afternoon, just before I went home from my work.'

"This calm reply, delivered without a tremor, positively made everyone gasp. For the moment coroner and jury were alike staggered.

"'But we have two witnesses here who saw you in the company of the deceased within a few minutes of twelve o'clock on the Sunday night!' the coroner managed to gasp out at last.

"'Pardon me,' again interposed the doctor, 'these witnesses were mistaken.'

"'Mistaken!'

"I think everyone would have shouted out the word in boundless astonishment had they dared to do so.

"'Dr. Earnshaw was mistaken,' reiterated Dr. Stapylton quietly. 'He neither saw me nor did he speak to me.'

"'You can substantiate that, of course?' queried the coroner.

"'Pardon me,' once more said the doctor, with utmost calm; 'it is surely Dr. Earnshaw who should substantiate *his* statement.'

"'There is Constable Fiske's corroborative evidence for that,' retorted the coroner, somewhat nettled.

"'Hardly, I think. You see, the constable states that he saw a gentleman in evening dress, etc., talking to the deceased at a minute or two before twelve o'clock, and that when he heard the clock of St. Mary Magdalen chime the hour of midnight he was just walking away from the footbridge. Now, just as that very church clock was chiming that hour, I was stepping into a cab at the corner of Harrow Road, not a hundred yards *in front* of Constable Fiske.'

"'You swear to that?' queried the coroner in amazement.

"'I can easily prove it,' said Dr. Stapylton. 'The cabman who drove me from there to my club is here and can corroborate my statement.'

"And amidst boundless excitement, John Smith, a hansom cabdriver, stated that he was hailed in the Harrow Road by the last witness, who told him to drive to the Royal Clinical Club, in Mardon Street. Just as he started off, St. Mary Magdalen's church, close by, struck the hour of midnight.

"At that very moment, if you remember, Constable Fiske had just crossed the footbridge, and was walking towards the Harrow Road, and he was quite sure (for he was closely questioned afterwards) that no one overtook him from behind. Now there would be no way of getting from one side of the canal to the other at this point except over that footbridge; the nearest bridge is fully 200 yards further down the Blomfield Road. The girl was alive a minute *before* the constable crossed the footbridge, and it would have been absolutely impossible for anyone to have murdered a girl, placed the knife in her hand, run a couple of hundred yards to the next bridge and another 300 to the corner of Harrow Road, all in the space of three minutes.

"This alibi, therefore, absolutely cleared Dr. Stapylton from any suspicion of having murdered Miss Elliott. And yet, looking on that man as he sat there, calm, cool, and contemptuous, no one could have had the slightest doubt but that he was lying—lying when he said he had not seen Miss Elliott that evening; lying when he denied Dr. Earnshaw's statement; lying when he professed himself ignorant of the poor girl's fate.

"Dr. Earnshaw repeated his statement with the same emphasis, but it was one man's word against another's, and as Dr. Stapylton was so glaringly innocent of the actual murder, there seemed no valid reason at all why he should have denied having seen her that night, and the point was allowed to drop. As for Nurse Dawson's story of his alleged quarrel with Miss Elliott on the Saturday night, Dr. Stapylton again had a simple and logical explanation.

"'People who listen at keyholes,' he said quietly, 'are apt to hear only fragments of conversation, and often mistake ordinary loud voices for quarrels. As a matter of fact, Miss Elliott and I were discussing the dismissal of certain nurses from the Home, whom she deemed incompetent. Nurse Dawson was among that number. She desired their immediate dismissal, and I tried to pacify her. That was the subject of my conversation with the deceased lady. I can swear to every word of it.'"

IV

The man in the corner had long ceased speaking, and was placing quietly before me a number of photographs. One by one I saw the series of faces which had been watched so eagerly in the coroner's court that memorable afternoon by an excited crowd.

"So the fate of poor Miss Elliott has remained wrapt in mystery?" I said thoughtfully at last.

"To everyone," rejoined the funny creature, "except to me."

"Ah! What is your theory, then?"

"A simple one, dear lady; so simple that it really amazes me that no one, not even you, my faithful pupil, ever thought of it."

"It may be so simple that it becomes idiotic," I retorted with lofty disdain.

"Well, that may be. Shall I at any rate try to make it clear?"

"If you like."

"For this I think the best way would be, if you were to follow me through what transpired before the inquest. But first tell me, what do you think of Dr. Earnshaw's statement?"

"Well," I replied, "a good many people thought that it was he who murdered Miss Elliott, and that his story of meeting Dr. Stapylton with her was a lie from beginning to end."

"Impossible," he retorted, making an elaborate knot in his bit of string. "Dr. Earnshaw's friends with whom he had been dining that night swore that he was *not* in evening dress, nor wore a high hat. And on that point—the evening dress, and the hat—Constable Fiske was most positive."

"Then Dr. Earnshaw was mistaken, and it was not Dr. Stapylton he met."

"Impossible!" he shrieked, whilst another knot went to join its fellows. "He spoke to Dr. Stapylton, and Dr. Stapylton spoke to him."

"Very well, then," I argued; "why should Dr. Stapylton tell a lie about it? He had such a conclusive alibi that there could be no object in his making a false statement about that."

"No object!" shrieked the excited creature. "Why, don't you *see* that he had to tell the lie in order to set police, coroner, and jury by the ears, because he did not wish it to be even remotely hinted at, that the man whom Dr. Earnshaw saw with Miss Elliott, and the man whom Constable Fiske saw with her ten minutes later were *two different persons.*"

"Two different persons!" I ejaculated.

"Aye! two confederates in this villainy. No one has ever attempted to deny the truth of the shaky finances of the Home; no one has really denied that Miss Elliott suspected certain defalcations and was trying to force the hands of the Honorary Treasurer towards a full inquiry. That the Honorary Treasurer knew where all the money went to was pretty clear all along—his magnificent house in Hamilton Terrace fully testifies to that. That the president of the institution was a party to these defalcations and largely profited by them I for one am equally convinced."

"Dr. Kinnaird?" I ejaculated in amazement.

"Aye, Dr. Kinnaird. Do you mean to tell me that he alone among the entire staff of that Home was ignorant of those defalcations? Impossible! And if he knew of them, and did neither inquire into them nor attempt to stop them, then he *must* have been a party to them. Do you admit that?"

"Yes, I admit that," I replied.

"Very well then. The rest is quite simple; those two men, unworthy to bear the noble appellation of doctor, must for years have quietly stolen the money subscribed by the benevolent for the Home, and converted it to their own use: then, they suddenly find themselves face to face with immediate discovery in the shape of a young girl determined to unmask the systematic frauds of the past few years. That meant exposure, disgrace, ruin for them both, and they determine to be rid of her.

"Under the pretence of an evening walk, her so-called lover entices her to a lonely and suitable spot; his confederate is close by, hidden in the shadows, ready to give him assistance if the girl struggles and screams. But suddenly Dr. Earnshaw appears. He recognises Stapylton and challenges him. For a moment the villains are nonplussed, then Kinnaird—the cleverer of the two—steps forward, greets the two lovers unconcernedly, and after two minutes' conversation casually reminds Stapylton of an appointment the latter is presumed to have at a club in St. James' Street.

"The latter understands and takes the hint, takes a quick farewell of the girl, leaving her in his friend's charge, then, as fast as he can, goes off, presently takes a cab, leaving his friend to do the deed, whilst the alibi he can prove, coupled with Dr. Earnshaw's statement, was sure to bewilder and mislead the police and the public.

"Thus it was that though Dr. Earnshaw saw and recognised Dr. Stapylton, Constable Fiske saw Dr. Kinnaird, whom he did *not* recognise, on whom no suspicion had fallen, and whose name had never been coupled with that of Miss Elliott. When Constable Fiske had turned his back, Kinnaird murdered the girl and went off quietly, whilst Dr. Stapylton, on whom all suspicions were bound to fasten sooner or later, was able to prove the most perfect alibi ever concocted.

"One day I feel certain that the frauds at the Home will be discovered, and then who knows what else may see the light?

"Think of it all quietly when I am gone, and tomorrow when we meet tell me whether if *I* am wrong what is *your* explanation of this extraordinary mystery."

Before I could reply he had gone, and I was left wondering, gazing at the photographs of two good-looking, highly respectable and respected men, whom an animated scarecrow had just boldly accused of committing one of the most dastardly crimes ever recorded in our annals.

THE LISSON GROVE MYSTERY

DRAMATIS PERSONAE

THE OLD MAN IN THE CORNER
who explains the mystery to
THE LADY JOURNALIST
who retells it.
MR. DYKE
(a crippled old man).
MISS AMELIA DYKE
(his daughter).
MRS. MARSH
(a neighbour of the Dykes').
MR. AND MRS. PITT
(other neighbours).
ALFRED WYATT
(fiancé of Amelia Dyke).
NICHOLSON
(a charwoman).
MESSRS. SNOW AND PATTERSON
(solicitors).
MR. PARLETT
(their clerk).
WILFRED POAD
(manager of a motor-car depôt).
CONSTABLE TURNER
(who was called in after Mr. Dyke's murder).
MR. AND MRS. OGDEN
(witnesses in the murder case).

I

The man in the corner ordered another glass of milk, and timidly asked for a second cheesecake at the same time.

"I am going down to the Marylebone Police Court, to see those people brought up before the 'Beak,'" he remarked.

"What people?" I queried.

"What people!" he exclaimed, in the greatest excitement. "You don't mean to say that you have not studied the Lisson Grove Mystery?"

I had to confess that my knowledge on that subject was of the most superficial character.

"One of the most interesting cases that has cropped up in recent years," he said, with an indescribable look of reproach.

"Perhaps. I did not study it in the papers because I preferred to hear *you* tell me all about it," I said.

"Oh, if that's it," he replied, as he settled himself down in his corner like a great bird after the rain, "then you showed more sense than lady journalists usually possess. I can, of course, give you a far clearer account than the newspapers have done; as for the police—well! I never saw such a muddle as they are making of this case."

"I daresay it is a peculiarly difficult one," I retorted, for I am ever a champion of that hardworking department.

"H'm!" he said, "so, so—it is a tragedy in a prologue and three acts. I am going down this afternoon to see the curtain fall for the third time on what, if I mistake not, will prove a good burlesque; but it all began dramatically enough. It was last Saturday, November 21st, that two boys, playing in the little spinney just outside Wembley Park Station, came across three large parcels done up in American cloth.

"With the curiosity natural to their age, they at once proceeded to undo these parcels, and what they found so upset the little beggars that they ran howling through the spinney and the polo ground, straight as a dart to Wembley Park Station. Half frantic with excitement, they told their tale to one of the porters on duty, who walked back to the spinney with them. The three parcels, in point of fact, contained the remains of a dismembered human body. The porter sent one of the boys for the local police, and the remains were duly conveyed to the mortuary, where they were kept for identification.

"Three days later—that is to say, on Tuesday, November 24th, Miss Amelia Dyke, residing at Lisson Grove Crescent, returned from Edinburgh, where she had spent three or four days with a friend. She drove up from St. Pancras in a cab, and carried her small box up herself to the door of the flat, at which she knocked loudly and repeatedly—so loudly and so persistently, in fact, that the inhabitants of the neighbouring flats came out onto their respective landings to see what the noise was about.

"Miss Amelia Dyke was getting anxious, Her father, she said, must be seriously ill, or else why did he not come and open the door to her. Her anxiety, however, reached its culminating point when Mr. and Mrs. Pitt, who reside in the flat immediately beneath that occupied by the Dykes, came forward with the alarming statement that, as a matter of fact, they had themselves been wondering if anything were wrong with old Mr. Dyke, as they had not heard any sound overhead for the last few days.

"Miss Amelia, now absolutely terrified, begged one of the neighbours to fetch either the police or a locksmith, or both. Mr. Pitt ran out at once, both police and locksmith were brought upon the scene, the door was forcibly opened, and amidst indescribable excitement Constable Turner, followed by Miss Dyke, who was faint and trembling with apprehension, effected an entrance into the flat.

"Everything in it was tidy and neat to a degree, all the fires were laid, the beds made, the floors were clean and washed, the brasses polished, only a slight, very slight layer of dust lay over everything, dust that could not have accumulated for more than a few days. The flat consisted of four rooms and a bathroom; in not one of them was there the faintest trace of old Mr. Dyke.

"In order fully to comprehend the consternation which all the neighbours felt at this discovery," continued the man in the corner, "you must understand that old Mr. Dyke was a helpless cripple; he had been a mining engineer in his young days, and a terrible blasting accident deprived him, at the age of forty, of both legs. They had been amputated just above the knee, and the unfortunate man—then a widower with one little girl—had spent the remainder of his life on crutches. He had a small—a very small—pension, which, as soon as his daughter Amelia was grown up, had enabled him to live in comparative comfort in the small flat in Lisson Grove Crescent.

"His misfortune, however, had left him terribly sensitive; he never could bear the looks of compassion thrown upon him, whenever he ventured out on his crutches, and even the kindliest sympathy was positive torture to him. Gradually, therefore, as he got on in life, he took to staying more and more at home, and after awhile gave up going out altogether. By the time he was sixty-five years old and Miss Amelia a fine young woman of seven-and-twenty, old Dyke had not been outside the door of his flat for at least five years.

"And yet, when Constable Turner aided by the locksmith entered the flat on that memorable November 24th, there was not a trace anywhere of the old man.

"Miss Amelia was in the last stages of despair, and at first she seemed far too upset and hysterical to give the police any coherent and definite information. At last, however, from amid the chaos of tears and of ejaculations, Constable Turner gathered the following facts:

"Miss Amelia had some great friends in Edinburgh whom she had long wished to visit, her father's crippled condition making this extremely difficult. A fortnight ago, however, in response to a very ur-

gent invitation, she at last decided to accept it, but, in order to leave
her father altogether comfortable, she advertised in the local paper for
a respectable woman who would come to the flat every day and see to
all the work, cook his dinner, make the bed, and so on.

"She had several applications in reply to this advertisement, and ultimately selected a very worthy-looking elderly person, who, for seven
shillings a week, undertook to come daily from seven in the morning
until about six in the afternoon, to see to all Mr. Dyke's comforts.

Miss Amelia was very favourably impressed with this person's
respectable and motherly appearance, and she left for Edinburgh by
the 5:15 A.M. train on the morning of Thursday, November 19th, feeling confident that her father would be well looked after. She certainly
had not heard from the old man while she was away, but she had not
expected to hear unless, indeed, something had been wrong.

Miss Amelia was quite sure that something dreadful had happened
to her father, as he could not possibly have walked downstairs and out
of the house alone; certainly his crutches were nowhere to be found,
but this only helped to deepen the mystery of the old man's disappearance.

"The constable, having got thus far with his notes, thought it best to
refer the whole matter at this stage to higher authority. He got from
Miss Amelia the name and address of the charwoman, and then went
back to the station.

"There, the very first news that greeted him was that the medical officer of the district had just sent round to the various police stations his
report on the human remains found in Wembley Park the previous
Saturday: they had proved to be the dismembered body of an old man
between sixty and seventy years of age, the immediate cause of whose
death had undoubtedly been a violent blow on the back of the head
with a heavy instrument, which had shattered the cranium. Expert
examination further revealed the fact that deceased had had in early
life both legs removed by a surgical operation just above the knee.

"That was the end of the prologue in the Lisson Grove tragedy,"
continued the man in the corner, after a slight and dramatic pause, "as
far as the public was concerned. When the curtain was subsequently
raised upon the first act, the situation had been considerably changed.

"The remains had been positively identified as those of old Mr.
Dyke, and a charge of wilful murder had been brought against Alfred
Wyatt, of no occupation, residing in Warlock Road, Lisson Grove, and
against Amelia Dyke for complicity in the crime. They are the two
people whom I am going to see this afternoon brought before the Beak
at the Marylebone Police Court."

II

"Two very important bits of evidence, I must tell you, had come to light, on the first day of the inquest and had decided the police to make this double arrest.

"In the first place, according to one or two of the neighbours, who happened to know something of the Dyke household, Miss Amelia had kept company for some time with a young man named Alfred Wyatt: he was an electrical engineer, resided in the neighbourhood, and was some years younger than Miss Dyke. As he was known not to be very steady, it was generally supposed that the old man did not altogether approve of his daughter's engagement.

"Mrs. Pitt, residing in the flat, immediately below the one occupied by the Dykes, had stated, moreover, that on Wednesday the 18th, at about midday, she heard very loud and angry voices proceeding from above; Miss Amelia's shrill tones being specially audible. Shortly afterwards she saw Wyatt go out of the house; but the quarrel continued for some little time without him, for the neighbours could still hear Miss Amelia's high-pitched voice, speaking very excitedly and volubly.

"'An hour later,' further explained Mrs. Pitt, 'I met Miss Dyke on the stairs; she seemed very flushed and looked as if she had been crying. I suppose she saw that I noticed this, for she stopped and said to me:

"'"All this fuss, you know, Mrs. Pitt, because Alfred asked me to go for a drive with him this afternoon, but I am going all the same."

"'Later in the afternoon, it must have been quite half-past four, for it was getting dark, young Wyatt drove up in a motorcar, and presently I heard Miss Dyke's voice on the stairs saying very pleasantly and cheerfully: "All right, daddy, we shan't be long." Then Mr. Dyke must have said something which I didn't hear, for she added, "Oh, that's all right; I am well wrapped up, and we have plenty of rugs!"'

"Mrs. Pitt then went to her window and saw Wyatt and Amelia Dyke start off in a motor. She concluded that the old man had been mollified, for both Amelia and Wyatt waved their hands affectionately up towards the window. They returned from their drive about six o'clock: Wyatt saw Amelia to the door, and then went off again. The next day Miss Dyke went to Scotland.

"As you see," continued the man in the corner, "Alfred Wyatt had become a very important personality in this case; he was Amelia's sweetheart, and it was strange—to say the least of it—that she had never as yet even mentioned his name. Therefore when she was recalled in order to give further evidence, you may be sure that she was pretty sharply questioned on the subject of Alfred Wyatt.

"In her evidence before the coroner, she adhered fairly closely to her original statement:

"'I did not mention Mr. Wyatt's name,' she explained, 'because I did not think it was of any importance; if he knew anything about my dear father's mysterious fate, he would have come forward at once, of course, and helped me to find out who the cowardly murderer was who could attack a poor, crippled old man. Mr. Wyatt was devoted to my father, and it is perfectly ridiculous to say that daddy objected to my engagement; on the contrary, he gave us his full consent, and we were going to be married directly after the New Year, and continue to live with father in the flat.'

"'But,' questioned the coroner, who had not by any means departed from his severity, 'what about this quarrel which the last witness overheard on the subject of your going out driving with Mr. Wyatt?'

"'Oh, that was nothing,' replied Miss Dyke very quietly. 'Daddy only objected because he thought that it was rather too late to start at four o'clock, and that I should be cold. When he saw that we had plenty of rugs he was quite pleased for me to go.'

"'Isn't it rather astonishing, then,' asked the coroner, 'seeing that Mr. Wyatt was on such good terms with your father, that he did not go to see him while you were away?'

"'Not at all,' she replied unconcernedly; 'Alfred went down to Edinburgh on the Thursday evening. He couldn't travel with me in the morning, for he had some business to see to in town that day; but he joined me at my friends' house on the Friday morning, having travelled all night.'

"'Ah!' remarked the coroner drily, 'then he had not seen your father since you left.'

"'Oh yes,' said Miss Amelia; 'he called round to see dad during the day, and found him looking well and cheerful.'

"Miss Amelia Dyke, as she gave this evidence, seemed absolutely unconscious of saying anything that might in any way incriminate her lover. She is a handsome, though somewhat coarse-looking woman, nearer thirty, I should say, than she would care to own. I was present at the inquest, mind you, for that case had too many mysteries about it from the first for it to have eluded my observation, and I watched her closely throughout. Her voice struck me as fine and rich, with—in this instance also—a shade of coarseness in it; certainly, it was very far from being high-pitched, as Mrs. Pitt had described it.

"When she had finished her evidence she went back to her seat, looking neither flustered nor uncomfortable, although many looks of contempt and even of suspicion were darted at her from every corner of the crowded court.

"Nor did she lose her composure in the slightest degree when Mr.

Parlett, clerk to Messrs. Snow and Patterson, solicitors, of Bedford
Row, in his turn came forward and gave evidence; only while the little
man spoke her full red lips curled and parted with a look of complete
contempt.

"Mr. Parlett's story was indeed a remarkable one, inasmuch as it
suddenly seemed to tear asunder the veil of mystery which so far had
surrounded the murder of old Dyke by supplying it with a motive—a
strong motive, too: the eternal greed of gain.

"In June last, namely, it appears that Messrs. Snow and Patterson
received intimation from a firm of Melbourne solicitors that a man of
the name of Dyke had died there recently, leaving a legacy of £4000 to
his only brother, James Arthur Dyke, a mining engineer, who in 1890
was residing at Lisson Grove Crescent. The Melbourne solicitors in
their communication asked for Messrs. Snow and Patterson's kind
assistance in helping them to find the legatee.

"The search was easy enough, since James Arthur Dyke, mining
engineer, had never ceased to reside at Lisson Grove Crescent. Armed,
therefore, with full instructions from their Melbourne correspondent,
Messrs. Snow and Patterson communicated with Dyke, and after a
little preliminary correspondence, the sum of £4000 in Bank of Aus-
tralia notes and various securities were handed over by Mr. Parlett to
the old cripple.

"The money and securities were—so Mr. Parlett understood—subsequently deposited by Mr. Dyke at the Portland Road Branch of the
London and South Western Bank; as the old man apparently died
intestate, the whole of the £4000 would naturally devolve upon his only
daughter and natural legatee.

"Mind you, all through the proceedings, the public had instinctively
felt that money was somewhere at the bottom of this gruesome and
mysterious crime. There is not much object in murdering an old cripple except for purposes of gain, but now Mr. Parlett's evidence had
indeed furnished a damning motive for the appalling murder.

"What more likely than that Alfred Wyatt wanting to finger that
£4000 had done away with the old man? And if Amelia Dyke did not
turn away from him in horror, after such a cowardly crime, then she
must have known of it and had perhaps connived in it.

"As for Nicholson, the charwoman, her evidence had certainly done
more to puzzle everybody all round than any other detail in this
strange and mysterious crime.

"She deposed that on Friday, November 13th, in answer to an advertisement in the *Marylebone Star,* she had called on Miss Dyke at
Lisson Grove, when it was arranged that she should do a week's work
at the flat, beginning Thursday, the 19th, from seven in the morning
until six in the afternoon. She was to keep the place clean, get Mr.

Dyke—who, she understood, was an invalid—all his meals, and make herself generally useful to him.

"Accordingly, Nicholson turned up on the Thursday morning. She let herself into the flat, as Miss Dyke had entrusted the latchkey to her, and went on with the work. Mr. Dyke was in bed, and she got him all his meals that day. She thought she was giving him satisfaction, and was very astonished when, at six o'clock, having cleared away his tea, he told her that he would not require her again. He gave her no explanation, asked her for the latchkey, and gave her her full week's money—seven shillings in full. Nicholson then put on her bonnet, and went away.

"Now," continued the man in the corner, leaning excitedly forward, and marking each sentence he uttered with an exquisitely complicated knot in his bit of string, "an hour later, another neighbour, Mrs. Marsh, who lived on the same floor as the Dykes, on starting to go out, met Alfred Wyatt on the landing. He took off his hat to her, and then knocked at the door of the Dyke's flat.

"When she came home at eight o'clock, she again passed him on the stairs; he was then going out. She stopped to ask him how Mr. Dyke was, and Wyatt replied: 'Oh, fairly well, but he misses his daughter, you know.'

"Mrs. Marsh, now closely questioned, said that she thought Wyatt was carrying a large parcel under his arm, but she could not distinguish the shape of the parcel as the angle of the stairs, where she met him, was very dark. She stated though that he was running down the stairs very fast.

"It was on all that evidence that the police felt justified in arresting Alfred Wyatt for the murder of James Arthur Dyke, and Amelia Dyke for connivance in the crime. And now this very morning, those two young people have been brought before the magistrate, and at this moment evidence—circumstantial, mind you, but positively damning—is being heaped upon them by the prosecution. The police did their work quickly. The very evening after the first day of the inquest, the warrant was out for their arrest."

He looked at a huge silver watch which he always carried in his waistcoat pocket.

"I don't want to miss the defence," he said, "for I know that it will be sensational. But I did not want to hear the police and medical evidence all over again. You'll excuse me, won't you? I shall be back here for five o'clock tea. I know you will be glad to hear all about it."

III

When I returned to the A.B.C. shop for my tea at five minutes past five, there he sat in his accustomed corner, with a cup of tea before him, another placed opposite to him, presumably for me, and a long piece of string between his bony fingers.

"What will you have with your tea?" he asked politely, the moment I was seated.

"A roll and butter and the end of the story," I replied.

"Oh, the story has no end," he said with a chuckle; "at least, not for the public. As for me, why. I never met a more simple 'mystery.' Perhaps that is why the police were so completely at sea."

"Well, and what happened?" I queried with some impatience.

"Why, the usual thing," he said, as he once more began to fidget nervously with his bit of string. "The prisoners had pleaded not guilty, and the evidence for the prosecution was gone into in full. Mr. Parlett repeated his story of the £4000 legacy, and all the neighbours had some story or other to tell about Alfred Wyatt, who, according to them, was altogether a most undesirable young man.

"I heard the fag end of Mrs. Marsh's evidence. When I reached the court she was repeating the story she had already told to the police.

"Someone else in the house had also heard Wyatt running helter-skelter downstairs at eight o'clock on the Thursday evening; this was a point, though a small one, in favour of the accused. A man cannot run downstairs when he is carrying the whole weight of a dead body, and the theory of the prosecution was that Wyatt had murdered old Dyke on that Thursday evening, got into his motorcar somewhere, scorched down to Wembley with the dismembered body of his victim, deposited it in the spinney where it was subsequently found, and finally had driven back to town, stabled his motorcar, and reached King's Cross in time for the 11:30 night express to Edinburgh. He would have time for all that, remember, for he would have three hours and a half to do it in.

"Besides which the prosecution had unearthed one more witness, who was able to add another tiny link to the already damning chain of evidence built up against the accused.

"Wilfred Poad, namely, manager of a large cycle and motorcar depôt in Euston Road, stated that on Thursday afternoon. November 19th, at about half-past six o'clock Alfred Wyatt, with whom he had had some business dealings before, had hired a small car from him, with the understanding that he need not bring it back until after eleven P.M. This was agreed to, Poad keeping the place open until just before eleven, when Wyatt drove up in the car, paid for the hire of it and then walked away from the shop in the direction of the Great Northern terminus.

"That was pretty strong against the male prisoner wasn't it? For, mind you, Wyatt had given no satisfactory account whatever of his time between eight P.M., when Mrs. Marsh had met him going out of Lisson Grove Crescent, and eleven P.M., when he brought back the car to the Euston Road shop. 'He had been driving about aimlessly,' so he said. Now one doesn't go out motoring for hours on a cold, drizzly night in November for no purpose whatever.

"As for the female prisoner, the charge against her was merely one of complicity.

"This closed the case for the prosecution," continued the funny creature with one of his inimitable chuckles, "leaving but one tiny point obscure, and that was, the murdered man's strange conduct in dismissing the woman Nicholson.

"Yes, the case was strong enough, and yet there stood both prisoners in the dock, with that sublime air of indifference and contempt which only complete innocence or hardened guilt could give.

"Then when the prosecution had had their say, Alfred Wyatt chose to enter the witness box and make a statement in his own defence. Quietly, and as if he were making the most casual observation he said:

"'I am not guilty of the murder of Mr. Dyke, and in proof of this I solemnly assert that on Thursday, November 19th, the day I am supposed to have committed the crime, the old man was still alive at half-past ten o'clock in the evening.'

"He paused a moment, like a born actor, watching the effect he had produced. I tell you, it was astounding.

"'I have three separate and independent witnesses here,' continued Wyatt, with the same deliberate calm, 'who heard and saw Mr. Dyke as late as half-past ten that night. Now, I understand that the dismembered body of the old man was found close to Wembley Park. How could I, between half-past ten and eleven o'clock, have killed Dyke, cut him up, cleaned and put the flat all tidy, carried the body to the car, driven on to Wembley, hidden the corpse in the spinney, and be back in Euston Road, all in the space of half-an-hour? I am absolutely innocent of this crime and, fortunately, it is easy for me now to prove my innocence.'

"Alfred Wyatt had made no idle boast. Mrs. Marsh had seen him running down stairs at 8 P.M. An hour after that, the Pitts in the flat beneath heard the old man moving about overhead.

"'Just as usual,' observed Mrs. Pitt. 'He always went to bed about nine, and we could always hear him most distinctly.'

"John Pitt, the husband, corroborated this statement; the old man's movements were quite unmistakable because of his crutches.

"Henry Ogden, on the other hand, who lived in the house facing the block of flats, saw the light in Dyke's window that evening, and the old man's silhouette upon the blind from time to time. The light was put out at half-past ten. This statement again was corroborated by Mrs. Ogden, who also had noticed the silhouette and the light being extinguished at half-past ten.

"But this was not all; both Mr. and Mrs. Ogden had seen old Dyke at his window, sitting in his accustomed armchair, between half-past eight and nine o'clock. He was gesticulating, and apparently talking to someone else in the room whom they could not see.

"Alfred Wyatt, therefore, was quite right when he said that he would have no difficulty in proving his innocence. The man whom he was supposed to have murdered was, according to the testimony, alive at six o'clock; according to Mr. and Mrs. Ogden he was alive and sitting in his window until nine; again, he was heard to move about until ten o'clock by both the Pitts, and at half-past ten only was the light put out in his flat. Obviously, therefore, as his dead body was found twelve miles away, Wyatt, who was out of the Crescent at eight, and in Euston Road at eleven, could not have done the deed.

"He was discharged, of course; the magistrate adding a very severe remark on the subject of 'carelessly collected evidence.' As for Miss Amelia, she sailed out of the court like a queen after her coronation, for with Wyatt's discharge the case against her naturally collapsed. As for me, I walked out too, with an elated feeling at the thought that the intelligence of the British race had not yet sunk so low as our friends on the Continent would have us believe."

IV

"But then, who murdered the old man?" I asked, for I confess the matter was puzzling me in an irritating kind of a way.

"Ah! who indeed?" he rejoined sarcastically, while an artistic knot went to join its fellows along that never-ending bit of string.

"I wish you'd tell me what's in your mind," I said, feeling peculiarly irritated with him just at that moment.

"What's in my mind?" he replied with a shrug of his thin shoulders. "Oh, only a certain degree of admiration!"

"Admiration at what?"

"At a pair of exceedingly clever criminals."

"Then you do think that Wyatt murdered Dyke?"

"I don't think—I am sure."

"But when did they do it?"

"Ah, that's more to the point. Personally, I should say between them on Wednesday morning, November 18th."

"The day they went for that motorcar ride?" I gasped.

"And carried away the old man's remains beneath a multiplicity of rugs," he added.

"But he was *alive* long after that!" I urged. "The woman, Nicholson——"

'The woman Nicholson saw and spoke to a man in bed, whom she *supposed* was old Mr. Dyke. Among the many questions put to her by those clever detectives, no one thought, of course, of asking her to describe the old man. But even if she had done so, Wyatt was far too great an artist in crime not to have contrived a makeup which, described by a witness who had never before seen Dyke, would easily pass as a description of the old man himself."

"Impossible!" I said, struck in spite of myself by the simplicity of his logic.

"Impossible, you say?" he shrieked excitedly. "Why, I call that crime a masterpiece from beginning to end; a display of ingenuity which, fortunately, the criminal classes seldom possess, or where would society be? Here was a crime committed, where everything was most beautifully stagemanaged, nothing left unforeseen. Shall I reconstruct it for you?"

"Do!" I said, handing across the table to him a brand new, beautiful bit of string, on which his talon-like fingers fastened as upon a prey.

"Very well," he said, marking each point with a scientific knot. "Here it is, scene by scene: there was Alfred Wyatt and Amelia Dyke—a pair of blackguards, eager to obtain that £4000 which only the man's death could secure for them. They decide upon killing him, and: Scene 1, Miss Amelia makes *her* arrangements. She advertises for a charwoman, and engages one, who is to be a very useful witness presently.

"Scene 2—The murder, brutal, horrible, on the person of an old cripple, whilst his own daughter stands by, and the dismembering of the body.

"Scene 3—The ride in the motorcar, after dark, remember, and with plenty of rugs, beneath which the gruesome burden is concealed. The scene is accompanied by the comedy of Miss Dyke speaking to her father, and waving her hand affectionately at him from below. I tell you, that woman must have had some nerve!

"Then, scene 4—The arrival at Wembley, and the hiding of the remains.

"Scene 5—Amelia goes to Edinburgh by the 5:15 A.M. train, and thus secures her own alibi. After that, the comedy begins in earnest. The impersonation of the dead man by Wyatt during the whole of that memorable Thursday. Mind you, that was not very difficult; it only needed the brain to invent, and the nerve to carry it through. The charwoman had never seen old Dyke before; she only knew that he was an invalid. What more natural than that she should accept as her new master the man who lay in bed all day, and only spoke a few words to her? A very slight makeup of hair and beard would complete the illusion.

"Then, at six o'clock, the woman gone, Wyatt steals out of the house, bespeaks the motorcar, leaves it in the street in a convenient spot, and is back in time to be seen by Mrs. Marsh at seven.

"The rest is simplicity itself. The silhouette at the window was easy enough to arrange; the sound of a man walking on crutches is easily imitated with a couple of umbrellas—the actual crutches were no doubt burned directly after the murder. Lastly, the putting out of the light at half-past ten was the crowning stroke of genius.

"One little thing might have upset the whole wonderful plan, but that one thing only, and that was if the body had been found *before* the great comedy scene of Thursday had been fully played. But that spinney near Wembley was well-chosen. People don't go wandering under trees and in woods on cold November days, and the remains were not found until the Saturday.

"Ah, it was cleverly stagemanaged, and no mistake. I couldn't have done it better myself. Won't you have another cup of tea? No? Don't look so upset. The world does not contain many such clever criminals as Alfred Wyatt and Amelia Dyke."

THE TRAGEDY IN DARTMOOR TERRACE

DRAMATIS PERSONAE

THE OLD MAN IN THE CORNER
who unravels the mystery to
THE LADY JOURNALIST
who retells it.
MRS. YULE
(*a rich widow who is found dead in her house*).
WILLIAM YULE
(*her son*).
MRS. WILLIAM YULE
(*his wife*).
WILLIAM BLOGGS
(*a gardener's son whom Mrs. Yule adopted*).
MR. STATHAM
(*a solicitor*).
ANNIE and JANE
(*servants*).

I

"It is not by any means the Law and Police Courts that form the only interesting reading in the daily papers," said the man in the corner airily, as he munched his eternal bit of cheesecake and sipped his glass of milk, like a frowsy old tomcat.

"You don't agree with me," he added, for I had offered no comment to his obvious remark.

"No?" I answered. "I suppose you were thinking——"

"Of the tragic death of Mrs. Yule, for instance," he replied eagerly. "Beyond the inquest, and its very unsatisfactory verdict, very few circumstances connected with that interesting case ever got into the papers at all."

"I forget what the verdict actually was," I said, eager, too, on my side to hear him talk about that mysterious tragedy, which, as a matter of fact, had puzzled a good many people.

"Oh, it was as vague and as wordy as the English language would allow. The jury found that 'Mrs. Yule had died through falling downstairs, in consequence of a fainting attack, but *how* she came to fall is not clearly shown.'"

"What had happened was this: Mrs. Yule was a rich and eccentric old lady, who lived very quietly in a small house in Kensington; No. 9, Dartmoor Terrace is, I believe, the correct address.

"She had no expensive tastes, for she lived, as I said before, very simply and quietly in a small Kensington house, with two female servants—a cook and a housemaid—and a young fellow whom she had adopted as her son.

"The story of this adoption is, of course, the pivot round which all the circumstances of the mysterious tragedy revolved. Mrs. Yule, namely, had an only son, William, to whom she was passionately attached; but, like many a fond mother, she had the desire of mapping out that son's future entirely according to her own ideas. William Yule, on the other hand, had his own views with regard to his own happiness, and one fine day went so far as to marry the girl of his choice, and that in direct opposition to his mother's wishes.

"Mrs. Yule's chagrin and horror at what she called her son's base ingratitude knew no bounds; at first it was even thought that she would never get over it.

"'He has gone in direct opposition to my fondest wishes, and chosen a wife whom I could never accept as a daughter; he shall have none of the property which has enriched me, and which I know he covets.'

"At first her friends imagined that she meant to leave all her money to charitable institutions; but oh! dear me, no! Mrs. Yule was one of those women who never did anything that other people expected her to. Within three years of her son's marriage she had filled up the place which he had vacated both in her house and in her heart. She had adopted a son, preferring, as she said, that her money should benefit an individual rather than an institution.

"Her choice had fallen upon the only son of a poor man—an ex-soldier—who used to come twice a week to Dartmoor Terrace to tidy up the small garden at the back: he was very respectable and very honest—was born in the same part of England as Mrs. Yule, and had an only son whose name happened to be William: he rejoiced in the surname of Bloggs.

"'It suits me in every way,' explained Mrs. Yule to old Mr. Statham, her friend and solicitor. 'You see, I am used to the name of William, and the boy is nice-looking and has done very well at the Board School. Moreover, old Bloggs will die within a year or two, and William will be left without any incumbrances.'

"Herein Mrs. Yule's prophecy proved to be correct. Old Bloggs did die very soon and his son was duly adopted by the rich and eccentric old lady, sent to a good school and finally given a berth in the Union Bank.

"I saw young Bloggs—it is not a euphonious name, is it?—at that memorable inquest later on. He was very young and unassuming, and used to keep very much out of the way of Mrs. Yule's friends, who, mind you, strongly disapproved of his presence in the rich old widow's house, to the detriment of the only legitimate son and heir.

"What happened within the intimate close circle of 9, Dartmoor Terrace during the next three years of course nobody can tell. Certain it is that by the time young Bloggs was nearing his twenty-first birthday, he had become the very apple of his adopted mother's eye.

"During those three years Mr. Statham and other old friends had worked hard in the interests of William Yule. Everyone felt that the latter was being very badly treated indeed. He had studied painting in his younger days, and now had set up a small studio in Hampstead, and was making perhaps a couple of hundred or so a year, and that, with much difficulty, whilst the gardener's son had supplanted him in his mother's affections, and, worse still, in his mother's purse.

"The old lady was more obdurate than ever. In deference to the strong feelings of her friends she had agreed to see her son occasionally, and William Yule would call upon his mother from time to time—in the middle of the day when Bloggs was out of the way at the Bank—stay to tea, and part from her in frigid, though otherwise amicable terms.

"'I have no ill-feeling against my son,' the old lady would say, 'but when he married against my wishes, he became a stranger to me—that is all—a stranger, however, whose pleasant acquaintanceship I am pleased to keep up.'

"That the old lady meant to carry her eccentricities in this respect to the bitter end, became all the more evident, when she sent for her old friend and lawyer, Mr. Statham, and explained to him that she wished to make over to young Bloggs the whole of her property by deed of gift, during her lifetime—on condition that on his twenty-first birthday he legally took up the name of Yule.

"Mr. Statham subsequently made public, as you know, the whole of this interview which he had with Mrs. Yule.

"'I tried to dissuade her, of course,' he said, 'for I thought it so terribly unfair on William Yule, and his children. Moreover, I had always hoped that when Mrs. Yule grew older and more feeble she would surely relent towards her only son. But she was terribly obstinate.'

"'It is because I may become weak in my dotage,' she said, 'that I want to make the whole thing absolutely final—I don't want to relent. I wish that William should suffer, where I think he will suffer most, for he was always overfond of money. If I make a will in favour of Bloggs, who knows I might repent it, and alter it at the eleventh hour? One is apt to become maudlin when one is dying, and has people weeping all round one. No!—I want the whole thing to be absolutely irrevocable; and I shall present the deed of gift to young Bloggs on his twenty-first birthday. I can always make it a condition that he keeps me in moderate comfort to the end of my days. He is too big a fool to be really ungrateful, and after all I don't think I should very much mind ending my life in the workhouse.'

"'What could I do?' added Mr. Statham. 'If I had refused to draw up that iniquitous deed of gift, she only would have employed some other lawyer to do it for her. As it is, I secured an annuity of £500 a year for the old lady, in consideration of a gift worth some £30,000 made over absolutely to Mr. William Bloggs.'

"The deed was drawn up," continued the man in the corner, "there is no doubt of that. Mr. Statham saw to it. The old lady even insisted on having two more legal opinions upon it, lest there should be the slightest flaw that might render the deed invalid. Moreover, she caused herself to be examined by two specialists in order that they might testify that she was absolutely sound in mind, and in full possession of all her faculties.

"When the deed was all that the law could wish, Mr. Statham handed it over to Mrs. Yule, who wished to keep it by her until April 3rd—young Bloggs' twenty-first birthday—on which day she meant to surprise him with it.

"Mr. Statham handed over the deed to Mrs. Yule on February 14th, and on March 28th—that is to say, six days before Bloggs' majority—the old lady was found dead at the foot of the stairs in Dartmoor Terrace, whilst her desk was found to have been broken open, and the deed of gift had disappeared."

II

"From the very first the public took a great interest in the sad death of Mrs. Yule. The old lady's eccentricities were pretty well known throughout all her neighbourhood, at any rate. Then, she had a large circle of friends, who all took sides, either for the disowned son or for the old lady's rigid and staunch principles of filial obedience.

"Directly, therefore, that the papers mentioned the sudden death of Mrs. Yule, tongues began to wag, and whilst some asserted 'Accident,' others had already begun to whisper 'Murder.'

"For the moment nothing definite was known. Mr. Bloggs had sent for Mr. Statham, and the most persevering and most inquisitive persons of both sexes could glean no information from the cautious old lawyer.

"The inquest was to be held on the following day, and perforce curiosity had to be bridled until then. But you may imagine how that coroner's court at Kensington was packed on that day. I, of course, was at my usual place—well to the front—for I was already keenly interested in the tragedy, and knew that a palpitating mystery lurked behind the old lady's death.

"Annie, the housemaid at Dartmoor Terrace, was the first, and I may say the only really important, witness during that interesting inquest. The story she told amounted to this: Mrs. Yule, it appears, was very religious, and, in spite of her advancing years and decided weakness of the heart, was in the habit of going to early morning service every day of her life at six o'clock. She would get up before anyone else in the house, and winter or summer, rain or snow, or fine, she would walk round to St. Matthias' Church, coming home at about a quarter to seven, just when her servants were getting up.

"On this sad morning (March 28th) Annie explained that she got up as usual and went downstairs (the servants slept at the top of the house) at seven o'clock. She noticed nothing wrong, her mistress's bedroom door was open as usual. Annie merely remarking to herself that the mistress was later than usual from church that morning. Then suddenly, in the hall at the foot of the stairs, she caught sight of Mrs. Yule lying head downwards, her head on the mat, motionless.

"'I ran downstairs as quickly as I could,' continued Annie, 'and I suppose I must 'ave screamed, for cook came out of 'er room upstairs, and Mr. Bloggs, too, shouted down to know what was the matter. At first we only thought Mrs. Yule was unconscious like. Me and Mr. Bloggs carried 'er to 'er room, and then Mr. Bloggs ran for the doctor.'

"The rest of Annie's story," continued the man in the corner, "was drowned in a deluge of tears. As for the doctor, he could add but little to what the public had already known and guessed. Mrs. Yule undoubtedly suffered from a weak heart, although she had never been known to faint. In this instance, however, she undoubtedly must have turned giddy, as she was about to go downstairs, and fallen headlong. She was of course, very much injured—the doctor explained—but she actually died of heart failure, brought on by the shock of the fall. She must have been on her way to church, for her prayer book was found on the floor close by her, also a candle—which she must have carried, as it was a dark morning—had rolled along and extinguished itself as it rolled. From these facts, therefore, it was gathered that the poor old lady came by this tragic death at about six o'clock, the hour at which she regularly started out for morning service. Both the servants and also Mr. Bloggs slept at the top of the house, and it is a known fact that sleep in most cases is always heaviest in the early morning hours; there was, therefore, nothing strange in the fact that no one heard either the fall or a scream, if Mrs. Yule uttered one, which is doubtful.

"So far you see," continued the man in the corner, after a slight pause, "there did not appear to be anything very out of the way or mysterious about Mrs. Yule's tragic death. But the public had expected interesting developments, and I must say their expectations were more than fully realised.

"Jane, the cook, was the first witness to give the public an inkling of the sensations to come.

"She deposed that on Thursday, the 27th, she was alone in the kitchen in the evening after dinner, as it was the housemaid's evening out, when, at about nine o'clock there was a ring at the bell.

"'I went to answer the door,' said Jane, 'and there was a lady, all dressed in black as far as I could see—as the 'all gas always did burn very badly—I still think she was dressed dark, and she 'ad on a big 'at and a veil with spots. She says to me: "Mrs. Yule lives 'ere?" I says "She do 'm," though I don't think she was quite the lady, so I don't know why I said 'm, but——'

"'Yes, yes!' here interrupted the coroner somewhat impatiently, 'it doesn't matter what you said. Tell us what happened.'

"'Yes, sir,' continued Jane, quite undisturbed, 'as I was saying, I asked the lady her name, and she says: "Tell Mrs. Yule I would wish to speak with her," then as she saw me 'esitating, for I didn't like leaving 'er all alone in the 'all, she said, "Tell Mrs. Yule, that Mrs. William Yule wishes to speak with 'er."'

"Jane paused to take breath, for she talked fast and volubly, and all eyes were turned to a corner of the room, where William Yule, dressed in the careless fashion affected by artists, sat watching and listening eagerly to everything that was going on. At the mention of his wife's name he shrugged his shoulders, and I thought for the moment that he would jump up and say something; but he evidently thought better of it, and remained as before, silent and quietly watching.

"'You showed the lady upstairs?' asked the coroner, after an instant's most dramatic pause.

"'Yes, sir,' replied Jane; 'but I went to ask the mistress first. Mrs. Yule was sitting in the drawing room reading. She says to me, "Show the lady up at once; and, Jane," she says, "ask Mr. Bloggs to kindly come to the drawing room." I showed the lady up, and I told Mr. Bloggs, who was smoking in the library, and 'e went to the drawing room.

"'When Annie come in,' continued Jane, with increased volubility, 'I told 'er 'oo 'ad come, and she and me was very astonished, because we 'ad often seen Mr. William Yule come to see 'is mother, but we 'ad never seen 'is wife. "Did you see what she was like, cook?" says Annie to me. "No," I says, "the 'all gas was burnin' that badly, and she 'ad a veil on." Then Annie ups and says "I must go up, cook," she says, "for my things is all wet. I never did see such rain in all my life. I tell you my boots and petticoats is all soaked through." Then up she runs, and I thought then that per'aps she meant to see if she couldn't 'ear anything that was goin' on upstairs. Presently she come down——'

"But at this point Jane's flow of eloquence received an unexpected check. The coroner preferred to hear from Annie herself whatever the latter may have overheard, and Jane, very wrathful and indignant, had to stand aside, while Annie, who was then recalled, completed the story.

"'I don't know what made me stop on the landing,' she explained timidly, 'and I'm sure I didn't mean to listen. I was going upstairs to change my things, and put on my cap and apron, in case the mistress wanted anything.

"'Then, I don't think I ever 'eard Mrs. Yule's voice so loud and angry.'

"'You stopped to listen?' asked the coroner.

"'I couldn't 'elp it, sir. Mrs. Yule was shoutin' at the top of 'er voice. "Out of my house," she says, "I never wish to see you or your precious husband inside my doors again."

"'You are quite sure that you heard those very words?' asked the coroner earnestly.

"'I'll take my Bible oath on every one of them sir,' said Annie emphatically. 'Then I could 'ear someone crying and moaning: "Oh! what have I done? Oh! what have I done?" I didn't like to stand on the landing then, for fear someone should come out, so I ran upstairs, and put on my cap and apron, for I was all in a tremble, what with what I'd 'eard, and the storm outside, which was coming down terrible.

"'When I went down again, I 'ardly durst stand on the landing, but the door of the drawing room was ajar, and I 'eard Mr. Bloggs say: "Surely you will not turn a human being, much less a woman, out on a night like this?" And the mistress said, still speaking very angry: "Very well, you may sleep here; but remember, I don't wish to see your face again. I go to church at six and come home again at seven; mind you are out of the house before then. There are plenty of trains after seven o'clock.'"

"After that," continued the man in the corner, "Mrs. Yule rang for the housemaid and gave orders that the spare room should be got ready, and that the visitor should have some tea and toast brought to her in the morning as soon as Annie was up.

"But Annie was rather late on that eventful morning of the 28th. She did not go downstairs till seven o'clock. When she did, she found her mistress lying dead at the foot of the stairs. It was not until after the doctor had been and gone that both the servants suddenly recollected the guest in the spare room. Annie knocked at her door, and receiving no answer, she walked in; the bed had not been slept in, and the spare room was empty.

"'There now!' was the housemaid's decisive comment, 'me and cook did 'ear someone cross the 'all, and the front door bang about an hour after everyone else was in bed.'

"Presumably, therefore, Mrs. William Yule had braved the elements and left the house at about midnight, leaving no trace behind her, save, perhaps, the broken lock of the desk that had held the deed of gift in favour of young Bloggs."

III

"Some say there's a Providence that watches over us," said the man in the corner, when he had looked at me keenly, and assured himself that I was really interested in his narrative, "others use the less poetic and more direct formula, that 'the devil takes care of his own.' The impression of the general public during this interesting coroner's inquest was that the devil was taking special care of his own ('his own' being in this instance represented by Mrs. William Yule, who, by the way, was not present).

"What the Evil One had done for her was this: He caused the hall gas to burn so badly on that eventful Thursday night, March 27th, that Jane, the cook, had not been able to see Mrs. William Yule at all distinctly. He, moreover, decreed that when Annie went into the drawing room later on to take her mistress's orders, with regard to the spare room, Mrs. William was apparently dissolved in tears, for she only presented the back of her head to the inquisitive glances of the young housemaid.

"After that the two servants went to bed, and heard someone cross the hall and leave the house about an hour or so later; but neither of them could swear positively that they would recognise the mysterious visitor if they set eyes on her again.

"Throughout all these proceedings, however, you may be sure that Mr. William Yule did not remain a passive spectator. In fact, I, who watched him, could see quite clearly that he had the greatest possible difficulty in controlling himself. Mind you, I knew by then exactly where the hitch lay, and I could, and will presently, tell you exactly all that occurred on Thursday evening, March 27th, at No. 9, Dartmoor Terrace, just as if I had spent that memorable night there myself; and I can assure you that it gave me great pleasure to watch the faces of the two men most interested in the verdict of this coroner's jury.

"Everyone's sympathy had by now entirely veered round to young Bloggs, who for years had been brought up to expect a fortune, and had then, at the last moment, been defrauded of it, through what looked already much like a crime. The deed of gift had, of course, not been what the lawyers call 'completed.' It had rested in Mrs. Yule's desk, and had never been 'delivered' by the donor to the donee, or even to another person on his behalf.

"Young Bloggs, therefore, saw himself suddenly destined to live his life as penniless as he had been when he was still the old gardener's son.

"No doubt the public felt that what lurked mostly in his mind was a desire for revenge, and I think everyone forgave him when he gave his evidence with a distinct tone of animosity against the woman, who had apparently succeeded in robbing him of a fortune.

"He had only met Mrs. William Yule once before, he explained, but he was ready to swear that it was she who called that night. As for the original motive of the quarrel between the two ladies, young Bloggs was inclined to think that it was mostly on the question of money.

"'Mrs. William,' continued the young man, 'made certain peremptory demands on Mrs. Yule, which the old lady bitterly resented.'

"But here there was an awful and sudden interruption. William Yule, now quite beside himself with rage, had with one bound reached the witness-box, and struck young Bloggs a violent blow in the face.

"'Liar and cheat!' he roared, 'take that!'

"And he prepared to deal the young man another even more vigorous blow, when he was overpowered and seized by the constables. Young Bloggs had become positively livid; his face looked grey and ashen, except there, where his powerful assailant's fist had left a deep purple mark.

"'You have done your wife's cause no good,' remarked the coroner drily, as William Yule, sullen and defiant, was forcibly dragged back to his place. 'I shall adjourn the inquest until Monday, and will expect Mrs. Yule to be present and to explain exactly what happened after her quarrel with the deceased, and why she left the house so suddenly and mysteriously that night.'

"William Yule tried an explanation even then. His wife had never left the studio in Sheriff Road, West Hampstead, the whole of that Thursday evening. It was a fearfully stormy night, and she never went outside the door. But the Yules kept no servant at the cheap little rooms; a charwoman used to come in every morning only for an hour or two, to do the rough work; there was no one, therefore, except the husband himself to prove Mrs. William Yule's alibi.

"At the adjourned inquest, on the Monday, Mrs. William Yule duly appeared; she was a young, delicate-looking woman with a patient and suffering face, that had not an atom of determination or vice in it.

"Her evidence was very simple; she merely swore solemnly that she had spent the whole evening indoors, she had never been to 9, Dartmoor Terrace in her life, and, as a matter of fact, would never have dared to call on her irreconcilable mother-in-law. Neither she nor her husband were specially in want of money either.

"'My husband had just sold a picture at the Water Colour Institute,' she explained, 'we were not hard up; and certainly I should never have attempted to make the slightest demand on Mrs. Yule.'

"There the matter had to rest with regard to the theft of the document, for that was no business of the coroner's or of the jury. According to medical evidence the old lady's death had been due to a very natural and possible accident—a sudden feeling of giddiness—and the verdict had to be in accordance with this.

"There was no real proof against Mrs. William Yule—only one man's word, that of young Bloggs; and it would no doubt always have been felt that his evidence might not be wholly unbiased. He was therefore well advised not to prosecute. The world was quite content to believe that the Yules had planned and executed the theft, but he never would have got a conviction against Mrs. William Yule just on his own evidence."

IV

"Then William Yule and his wife were left in full possession of their fortune?" I asked eagerly.

"Yes, they were," he replied; "but they had to go and travel abroad for a while; feeling was so high against them. The deed, of course, not having been 'delivered,' could not be upheld in a court of law; that was the opinion of several eminent counsel whom Mr. Statham, with a lofty sense of justice, consulted on behalf of young Bloggs."

"And young Bloggs was left penniless?"

"No," said the man in the corner, as, with a weird and satisfied smile, he pulled a piece of string out of his pocket; "the friends of the late Mrs. Yule subscribed the sum of £1000 for him, for they all thought he had been so terribly badly treated, and Mr. Statham has taken him in his office as articled pupil. No! no! young Bloggs has not done so badly either——"

"What seems strange to me," I remarked, "is that, for ought she knew, Mrs. William Yule might have committed only a silly and purposeless theft. If Mrs. Yule had not died suddenly and accidentally the next morning, she would, no doubt, have executed a fresh deed of gift, and all would have been *in statu quo*."

"Exactly," he replied drily, whilst his fingers fidgeted nervously with his bit of string.

"Of course," I suggested, for I felt that the funny creature wanted to be drawn out; "she may have reckoned on the old lady's weak heart, and the shock to her generally, but it was, after all, very problematical."

"Very," he said, "and surely you are not still under the impression that Mrs. Yule's death was purely the result of an accident?"

"What else could it be?" I urged.

"The result of a slight push from the top of the stairs," he remarked placidly, whilst a complicated knot went to join a row of its fellows.

"But Mrs. William Yule had left the house before midnight—or, at any rate, someone had. Do you think she had an accomplice?"

"I think," he said excitedly, "that the mysterious visitor who left the house that night had an instigator whose name was William Bloggs."

"I don't understand," I gasped in amazement.

"Point No. 1," he shrieked, while the row of knots followed each other in rapid succession, "young Bloggs swore a lie when he swore that it was Mrs. William Yule who called at Dartmoor Terrace that night."

"What makes you say that?" I retorted.

"One very simple fact," he replied, "so simple that it was, of course, overlooked. Do you remember that one of the things which Annie overheard was old Mrs. Yule's irate words.'Very well, you may sleep here; but, remember, I do not wish to see your face again. You can leave my house before I return from church; you can get plenty of trains after seven o'clock.' Now what do you make of that?" he added triumphantly.

"Nothing in particular," I rejoined; "it was an awfully wet night, and——"

"And High Street Kensington Station within two minutes' walk of Dartmoor Terrace, with plenty of trains to West Hampstead, and Sheriff Road within two minutes of this latter station," he shrieked, getting more and more excited, "and the hour only about ten o'clock, when there *are* plenty of trains, from one part of London to another? Old Mrs. Yule, with her irascible temper, and obstinate ways would have said: 'There's the station, not two minutes walk, get out of my house, and don't ever let me see your face again.' Wouldn't she now?"

"It certainly seems more likely."

"Of course it does. She only allowed the woman to stay because the woman had either a very long way to go to get a train, or perhaps had missed her last train—a connection on a branch line presumably—and could not possibly get home at all that night."

"Yes, that sounds logical," I admitted.

"Point No. 2," he shrieked, "young Bloggs having told a lie, had some object in telling it. That was my starting point; from there I worked steadily until I had reconstructed the events of that Thursday night—nay more, until I knew something more about young Bloggs' immediate future, in order that I might then imagine his past.

"And this is what I found.

"After the tragic death of Mrs. Yule, young Bloggs went abroad at the expense of some kind friends, and came home with a wife, whom he is supposed to have met and married in Switzerland. From that point everything became clear to me. Young Bloggs had told a lie when he swore that it was Mrs. William Yule who called that night—it was certainly *not* Mrs. William Yule; therefore it was somebody who either represented herself as such, or who believed herself to be Mrs. William Yule.

"The first supposition," continued the funny creature, "I soon dismissed as impossible; young Bloggs knew Mrs. William Yule by sight—and since he had lied, he had done so deliberately. Therefore to my mind the lady who called herself Mrs. William Yule did so because she believed that she had a right to that name; that she had married a man, who, for purposes of his own, had chosen to call himself by that name. From this point to that of guessing who that man was was simple enough."

"Do you mean young Bloggs himself?" I asked in amazement.

"And whom else?" he replied. "Isn't that sort of thing done every day? Bloggs was a hideous name, and Yule was eventually to be his own. With William Yule's example before him, he must have known that it would be dangerous to broach the marriage question at all before the old lady, and probably only meant to wait for a favourable opportunity of doing so. But after a while the young wife would naturally become troubled and anxious, and, like most women under the same circumstances, would become jealous and inquisitive as well.

"She soon found out where he lived, and no doubt called there thinking that old Mrs. Yule was her husband's own fond mother.

"You can picture the rest. Mrs. Yule, furious at having been deceived, herself destroys the deed of gift which she meant to present to her adopted son, and from that hour young Bloggs sees himself penniless.

"The false Mrs. Yule left the house, and young Bloggs waited for his opportunity on the dark landing of a small London house. One push and the deed was done. With her weak heart, Mrs. Yule was sure to die of the shock if not of the fall.

"Before that, already the desk had been broken open and every appearance of a theft given to it. After the tragedy, then, young Bloggs retired quietly to his room. The whole thing looked so like an accident that, even had the servants heard the fall at once, there would still have been time enough for the young villain to sneak into his room, and then to reappear at his door, as if he, too, had been just awakened by the noise.

"The result turned out just as he expected. The William Yules have been and still are suspected of the theft; and young Bloggs is a hero of romance, with whom everyone is in sympathy."

THE TREMARN CASE

DRAMATIS PERSONAE

THE OLD MAN IN THE CORNER
who unravels the mystery to
THE LADY JOURNALIST
who relates it.
EARL OF TREMARN
(*uncle of the murdered man*).
PHILIP LE CHEMINANT
(*heir to the Tremarn earldom*).
HAROLD LE CHEMINANT
(*the deposed heir*).
JAMES TOVEY
(*butler to the Earl*).
THOMAS SAWYER
(*porter at the Junior Grosvenor Club*).
CHARLES COLLINS
(*witness at the inquest*).

I

"Well, it certainly is most amazing!" I said that day, when I had finished reading about it all in the *Daily Telegraph*.

"Yet the most natural thing in the world," retorted the man in the corner, as soon as he had ordered his lunch. "Crime invariably begets crime. No sooner is a murder, theft, or fraud committed in a novel or striking way, than this method is aped—probably within the next few days—by some other less imaginative scoundrel.

"Take this case, for instance," he continued, as he slowly began sipping his glass of milk, "which seems to amaze you so much. It was less than a year ago, was it not? that in Paris a man was found dead in a cab, stabbed in a most peculiar way—right through the neck from ear to ear—with, presumably, a long, sharp instrument of the type of an Italian stiletto.

"No one in England took much count of the crime, beyond a contemptuous shrug of the shoulders at the want of safety of the Paris streets, and the incapacity of the French detectives, who not only never discovered the murderer, who had managed to slip out of the cab unperceived, but who did not even succeed in establishing the identity of the victim.

"But this case," he added, pointing once more to my daily paper, "strikes nearer home. Less than a year has passed, and last week, in the very midst of our much vaunted London streets, a crime of a similar nature has been committed. I do not know if your paper gives full details, but this is what happened: last Monday evening two gentlemen, both in evening dress and wearing opera hats, hailed a hansom in Shaftesbury Avenue. It was about a quarter past eleven, and the night, if you remember, was a typical November one—dark, drizzly, and foggy. The various theatres in the immediate neighborhood were disgorging a continuous stream of people after the evening performance.

"The cabman did not take special notice of his fares. They jumped in very quickly, and one of them, through the little trap above, gave him an address in Cromwell Road. He drove there as quickly as the fog would permit him, and pulled up at the number given. One of the gentlemen then handed him up a very liberal fare—again through the little trap—and told him to drive his friend on to Westminster Chambers, Victoria Street.

"Cabby noticed that 'the swell,' when he got out of the hansom, stopped for a moment to say a few words to his friend, who had remained inside; then he crossed over the road and walked quickly in the direction of the Natural History Museum.

"When the cabman pulled up at Westminster Chambers, he waited for the second fare to get out; the latter seemingly making no movement that way, cabby looked down at him through the trap.

"'I thought 'e was asleep,' he explained to the police later on. ''E was leaning back in 'is corner and 'is 'ead was turned towards the window. I gets down and calls to 'im, but 'e don't move. Then I gets on to the step and give 'im a shake. . . . There!—I'll say no more. . . . We was near a lamppost, the mare took a step forward, and the light fell full on the gent's face. 'E was dead, and no mistake. I saw the wound just underneath 'is ear, and "Murder!" I says to myself at once.'

"Cabby lost no time in whistling for the nearest point policeman, then he called the night porter of the Westminster Chambers. The latter looked at the murdered man, and declared that he knew nothing of him; certainly he was not a tenant of the Chambers.

"By the time a couple of policemen arrived upon the scene, quite a crowd had gathered around the cab, in spite of the lateness of the hour and the darkness of the night. The matter was such an important one that one of the constables thought it best at once to jump into the hansom beside the murdered man and to order the cabman to drive to the nearest police station.

"There the cause of death was soon ascertained; the victim of this daring outrage had been stabbed through the neck from ear to ear with a long, sharp instrument, in shape like an antique stiletto, which, I may tell you, was subsequently found under the cushions of the hansom. The murderer must have watched his opportunity, when his victim's head was turned away from him, and then dealt the blow, just below the left ear, with amazing swiftness and precision.

"Of course the papers were full of it the next day; this was such a lovely opportunity for driving home a moral lesson, of how one crime engenders another, and how—but for that murder in Paris a year ago—we should not now have to deplore a crime committed in the very centre of fashionable London, the detection of which seems likely to completely baffle the police.

"Plenty more in that strain, of course, from which the reading public quickly jumped to the conclusion that the police held absolutely no clue as to the identity of the daring and mysterious miscreant.

"A most usual and natural thing had happened; cabby could only give a very vague description of his other 'fare,' of the 'swell' who had got out at Cromwell Road, and been lost to sight after having committed so dastardly and so daring a crime.

"This was scarely to be wondered at, for the night had been very foggy, and the murderer had been careful to pull his opera hat well over his face, thus hiding the whole of his forehead and eyes; moreover, he had always taken the additional precaution of only communicating with the cabman through the little trapdoor.

"All cabby had seen of him was a clean-shaven chin. As to the murdered man, it was not until about noon, when the early editions of the evening papers came out with a fuller account of the crime and a description of the victim, that his identity was at last established.

"Then the news spread like wildfire, and the evening papers came out with some of the most sensational headlines it had ever been their good fortune to print. The man who had been so mysteriously murdered in the cab was none other than Mr. Philip Le Cheminant, the nephew and heir-presumptive of the Earl of Tremarn."

II

"In order fully to realise the interest created by this extraordinary news, you must be acquainted with the various details of that remarkable case, popularly known as the 'Tremarn Peerage Case,'" continued the man in the corner, as he placidly munched his cheesecake. "I do not know if you followed it in its earlier stages, when its many details—which read like a romance—were first made public."

I looked so interested and so eager that he did not wait for my reply.

"I must try and put it all clearly before you," he said; "I was interested in it all from the beginning, and from the numerous wild stories afloat I have sifted only what was undeniably true. Some points of the case are still in dispute, and will, perhaps, now forever remain a mystery. But I must take you back some five-and-twenty years. The Hon. Arthur Le Cheminant, second son of the late Earl of Tremarn, was then travelling round the world for health and pleasure.

"In the course of his wanderings he touched at Martinique, one of the French West Indian islands, which was devastated by volcanic eruptions about two years ago. There he met and fell in love with a beautiful half-caste girl named Lucie Legrand, who had French blood in her veins, and was a Christian, but who, otherwise, was only partially civilised, and not at all educated.

"How it all came about it is difficult to conjecture, but one thing is absolutely certain, and that is that the Hon. Arthur Le Cheminant, the son of one of our English peers, married this half-caste girl at the parish church of St. Pierre, in Martinique, according to the forms prescribed by French laws, both parties being of the same religion.

"I suppose now no one will ever know whether that marriage was absolutely and undisputably a legal one—but, in view of subsequent events, we must presume that it was. The Hon. Arthur, however, in any case, behaved like a young scoundrel. He only spent a very little time with his wife, quickly tired of her, and within two years of his marriage collously abandoned her and his child, then a boy about a year old.

"He lodged a sum of £2000 in the local bank in the name of Mme. Le Cheminant, the interest of which was to be paid to her regularly for the maintenance of herself and child, then he calmly sailed for England, with the intention never to return. This intention fate itself helped him to carry out, for he died very shortly afterwards, taking the secret of his incongruous marriage with him to his grave.

"Mme. Lecheminant, as she was called out there, seems to have accepted her own fate with perfect equanimity. She had never known anything about her husband's social position in his own country, and he had left her what, in Martinique amongst the coloured population, was considered a very fair competence for herself and child.

"The grandson of an English Earl was taught to read and write by the worthy curé of St. Pierre, and during the whole of her life Lucie never once tried to find out who her husband was, and what had become of him.

"But here the dramatic scene comes in this strange story," continued the man in the corner, with growing excitement; "two years ago St. Pierre, if you remember, was completely destroyed by volcanic eruptions. Nearly the entire population perished, and every house and building was in ruins. Among those who fell a victim to the awful catastrophe was Mme. Lecheminant, otherwise the Hon. Mrs. Arthur Le Cheminant, whilst amongst those who managed to escape, and ultimately found refuge in the English colony of St. Vincent, was her son, Philip.

"Well!—you can easily guess what happened, can't you? In that English-speaking colony the name of Lecheminant was, of course, well-known, and Philip had not been in St. Vincent many weeks, before he learned that his father was none other than a younger brother of the present Earl of Tremarn, and that he himself—seeing that the present peer was over fifty and still unmarried—was heir-presumptive to the title and estates.

"You know the rest. Within two or three months of the memorable St. Pierre catastrophe Philip Le Cheminant had written to his uncle, Lord Tremarn, demanding his rights. Then he took passage on board a French liner and crossed over to Havre *en route* for Paris and London.

"He and his mother—both brought up as French subjects—had, mind you, all the respect which French people have for their papers of identification; and when the house in which they had lived for twenty years was tumbling about the young man's ears, when his mother had already perished in the flames, he made a final and successful effort to rescue the papers which proved him to be a French citizen, the son of Lucie Legrand, by her lawful marriage with Arthur Le Cheminant at the church of the Immaculate Conception of St. Pierre.

"What happened immediately afterwards it is difficult to conjecture. Certain it is, however, that over here the newspapers soon were full of vague allusions about the newly-found heir to the Earldom of Tremarn, and within a few weeks the whole of the story of the secret marriage at St. Pierre was in everybody's mouth.

"It created an immense sensation; the Hon. Arthur Le Cheminant had lived a few years in England after his return from abroad, and no one, not even his brother, seemed to have had the slightest inkling of his marriage.

"The late Lord Tremarn, you must remember, had three sons, the eldest of whom is the present peer, the second was the romantic Arthur, and the third, the Hon. Reginald, who also died some years ago, leaving four sons, the eldest of whom, Harold, was just twenty-three, and had always been styled heir-presumptive to the Earldom.

"Lord Tremarn had brought up these four nephews of his, who had lost both father and mother, just as if they had been his own children, and his affection for them, and notably for the eldest boy, was a very beautiful trait in his otherwise unattractive character.

"The news of the existence and claim of this unknown nephew must have come upon Lord Tremarn as a thunderbolt. His attitude, however, was one of uncompromising incredulity. He refused to believe the story of the marriage, called the whole tale a tissue of falsehoods, and denounced the claimant as a barefaced and impudent impostor.

"Two or three months more went by; the public were eagerly awaiting the arrival of this semiexotic claimant to an English peerage, and sensations, surpassing those of the Tichborne case, were looked forward to with palpitating interest.

"But in the romances of real life it is always the unexpected that happens. The claimant did arrive in London about a year ago. He was alone, friendless, and moneyless, since the £2000 lay buried somewhere beneath the ruins of the St. Pierre bank. However, he called upon a well-known London solicitor, who advanced him some money and took charge of all the papers relating to his claim.

"Philip Le Cheminant then seems to have made up his mind to make a personal appeal to his uncle, trusting apparently in the old adage that 'blood is thicker than water.'

"As was only to be expected, Lord Tremarn flatly refused to see the claimant, whom he was still denouncing as an impostor. It was by stealth, and by bribing the servants at the Grosvenor Square mansion, that the young man at last obtained an interview with his uncle.

"Last New Year's Day, he gave James Tovey, Lord Tremarn's butler, a five-pound note, to introduce him, surreptitiously, into his master's study. There uncle and nephew at last met face to face.

"What happened at that interview nobody knows; was the cry of blood and of justice so convincing that Lord Tremarn dare not resist it? Perhaps.

"Anyway, from that moment, the new heir-presumptive was installed within his rights. After a single interview with Philip Le Cheminant's solicitor, Lord Tremarn openly acknowledged the claimant to be his brother Arthur's only son, and therefore his own nephew and heir.

"Nay, more, everyone noticed that the proud, bad-tempered old man, was as wax in the hands of this newly-found nephew. He seemed even to have withdrawn his affection from the four other young nephews, whom hitherto he had brought up as his own children, and bestowed it all upon his brother Arthur's son—some people said in compensation for all the wrong that had been done to the boy in the past.

"But the scandal around his dead brother's name had wounded the old man's pride very deeply, and from this he never recovered. He shut himself away from all his friends, living alone with his newly-found nephew in his gloomy house in Grosvenor Square. The other boys, the eldest of whom, Harold, was just twenty-three, decided very soon to leave a house where they were no longer welcome. They had a small private fortune of their own, from their father and mother; the youngest boy was still at college, two others had made a start in their respective professions.

"Harold had been brought up as an idle young man about town, and on him the sudden change of fortune fell most heavily. He was undecided what to do in the future, but in the meanwhile, partly from a spirit of independence, and partly from a desire to keep a home for his younger brothers, he took and furnished a small flat, which, it is interesting to note, is just off Exhibition Road, not far from the Natural History Museum in Kensington.

"This was less than a year ago. Ten months later the newly-found heir to the peerage of Tremarn was found murdered in a hansom cab, and Harold Le Cheminant is once more the future Earl."

III

"The papers, as you know, talked of nothing else but the mysterious murder in the hansom cab. Everyone's sympathy went out at once to Lord Tremarn, who, on hearing the terrible news, had completely broken down, and was now lying on a bed of sickness, from which they say he may never recover.

"From the first there had been many rumours of the terrible enmity which existed between Harold Le Cheminant and the man who had so easily captured Lord Tremarn's heart, as well as the foremost place in the Grosvenor Square household.

"The servants in the great and gloomy mansion told the detectives in charge of the case many stories of terrible rows which occurred at first between at first between the cousins. And now everyone's eyes were already turned with suspicion on the one man who could most benefit by the death of Philip Le Cheminant.

"However careful and reticent the police may be, details in connection with so interesting a case have a wonderful way of leaking out. Already one other most important fact had found its way into the papers. It appears that in their endeavours to reconstruct the last day spent by the murdered man the detectives had come upon most important evidence.

"It was Thomas Sawyer, hall-porter of the Junior Grosvenor Club, who first told the following interesting story. He stated that deceased was a member of the Club, and had dined there on the evening preceding his death.

"'Mr. Le Cheminant was just coming downstairs after his dinner,' explained Thomas Sawyer to the detectives, 'when a stranger comes into the hall of the club; Mr. Le Cheminant saw him as soon as I did, and appeared very astonished. "What do you want?" he says rather sharply. "A word with you," replies the stranger. Mr. Le Cheminant seemed to hesitate for a moment. He lights a cigar, whilst the stranger stands there glaring at him, with a look in his eye I certainly didn't like.

"'Mind you,' added Thomas Sawyer, 'the stranger was a gentleman, in evening dress, and all that. Presently Mr. Le Cheminant says to him: "This way, then," and takes him along into one of the club rooms. Half-an-hour later the stranger comes out again. He looked flushed and excited. Soon after Mr. Le Cheminant comes out too; but he was quite calm, and smoking a cigar. He asks for a cab, and tells the driver to take him to the Lyric Theatre.'

"This was all that the hall-porter had to say, but his evidence was corroborated by one of the waiters of the club who saw Mr. Le Cheminant and the stranger subsequently enter the dining room, which was quite deserted at the time.

"'They 'adn't been in the room a minute,' said the waiter, 'when I 'eard loud voices, as if they was quarrelling frightful. I couldn't 'ear what they said, though I tried, but they was shouting so, and drowning each other's voices. Presently there's a ring at my bell, and I goes into the room. Mr. Le Cheminant was sitting beside one of the tables, quietly lighting a cigar. "Show this—er—gentleman out of the club," 'e says to me. The stranger looked as if 'e would strike 'im. "You'll pay for this," 'e says, then 'e picks up 'is 'at, and dashes out of the club helter-skelter. "One is always pestered by these beggars," says Mr. Le Cheminant to me, as 'e stalks out of the room.'

"Later on it was arranged that both Thomas Sawyer and the waiter should catch sight of Harold Le Cheminant, as he went out of his house in Exhibition Road. Neither of them had the slightest hesitation in recognising in him the stranger who had called at the club that night.

"Now that they held this definite clue, the detectives continued their work with a will. They made inquiries at the Lyric Theatre, but there they only obtained very vague testimony; one point, however, was of great value, the commissionaire outside one of the neighbouring theatres stated that, some time after the performance had begun, he noticed a gentleman in evening dress walking rapidly past him.

"He seemed strangely excited, for as he went by he muttered quite audibly to himself: 'I can stand it no longer, it must be he or I.' Then he disappeared in the fog, walking away towards Shaftesbury Avenue. Unfortunately the commissionaire, just like the cabman, was not prepared to swear to the identity of this man, whom he had only seen momentarily through the fog.

"But add to all this testimony the very strong motive there was for the crime, and you will not wonder that, within twenty-four hours of the murder, the strongest suspicions had already fastened on Harold Le Cheminant, and it was generally understood that, even before the inquest, the police already had in readiness a warrant for his arrest on the capital charge."

IV

"It would be difficult, I think, for anyone who was not present at that memorable inquest to have the least idea of the sensation which its varied and dramatic incidents caused among the crowd of spectators there.

"At first the proceedings were of the usual kind. The medical officer gave his testimony as to the cause of death; this was, of course, not in dispute. The stiletto was produced; it was of an antique and foreign pattern, probably of Eastern or else Spanish origin. In England, it could only have been purchased at some bric-à-brac shop.

"Then it was the turn of the servants at Grosvenor Square, of the cabman, and of the commissionaire. Lord Tremarn's evidence, which he had sworn to on his sickbed, was also read. It added nothing to the known facts of the case, for he had last seen his favourite nephew alive in the course of the afternoon preceding the latter's tragic end.

"After that the employees of the Junior Grosvenor Club retold their story, and they were the first to strike the note of sensation which was afterwards raised to its highest possible pitch.

"Both of them namely, were asked each in their turn, to look round the court and see if they could recognise the stranger who had called at the club that memorable evening. Without the slightest hesitation, both the hall-porter and the waiter pointed to Harold Le Cheminant, who sat with his solicitor in the body of the court.

"But already an inkling of what was to come had gradually spread through that crowded court—instinctively everyone felt that behind the apparent simplicity of this tragic case there lurked another mystery, more strange even than that murder in the hansom cab.

"Evidence was being taken as to the previous history of the deceased, his first appearance in London, his relationship with his uncle, and subsequently his enmity with his cousin Harold. At this point a man was brought forward as a witness, who it was understood had communicated with the police at the very last moment, offering to make a statement which he thought would throw considerable light upon the mysterious affair.

"He was a man of about fifty years of age, who looked like a very seedy, superannuated clerk of some insurance office.

"He gave his name as Charles Collins, and said that he resided in Caxton Road, Clapham.

"In a perfectly level tone of voice, he then explained that some three years ago, his son William, who had always been idle and good-for-nothing, had suddenly disappeared from home.

"'We heard nothing of him for over two years,' continued Charles Collins in that same cheerless and even voice which spoke of a monotonous existence of ceaseless, patient grind, 'but some few weeks ago my daughter went up to the West End to see about an engagement—she plays dance music at parties sometimes—when, in Regent Street, she came face to face with her brother William. He was no longer wretched, as we all are,' added the old man pathetically, 'he was dressed like a swell, and when his sister spoke to him, he pretended not to know her. But she's a sharp girl, and guessed at once that there was something strange there which William wished to hide. She followed him from a distance, and never lost sight of him that day, until she saw him about six o'clock in the evening go into one of the fine houses in Grosvenor Square. Then she came home and told her mother and me all about it.'

"I can assure you," continued the man in the corner, "that you might have heard a pin drop in that crowded court whilst the old man spoke. That he was stating the truth no one doubted for a moment. The very fact that he was brought forward as a witness showed that his story had been proved, at any rate, to the satisfaction of the police.

"The Collins's seem to have been very simple, good-natured people. It never struck any of them to interfere with William, who appeared, in their own words, to have 'bettered himself.' They concluded that he had obtained some sort of position in a rich family, and was now ashamed of his poor relations at Clapham.

"Then one morning they read in the papers the story of the mysterious murder in the hansom cab, together with a description of the victim, who had not yet been identified. 'William,' they said with one accord. Michael Collins, one of the younger sons, went up to London to view the murdered man at the mortuary. There was no doubt whatever that it was William, and yet all the papers persisted in saying that the deceased was the heir to some grand peerage.

"'So I wrote to the police,' concluded Charles Collins, 'and my wife and children were all allowed to view the body, and we are all prepared to swear that it is that of my son, William Collins, who was no more heir to a peerage than your worship.'

"And mopping his forehead with a large coloured handkerchief, the old man stepped down from the box.

"Well, you may imagine what this bombshell was in the midst of that coroner's court. Everyone looked at his neighbour, wondering if this was real life, or some romantic play being acted upon a stage. Amidst indescribable excitement, various other members of the Collins family corroborated the old man's testimony, as did also one or two friends from Clapham. All those who had been allowed to view the body of the murdered man pronounced it without hesitation to be that of William Collins, who had disappeared from home three years ago.

"You see, it was like a repetition of the Tichborne case, only with this strange difference: this claimant was dead, but all his papers were in perfect order, the certificate of marriage between Lucie Legrand and Arthur Le Cheminant at Martinique, as well as the birth and baptismal certificate of Philip Le Cheminant, their son. Yet there were all those simple, honest folk swearing that the deceased had been born in Clapham, and the mother, surely, could not have been mistaken.

"That is where the difference with the other noteworthy case came in, for in this instance, as far as the general public is concerned, the actual identity of the murdered man will always remain a matter of doubt—Philip Le Cheminant or William Collins took that part of his secret, at any rate, with him to his grave."

V

"But the murder?" I asked eagerly, for the man in the corner had paused, intent upon the manufacture of innumerable knots in a long piece of string.

"Ah, yes, the murder, of course," he replied with a chuckle, "the second mystery in this extraordinary case. Well, of course, whatever the identity of the deceased really was, there was no doubt in the minds of the police that Harold Le Cheminant had murdered him. To him, at any rate, the Collins family were unknown; he only knew the man who had supplanted him in his uncle's affections, and snatched a rich inheritance away from him. The charge brought against him at the Westminster Court was also one of the greatest sensations of this truly remarkable case.

"It looked, indeed, as if the unfortunate young man had committed a crime which was as appalling as it was useless. Instead of murdering the impostor—if impostor he was—how much more simple it would have been to have tried to unmask him. But, strange to say, this he never seems to have done, at any rate as far as the public knew.

"But here again mystery stepped in. When brought before the magistrate, Harold Le Cheminant was able to refute the terrible charge brought against him by the simple means of a complete alibi. After the stormy episode at the Junior Grosvenor Club he had gone to his own club in Pall Mall, and fortunately for him did not leave it until twenty minutes past eleven, some few minutes *after* the two men in evening dress got into the hansom in Shaftesbury Avenue.

"But for this lucky fact, for which he had one or two witnesses, it might have fared ill with him, for feeling unduly excited he walked all the way home afterwards; and had he left his club earlier, he might have found it difficult to account for his time. As it was, he was of course discharged.

"But one more strange fact came out during the course of the magisterial investigation, and that was that Harold Le Cheminant, on the very day preceding the murder, had booked a passage for St. Vincent. He admitted in court that he meant to conduct certain investigations there with regard to the identity of the supposed heir to the Tremarn peerage.

"And thus the curtain came down on the last act of that extraordinary drama, leaving two great mysteries unsolved: the real identity of the murdered man, and that of the man who killed him. Some people still persist in thinking it was Harold Le Cheminant. Well, we may easily dismiss *that* supposition. Harold had decided to investigate the matter for himself, he was on his way to St. Vincent.

"Surely common sense would assert that, having gone so far, he would assure himself first whether the man was an impostor or not, before he resorted to crime in order to rid himself of him. Moreover, the witnesses who saw him leave his own club at twenty minutes past eleven were quite independent and very emphatic.

"Another theory is that the Collins' gang tried to blackmail Philip Le Cheminant—or William Collins, whichever we like to call him— and that it was one of them who murdered him out of spite when he refused to submit to the blackmailing process.

"Against that theory, however, there are two unanswerable arguments—firstly, the weapon used, which certainly was not one that would commend itself to the average British middle-class man on murder intent—a razor or knife would be more in his line; secondly, there is no doubt whatever that the murderer wore evening dress and an opera hat, a costume not likely to have been worn by any member of the Collins' family, or their friends. We may, therefore, dismiss that theory also with equal certainty."

And he surveyed placidly the row of fine knots in his bit of string.

"But then, according to you, who was the man in evening dress, and who but Harold Le Cheminant had any interest in getting rid of the claimant?" I asked at last.

"Who, indeed?" he replied with a chuckle, "who but the man who was as wax in the hands of that impostor."

"Whom do you mean?" I gasped.

"Let us take things from the beginning," he said with ever growing excitement, "and take the one thing which is absolutely beyond dispute, and that is the authenticity of the *papers*—the marriage certificate of Lucie Legrand, etc.—as against the authenticity of the *man*. Let us admit that the real Philip Le Cheminant was a refugee at St. Vincent, that he found out about his parentage, and determined to go to England. He writes to his uncle, then sails for Europe, lands at Havre, and arrives in Paris."

"Why Paris?" I asked.

"Because you, like the police and like the public, have persistently shut your eyes to an event which, to my mind, has bearing upon the whole of this mysterious case, and that is the original murder committed in Paris a year ago, also in a cab, also with a stiletto—which that time was *not* found—in fact, in the selfsame manner as this murder a week ago."

"Well, that crime was never brought home to its perpetrator any more than this one will be. But my contention is, that the man who committed that murder a year ago, repeated this crime last week—that the man who was murdered in Paris was the real Philip Le Cheminant, whilst the man who was murdered in London was some friend to whom he had confided his story, and probably his papers, and who then hit upon the bold plan of assuming the personality of the Martinique creole, heir to an English peerage."

"But what in the world makes you imagine such a preposterous thing?" I gasped.

"One tiny, unanswerable fact," he replied quietly. "William Collins, the impostor, when he came to London, called upon a solicitor, and deposited with him the valuable papers, *after that* he obtained his interview with Lord Tremarn. Then mark what happens. Without any question, immediately after that interview, and, therefore, without even having seen the papers of identification, Lord Tremarn accepts the claimant as his newly-found nephew.

"And why?"

"Only because that claimant has a tremendous hold over the Earl, which makes the old man as wax in his hands, and it is only logical to conclude that that hold was none other than that Lord Tremarn had met his real nephew in Paris, and had killed him, sooner than to see him supplant his beloved heir, Harold.

"I followed up the subsequent history of that Paris crime, and found that the Paris police had never established the identity of the murdered man. Being a stranger and moneyless, he had apparently lodged in one of those innumerable ill-famed little hotels that abound in Paris, the proprietors of which have very good cause to shun the police, and therefore would not even venture so far as to go and identify the body when it lay in the Morgue.

"But William Collins knew who the murdered man was; no doubt he lodged at the same hotel, and could lay his hands on the all-important papers. I imagine that the two young men originally met in St. Vincent, or perhaps on board ship. He assumed the personality of the deceased; crossed over to England and confronted Lord Tremarn, with the threat to bring the murder home to him if he ventured to dispute his claim.

"Think of it all, and you will see that I am right. When Lord Tremarn first heard from his brother Arthur's son, he went to Paris in order to assure himself of the validity of his claim. Seeing that there was no doubt of that, he assumed a friendly attitude towards the young man, and one evening took him out for a drive in a cab and murdered him on the way.

"Then came Nemesis in the shape of William Collins, whom he dared not denounce, lest his crime be brought home to him. How could he come forward and say: 'I know that this man is an impostor, as I happened to have murdered my nephew myself'?

"No; he preferred to temporise, and bide his time until, perhaps, chance would give him his opportunity. It took a year in coming. The yoke had become too heavy. 'It must be he or I!' he said to himself that very night. Apparently he was on the best of terms with his tormentor, but in his heart of hearts he had always meant to be even with him at the last.

"Everything favoured him; the foggy night, even the dispute between Harold and the impostor at the club. Can you not picture him meeting William Collins outside the theatre, hearing from him the story of the quarrel, and then saying, 'Come with me to Harold's; I'll soon make the young jackanapes apologise to you'?

"Mind you, a year had passed by since the original crime. William Collins, no doubt, never thought he had anything to fear from the old man. He got into the cab with him, and thus this remarkable story has closed, and Harold Le Cheminant is once more heir to the Earldom of Tremarn.

"Think it all over, and bear in mind that Lord Tremarn *never* made the slightest attempt to prove the rights or wrongs of the impostor's claim. On this base your own conclusions, and then see if they do not inevitably lead you to admit mine as the only possible solution of this double mystery."

He was gone, leaving me bewildered and amazed, staring at my *Daily Telegraph,* where, side by side with a long recapitulation of the mysterious claimant to the Earldom, there was the following brief announcement:

"We regret to say that the condition of Lord Tremarn is decidedly worse today, and that but little hope is entertained of his recovery. Mr. Harold Le Cheminant has been his uncle's constant and devoted companion during the noble Earl's illness."

THE MURDER OF MISS PEBMARSH

DRAMATIS PERSONAE

THE OLD MAN IN THE CORNER
who unravels the mystery to
THE LADY JOURNALIST
who relates it.
LADY DE CHAVASSE
(a society lady).
SIR PERCIVAL DE CHAVASSE
(her husband).
SERGEANT EVANS
(a constable).
MISS LUCY PEBMARSH
(an old maid).
MISS PAMELA PEBMARSH
(her niece).
JEMIMA GADD
(a servant).
MR. MILLER
(a greengrocer).
INSPECTOR ROBINSON
(a detective).

I

"You must admit," said the man in the corner to me one day, as I folded up and put aside my *Daily Telegraph,* which I had been reading with great care, "that it would be difficult to find a more interesting plot, or more thrilling situations than occurred during the case of Miss Pamela Pebmarsh. As for downright cold-blooded villainy, commend me to some of the actors in that real drama.

"The facts were simple enough: Miss Lucy Ann Pebmarsh was an old maid who lived with her young niece Pamela and an elderly servant in one of the small, newly-built houses not far from the railway station at Boreham Wood. The fact that she kept a servant at all, and that the little house always looked very spick and span, was taken by the neighbours to mean that Miss Pebmarsh was a lady of means; but she kept very much to herself, seldom went to church and never attended any of the mothers' meetings, parochial teas, and other social gatherings for which that popular neighborhood has long been famous.

"Very little, therefore, was known of the Pebmarsh household, save that the old lady had seen better days, that she had taken her niece to live with her recently, and that the latter had had a somewhat checkered career before she had found her present haven of refuge; some more venturesome gossips went so far as to hint—but only just above a whisper—that Miss Pamela Pebmarsh had been on the stage.

"Certain it is that that young lady seemed to chafe very much under the restraint imposed upon her by her aunt, who seldom allowed her out of her sight, and evidently kept her very short of money, for, in spite of Miss Pamela's obvious love of fine clothes, she had latterly been constrained to wear the plainest of frocks and most unbecoming of hats.

"All very commonplace and uninteresting, you see, until that memorable Wednesday in October, after which the little house in Boreham Wood became a nine days' wonder throughout newspaper-reading England.

"On that day Miss Pebmarsh's servant, Jemima Gadd, went over to Luton to see a sick sister; she was not expected back until the next morning. On that same afternoon Miss Pamela—strangely enough—seems also to have elected to go up to town, leaving her aunt all alone in the house, and not returning home until the late train, which reaches Boreham Wood a few minutes before one.

"It was about five minutes past one that the neighbours in the quiet little street were roused from their slumbers by most frantic and agonised shrieks. The next moment Miss Pamela was seen to rush out of her aunt's house and then to hammer violently at the door of one of her neighbours, still uttering piercing shrieks. You may imagine what a commotion such a scene at midnight would cause in a place like Boreham Wood. Heads were thrust out of the windows; one or two neighbours in hastily-donned miscellaneous attire came running out; and very soon the news spread round like wildfire that Miss Pamela on coming home had found her aunt lying dead in the sitting room.

"Mr. Miller, the local greengrocer, was the first to pluck up sufficient courage to effect an entrance into the house. Miss Pamela dared not follow him; she had become quite hysterical, and was shrieking at the top of her voice that her aunt had been murdered. The sight that greeted Mr. Miller and those who had been venturesome enough to follow him, was certainly calculated to unhinge any young girl's mind.

"In the small bow window of the sitting room stood a writing table, with drawers open and papers scattered all over and around it; in a

chair in front of it, half sitting and half lying across the table, face
downwards, and with arms outstretched, was the dead body of Miss
Pebmarsh. There were sufficient indications to show to the most casual
observer that, undoubtedly, the unfortunate lady had been murdered.

"One of the neighbours, who possessed a bicycle, had in the meanwhile had the good sense to ride over to the police station. Very soon
two constables were on the spot; they quickly cleared the room of
gossiping neighbours, and then endeavoured to obtain from Miss
Pamela some lucid information as to the terrible event.

"At first she seemed quite unable to answer coherently the many
questions which were being put to her; however, with infinite patience
and wonderful kindness, Sergeant Evans at last managed to obtain
from her the following statement:

"'I had had an invitation to go to the theatre this evening; it was an
old invitation, and my aunt had said long ago that I might accept it.
When Jemima Gadd wanted to go to Luton, I didn't see why I should
give up the theatre and offend my friend, just because of her. My aunt
and I had some words about it, but I went. . . . I came back by the last
train and walked straight home from the station. I had taken the
latchkey with me, and went straight into the sitting room; the lamp was
alight, and—and——'

"The rest was chaos in the poor girl's mind; she was only conscious
of having seen something awful and terrible, and of having rushed out
screaming for help. Sergeant Evans asked her no further questions
then; a kind neighbour had offered to take charge of Pamela for the
night, and took her away with her, the constable remaining in charge of
the body and the house until the arrival of higher authorities."

II

"Although, as you may well suppose," continued the man in the corner
after a pause, "the excitement was intense at Boreham Wood, it had
not as yet reached the general newspaper-reading public. As the tragic
event had occurred at one o'clock in the morning, the papers the
following day only contained a brief announcement that an old lady
had been found murdered at Boreham Wood under somewhat mysterious circumstances. Later on, the evening editions added that the
police were extremely reticent, but that it was generally understood
that they held an important clue.

"The following day had been fixed for the inquest, and I went down
myself in the morning, for somehow I felt that this case was going to be
an interesting one. A murder which at first seems absolutely purpose-

less always, in my experience, reveals, sooner or later, an interesting trait in human nature.

"As soon as I arrived at Boreham Wood, I found that the murder of Miss Pebmarsh and the forthcoming inquest seemed to be the sole subjects of gossip and conversation. After I had been in the place half an hour the news began to spread like wildfire that the murderer had been arrested; five minutes later the name of the murderer was on everybody's lips.

"It was that of the murdered woman's niece, Miss Pamela Pebmarsh.

"'Oh—oh!' I said to myself, 'my instincts have not deceived me: this case is indeed going to be interesting.'

"It was about two o'clock in the afternoon when I at last managed to find my way to the little police station, where the inquest was to be held. There was scarcely standing room, I can tell you, and I had some difficulty in getting a front place from which I could see the principal actors in this village drama.

"Pamela Pebmarsh was there in the custody of two constables—she, a young girl scarcely five-and-twenty, stood there accused of having murdered, in a peculiarly brutal way, an old lady of seventy, her relative who had befriended her and given her a home."

The man in the corner paused for a moment, and from the capacious pocket of his magnificent ulster he drew two or three small photos, which he placed before me.

"This is Miss Pamela Pebmarsh," he said, pointing to one of these; "tall and good-looking, in spite of the shabby bit of mourning with which she had contrived to deck herself. Of course, this photo does not give you an idea of what she looked like that day at the inquest. Her face then was almost ashen in colour; her large eyes were staring before her with a look of horror and of fear; and her hands were twitching incessantly, with spasmodic and painful nervousness.

"It was pretty clear that public feeling went dead against her from the very first. A murmur of disapproval greeted her appearance, to which she seemed to reply with a look of defiance. I could hear many uncharitable remarks spoken all round me; Boreham Wood found it evidently hard to forgive Miss Pamela her good looks and her unavowed past.

"The medical evidence was brief and simple. Miss Pebmarsh had been stabbed in the back with some sharp instrument, the blade of which had pierced the left lung. She had evidently been sitting in the chair in front of her writing table when the murderer had caught her unawares. Death had ensued within the next few seconds.

"The medical officer was very closely questioned upon this point by the coroner; it was evident that the latter had something very serious in his mind, to which the doctor's replies would give confirmation.

"'In your opinion.' he asked, 'would it have been possible for Miss Pebmarsh to do anything after she was stabbed. Could she have moved, for instance?'

"'Slightly, perhaps,' replied the doctor; 'but she did not attempt to rise from her chair.'

"'No; but could she have tried to reach the hand bell, for instance, which was on the table, or—the pen and ink—and written a word or two?'

"'Well, yes,' said the doctor thoughtfully; 'she might have done that, if pen and ink, or the hand bell, were *very* close to her hand. I doubt, though, if she could have written anything very clearly, but still it is impossible to say quite definitely—anyhow, it could only have been a matter of a few seconds.'

"Delightfully vague, you see," continued the man in the corner, "as these learned gentlemen's evidence usually is.

"Sergeant Evans then repeated the story which Pamela Pebmarsh had originally told him, and from which she had never departed in any detail. She had gone to the theatre, leaving her aunt all alone in the house; she had arrived home at one o'clock by the late Wednesday night train, and had gone straight into the sitting room, where she had found her aunt dead before her writing table.

"That she travelled up to London in the afternoon was easily proved; the station master and the porters had seen her go. Unfortunately for her alibi, however, those late 'theatre' trains on that line are always very crowded; the night had been dark and foggy, and no one at or near the station could swear positively to having seen her arrive home again by the train she named.

"There was one thing more; although the importance of it had been firmly impressed upon Pamela Pebmarsh, she absolutely refused to name the friends with whom she had been to the theatre that night, and who, presumably, might have helped her to prove at what hour she left London for home.

"Whilst all this was going on, I was watching Pamela's face intently. That the girl was frightened—nay more, terrified—there could be no doubt; the twitching of her hands, her eyes dilated with terror, spoke of some awful secret which she dared not reveal, but which she felt was being gradually brought to light. Was that secret the secret of a crime—a crime so horrible, so gruesome, that surely so young a girl would be incapable of committing?

"So far, however, what struck everyone mostly during this inquest was the seeming purposelessness of this cruel murder. The old lady, as far as could be ascertained, had no money to leave, so why should Pamela Pebmarsh have deliberately murdered the aunt who provided her, at any rate, with the comforts of a home? But the police, assisted by one of the most able detectives on the staff, had not effected so sensational an arrest without due cause; they had a formidable array of witnesses to prove their case up to the hilt. One of these was Jemima Gadd, the late Miss Pebmarsh's servant.

"She came forward attired in deep black, and wearing a monumental crape bonnet crowned with a quantity of glistening black beads. With her face the colour of yellow wax, and her thin lips pinched tightly together, she stood as the very personification of puritanism and uncharitableness.

"She did not look once towards Pamela, who gazed at her like some wretched bird caught in a net, which sees the meshes tightening round it more and more.

"Replying to the coroner, Jemima Gadd explained that on the Wednesday morning she had had a letter from her sister at Luton, asking her to come over and see her some day.

"'As there was plenty of cold meat in the 'ouse,' she said, 'I asked the mistress if she could spare me until the next day, and she said yes, she could. Miss Pamela and she could manage quite well.'

"'She said nothing about her niece going out, too, on the same day?' asked the coroner.

"'No,' replied Jemima acidly, 'she did not. And later on, at breakfast, Miss Pebmarsh said to Miss Pamela before me: "Pamela," she says, "Jemima is going to Luton and won't be back until tomorrow. You and I will be alone in the 'ouse until then."'

"'And what did the accused say?'

"'She says "All right, aunt."'

"'Nothing more?'

"'No, nothing more.'

"'There was no question, then, of the accused going out also, and leaving Miss Pebmarsh all alone in the house?'

"'None at all,' said Jemima emphatically. 'If there 'ad been I'd 'ave 'eard of it. I needn't 'ave gone that day. Any day would 'ave done for me.'

"She closed her thin lips with a snap, and darted a vicious look at Pamela. There was obviously some old animosity lurking beneath that gigantic crape monument on the top of Jemima's wax-coloured head.

"'You know nothing, then, about any disagreement between the deceased and the accused on the subject of her going to the theatre that day?' asked the coroner after a while.

"'No, not about *that*,' said Jemima curtly; 'but there was plenty of disagreements between those two, I can tell you.'

"'Ah? what about?'

"'Money mostly. Miss Pamela was overfond of fine clothes, but Miss Pebmarsh, who was giving 'er a 'ome and 'er daily bread, 'adn't much money to spare for fallalery. Miss Pebmarsh 'ad a small pension from a lady of the haristocracy, but it wasn't much—a pound a week it was. Miss Pebmarsh might 'ave 'ad a lot more if she'd wanted to.'

"'Oh?' queried the coroner, 'how was that?'

"'Well, you see, that fine lady 'ad not always been as good as she ought to be. She'd been Miss Pamela's friend when they were both on the stage together, and pretty goings on, I can tell you, those two were up to, and——'

"'That'll do,' interrupted the coroner sternly. 'Confine yourself, please, to telling the jury about the pension Miss Pebmarsh had from a lady.'

"'I was speaking about that,' said Jemima, with another snap of her thin lips. 'Miss Pebmarsh knew a thing or two about this fine lady, and she had some letters which she often told me that fine lady would not care for her 'usband or her fine friends to read. Miss Pamela got to know about these letters, and she worried her poor aunt to death, for she wanted to get those letters and sell them to the fine lady for 'undreds of pounds. I 'ave 'eard 'er ask for those letters times and again, but Miss Pebmarsh wouldn't give them to 'er, and they was locked up in the writing-table drawer, and Miss Pamela wanted those letters, for she wanted to get 'undreds of pounds from the fine lady, and my poor mistress was murdered for those letters—and she was murdered by that wicked girl 'oo eat her bread and 'oo would 'ave starved but for 'er. And so I tell you, and I don't care 'oo 'ears me say it.'

"No one had attempted to interrupt Jemima Gadd as she delivered herself of this extraordinary tale, which so suddenly threw an unexpected and lurid light upon the mystery of poor Miss Pebmarsh's death.

"That the tale was a true one, no one doubted for a single instant. One look at the face of the accused was sufficient to prove it beyond question. Pamela Pebmarsh had become absolutely livid; she tottered almost as if she would fall, and the constable had to support her until a chair was brought forward for her.

"As for Jemima Gadd, she remained absolutely impassive. Having given her evidence, she stepped aside automatically like a yellow waxen image, which had been wound up and had now run down. There was silence for awhile. Pamela Pebmarsh, more dead than alive, was sipping a glass of brandy and water, which alone prevented her from falling in a dead faint.

"Detective Inspector Robinson now stepped forward. All the spectators there could read on his face the consciousness that his evidence would be of the most supreme import.

"'I was telegraphed for from the Yard,' he said in reply to the coroner, 'and came down here by the first train on the Thursday morning. Beyond the short medical examination the body had not been touched: as the constables know, we don't like things interfered with in cases of this kind. When I went up to look at deceased, the first thing I saw was a piece of paper just under her right hand. Sergeant Evans had seen it before and pointed it out to me. Deceased had a pen in her hand, and the ink bottle was close by. This is the paper I found, sir.'

"And amidst a deadly silence, during which nothing could be heard but the scarcely-perceptible rustle of the paper, the inspector handed a small note across to the coroner. The latter glanced at it for a moment, and his face became very grave and solemn as he turned towards the jury.

"'Gentlemen of the jury,' he said, 'these are the contents of the paper which the inspector found under the hand of the deceased.'

"He paused once more before he began to read, whilst we all in that crowded court held our breath to listen:

"'*I am dying. My murderess is my niece, Pam——*'

"'That is all, gentlemen,' added the coroner, as he folded up the note. 'Death overtook the unfortunate woman in the very act of writing down the name of her murderess.'

"Then there was a wild, an agonised shriek of horror. Pamela Pebmarsh, with hair dishevelled and eyes in which the light of madness had begun to gleam, threw up her hands, and without a word, and without a groan, fell down senseless upon the floor."

III

"Yes," said the man in the corner with a chuckle, "there was enough evidence there to hang twenty people, let alone that one fool of a girl who had run her neck so madly into a noose. I don't suppose that anyone left the court that day with the slightest doubt in their minds as to what the verdict would be; for the coroner had adjourned the inquest, much to the annoyance of the jury, who had fully made up their minds and had their verdict pat on the tips of their tongues: 'Wilful murder against Pamela Pebmarsh.'

"But this was a case which to the last kept up its reputation for surprises. By the next morning rumour had got about that 'the lady of the aristocracy,' referred to by Jemima Gadd, and who was supposed to have paid a regular pension to Miss Pebmarsh, was none other than Lady de Chavasse.

"When the name was first mentioned, everyone—especially the fair sex—shrugged their shoulders and said: 'Of course, what else *could* one expect?'

"As a matter of fact, Lady de Chavasse, *née* Birdie Fay, was one of the most fashionable women in society; she was at the head of a dozen benevolent institutions, was a generous patron of hospitals, and her house was one of the most exclusive ones in London. True, she had been on the stage in her younger days, and when Sir Percival de Chavasse married her, his own relations looked somewhat askance at the showy, handsome girl who had so daringly entered the ancient county family.

"Sir Percival himself was an extraordinarily proud man—proud of his lineage, of his social status, of the honour of his name. His very pride had forced his relations, had forced society to accept his beautiful young wife, and to Lady de Chavasse's credit be it said, not one breath of scandal as to her past life had ever become public gossip. No one could assert that they *knew* anything derogatory to Birdie Fay before she became the proud baronet's wife. As a matter of fact, all society asserted that Sir Percival would never have married her and introduced her to his own family circle if there had been any gossip about her.

"Now suddenly the name of Lady de Chavasse was on everybody's tongue. People at first spoke it under their breath, for everyone felt great sympathy with her. She was so rich, and entertained so lavishly. She was very charming, too; most fascinating in her ways; deferential to her austere mother-in-law; not a little afraid of her proud husband; very careful lest by word or look she betrayed her early connection with the stage before him.

"On the following day, however, we had further surprises in store for us. Pamela Pebmarsh, advised by a shrewd and clearheaded solicitor, had at last made up her mind to view her danger a little more coolly and to speak rather more of the truth than she had done hitherto.

"Still looking very haggard, but perhaps a little less scared, she now made a statement which, when it was fully substantiated, as she stated it could be, would go far towards clearing her of the terrible imputation against her. Her story was this: On the memorable day in question, she did go up to town, intending to go to the theatre. At the station she purchased an evening paper, which she began to read. This paper in its fashionable columns contained an announcement which arrested her attention; this was that Sir Percival and Lady de Chavasse had returned to their flat in town at 51, Marsden Mansions, Belgravia, from "The Chase," Melton Mowbray.

"'De Chavasse,' continued Pamela, 'was the name of the lady who paid my aunt the small pension on which she lived. I knew her years ago, when she was on the stage, and I suddenly thought I would like to go and see her, just to have a chat over old times. Instead of going to the theatre, I went and had some dinner at Slater's, in Piccadilly, and then I thought I would take my chance, and go and see if Lady de Chavasse was at home. I got to 51, Marsden Mansions, about eight o'clock, and was fortunate enough to see Lady de Chavasse at once. She kept me talking some considerable time; so much so, in fact, that I missed the 11 from St. Pancras. I only left Marsden Mansions at a quarter to eleven, and had to wait at St. Pancras until twenty minutes past midnight.'

"This was all reasonable and clear enough, and, as her legal adviser had subpoenaed Lady de Chavasse as a witness, Pamela Pebmarsh seemed to have found an excellent way out of her terrible difficulties, the only question being whether Lady de Chavasse's testimony alone would, in view of her being Pamela's friend, be sufficient to weigh against the terribly overwhelming evidence of Miss Pebmarsh's dying accusation.

"But Lady de Chavasse settled this doubtful point in a way least expected by anyone. Exquisitely dressed, golden-haired, and brilliant complexioned, she looked strangely out of place in this fusty little village court, amidst the local dames in their plain gowns and antiquated bonnets. She was, moreover, extremely self-possessed, and only cast a short, very haughty, look at the unfortunate girl whose life probably hung upon that fashionable woman's word.

"'Yes,' she said sweetly in reply to the coroner, 'she was the wife of Sir Percival de Chavasse, and resided at 51, Marsden Mansions, Belgravia.'

"'The accused, I understand, has been known to you for some time?' continued the coroner.

"'Pardon me,' rejoined Lady de Chavasse, speaking in a beautifully modulated voice, 'I did know this young—hem—person, years ago, when I was on the stage, but, of course, I had not seen her for years.'

"'She called on you on Wednesday last at about nine o'clock?'

"'Yes, she did, for the purpose of levying blackmail upon me.'

"There was no mistaking the look of profound aversion and contempt which the fashionable lady now threw upon the poor girl before her.

"'She had some preposterous story about some letters which she alleged would be compromising to my reputation,' continued Lady de Chavasse quietly. 'These she had the kindness to offer me for sale, for a few hundred pounds. At first her impudence staggered me, as, of course, I had no knowledge of any such letters. She threatened to take them to my husband, however, and I then—rather foolishly, perhaps— suggested that she should bring them to me first. I forget how the conversation went on, but she left me with the understanding that she would get the letters from her aunt, Miss Pebmarsh, who, by the way, had been my governess when I was a child, and to whom I paid a small pension in consideration of her having been left absolutely without means.'

"And Lady de Chavasse, conscious of her own disinterested benevolence, pressed a highly-scented bit of cambric to her delicate nose.

"'Then the accused did spend the evening with you on that Wednesday?' asked the coroner, while a great sigh of relief seemed to come from poor Pamela's breast.

"'Pardon me,' said Lady de Chavasse, 'she spent a little time with me. She came about nine o'clock.'

"'Yes. And when did she leave?'

"'I really couldn't tell you—about ten o'clock I think.'

"'You are not sure?' persisted the coroner. 'Think, Lady de Chavasse,' he added earnestly, 'try to think—the life of a fellow creature may, perhaps, depend upon your memory.'

"'I am indeed sorry,' she replied in the same musical voice. 'I could not swear without being positive, could I? And I am not quite positive.'

"'But your servants?'

"'They were at the back of the flat—the girl let herself out.'

"'But your husband?'

"'Oh! when he saw me engaged with the girl he went out to his club, and was not yet home when she left.'

"'Birdie! Birdie! won't you try and remember?' here came in an agonised cry from the unfortunate girl, who thus saw her last hope vanish before her eyes.

"But Lady de Chavasse only lifted a little higher a pair of very prettily-arched eyebrows, and having finished her evidence she stepped on one side and presently left the court, leaving behind her a faint aroma of violet sachet powder, and taking away with her, perhaps, the last hope of an innocent fellow creature."

IV

"But Pamela Pebmarsh?" I asked after a while, for he had paused and was gazing attentively at the photograph of a very beautiful and exquisitely-gowned woman.

"Ah, yes, Pamela Pebmarsh," he said with a smile. "There was yet another act in that palpitating drama of her life—one act—the *dénouement* as unexpected as it was thrilling. Salvation came where it was least expected—from Jemima Gadd, who seemed to have made up her mind that Pamela had killed her aunt, and yet who was the first to prove her innocence.

"She had been shown the few words which the murdered woman was alleged to have written after she had been stabbed. Jemima, not a very good scholar, found it difficult to decipher the words herself.

"'Ah, well, poor dear,' she said after a while, with a deep sigh, "'er 'andwriting was always peculiar, seein' as 'ow she wrote always with 'er left 'and.'

"'*Her left hand!!!*' gasped the coroner, while public and jury alike, hardly liking to credit their ears, hung upon the woman's thin lips, amazed, aghast, puzzled.

"'Why yes!' said Jemima placidly. 'Didn't you know she 'ad a bad accident to 'er right 'and when she was a child, and never could 'old anything in it? 'er fingers were like paralysed; the ink pot was always on the left of 'er writing table. Oh! she couldn't write with 'er right 'and at all.'

"Then a strange revulsion of feeling came over everyone there.

"Stabbed in the back, with her lung pierced through and through, how could she have done, dying, what she never did in life?

"Impossible!

"The murderer, whoever it was, had placed pen and paper to her hand, and had written on it the cruel words which were intended to delude justice and to send an innocent fellow creature—a young girl not five-and-twenty—to an unjust and ignominious death. But, fortunately for that innocent girl, the cowardly miscreant had ignored the fact that Miss Pebmarsh's right hand had been paralysed for years.

"The inquest was adjourned for a week," continued the man in the corner, "which enabled Pamela's solicitor to obtain further evidence of her innocence. Fortunately for her, he was enabled to find two witnesses who had seen her in an omnibus going towards St. Pancras at about 11:15 P.M., and a passenger on the 12:25 train who had travelled down with her as far as Hendon. Thus, when the inquest was resumed Pamela Pebmarsh left the court without a stain upon her character.

"But the murder of Miss Pebmarsh has remained a mystery to this day—as has also the secret history of the compromising letters. Did they exist or not? is a question the interested spectators at that memorable inquest have often asked themselves. Certain is it that failing Pamela Pebmarsh, who might have wanted them for purposes of blackmail, no one else could be interested in them except Lady de Chavasse."

"Lady de Chavasse!" I ejaculated in surprise. "Surely you are not going to pretend that that elegant lady went down to Boreham Wood in the middle of the night in order to murder Miss Pebmarsh, and then to lay the crime at another woman's door?"

"I only pretend what's logic," replied the man in the corner with inimitable conceit; "and in Pamela Pebmarsh's own statement, she was with Lady de Chavasse at 51, Marsden Mansions, until eleven o'clock, and there is no train from St. Pancras to Boreham Wood between eleven and twenty-five minutes past midnight. Pamela's alibi becomes that of Lady de Chavasse, and is quite conclusive. Besides, that elegant lady was not one to do that sort of work for herself."

"What do you mean?" I asked.

"Do you mean to say you never thought of the real solution of this mystery?" he retorted sarcastically.

"I confess——" I began a little irritably.

"Confess that I have not yet taught you to think logically, and to look at the beginning of things."

"What do you call the beginning of this case, then?"

"Why! the compromising letters, of course."

"But," I argued.

"Wait a minute!" he shrieked excitedly, whilst with frantic haste he began fidgeting, fidgeting again at that eternal bit of string. "These did exist, otherwise why did Lady de Chavasse parley with Pamela Pebmarsh? Why did she not order her out of the house then and there if she had nothing to fear from her?"

"I admit that," I said.

"Very well; then, as she was too fine, too delicate, to commit the villainous murder of which she afterwards accused poor Miss Pamela, who was there sufficiently interested in those letters to try and gain possession of them for her?"

"Who, indeed?" I queried, still puzzled, still not understanding.

"Aye! who but her husband," shrieked the funny creature, as with a sharp snap he broke his beloved string in two.

"Her husband!" I gasped.

"Why not? He had plenty of time, plenty of pluck. In a flat it is easy enough to overhear conversations that take place in the next room—he was in the house at the time, remember, for Lady de Chavasse said herself that he went out afterwards. No doubt he overheard every-thing—the compromising letters, and Pamela's attempt at levying blackmail. What the effect of such a discovery must have been upon the proud man I leave you to imagine—his wife's social position ruined, a stain upon his ancient name, his relations pointing the finger of scorn at his folly.

"Can't you picture him, hearing the two women's talk in the next room, and then resolving at all costs to possess himself of those com-promising letters? He had just time to catch the 10:00 train to Boreham Wood.

"Mind you, I don't suppose that he went down there with any evil intent. Most likely he only meant to buy those letters from Miss

Pebmarsh. What happened, however, nobody can say but the murderer himself.

"Who knows? But the deed done, imagine the horror of a refined, aristocratic man face to face with such a crime as that.

"Was it this terror, or merely rage at the girl who had been the original cause of all this, that prompted him to commit the final villainy of writing out a false accusation and placing it under the dead woman's hand? Who can tell?

"Then, the deed done, and the *mise-en-scène* complete, he is able to catch the last train—11:23—back to town. A man travelling alone would pass practically unperceived.

"Pamela's innocence was proved, and the murder of Miss Pebmarsh has remained a mystery, but if you will reflect on my conclusions you will admit that no one else—*no one else*—could have committed that murder, for no one else had a greater interest in the destruction of those letters."

THE AFFAIR AT THE NOVELTY THEATRE

DRAMATIS PERSONAE

THE OLD MAN IN THE CORNER
who explains the mystery to
THE LADY JOURNALIST
who retells it.
MISS PHYLLIS MORGAN
(*a popular actress*).
MR. HOWARD DENNIS
(*her fiancé*).
GEORGE FINCH
(*doorkeeper at the Novelty Theatre*).
CLARA KNIGHT
(*dresser to Miss Morgan*).
MESSRS. KIDD AND CO.
(*Bond Street jewellers*).
MR. THOMAS KIDD
(*one of the firm*).
JAMES RUMFORD
(*a skilled working jeweller*).
MACPHERSON
(*a detective*).

I

"Talking of mysteries," said the man in the corner, rather irrelevantly, for he had not opened his mouth since he sat down and ordered his lunch, "talking of mysteries, it is always a puzzle to me how few thefts are committed in the dressing rooms of fashionable actresses during a performance."

"There have been one or two," I suggested, "but nothing of any value was stolen."

"Yet you remember that affair at the Novelty Theatre a year or two ago, don't you?" he added. "It created a great deal of sensation at the time. You see, Miss Phyllis Morgan was and still is a very fashionable and popular actress, and her pearls are quite amongst the wonders of the world. She herself valued them at £10,000, and several experts who remember the pearls quite concur with that valuation.

"During the period of her short tenancy of the Novelty Theatre last season, she entrusted those beautiful pearls to Mr. Kidd, the well-known Bond Street jeweller, to be restrung. There were seven rows of perfectly matched pearls, held together by a small diamond clasp of 'art-nouveau' design.

"Kidd and Co. are, as you know, a very eminent and old-established firm of jewellers. Mr. Thomas Kidd, its present sole representative, was sometime president of the London Chamber of Commerce, and a man whose integrity has always been held to be above suspicion. His clerks, salesmen, and bookkeeper had all been in his employ for years, and most of the work was executed on the premises.

"In the case of Miss Phyllis Morgan's valuable pearls, they were restrung and reset in the back shop by Mr. Kidd's most valued and most trusted workman, a man named James Rumford, who is justly considered to be one of the cleverest craftsmen here in England.

"When the pearls were ready, Mr. Kidd himself took them down to the theatre, and delivered them into Miss Morgan's own hands.

"It appears that the worthy jeweller was extremely fond of the theatre; but, like so many persons in affluent circumstances, he was also very fond of getting a free seat when he could.

"All along he had made up his mind to take the pearls down to the Novelty Theatre one night, and to see Miss Morgan for a moment before the performance; she would then, he hoped, place a stall at his disposal.

"His previsions were correct. Miss Morgan received the pearls, and Mr. Kidd was on that celebrated night accommodated with a seat in the stalls.

"I don't know if you remember all the circumstances connected with that case, but, to make my point clear, I must remind you of one or two of the most salient details.

"In the drama in which Miss Phyllis Morgan was acting at the time, there is a brilliant masked ball scene which is the crux of the whole play; it occurs in the second act, and Miss Phyllis Morgan, as the hapless heroine dressed in the shabbiest of clothes, appears in the midst of a gay and giddy throng; she apostrophises all and sundry there, including the villain, and has a magnificent scene which always brings down the house, and nightly adds to her histrionic laurels.

"For this scene a large number of supers are engaged, and in order to further swell the crowd, practically all the available stagehands have to 'walk on' dressed in various coloured dominos, and all wearing masks.

"You have, of course, heard the name of Mr. Howard Dennis in connection with this extraordinary mystery. He is what is usually called 'a young man about town,' and was one of Miss Phyllis Morgan's most favoured admirers. As a matter of fact, he was generally understood to be the popular actress' *fiancé*, and as such, had of course the *entrée* of the Novelty Theatre.

"Like many another idle young man about town, Mr. Howard Dennis was stage-mad, and one of his greatest delights was to don nightly a mask and a blue domino, and to 'walk on' in the second act, not so much in order to gratify his love for the stage, as to watch Miss Phyllis Morgan in her great scene, and to be present, close by her, when she received her usual salvo of enthusiastic applause from a delighted public.

"On this eventful night, it was on July 20th last, the second act was in full swing, the supers, the stagehands, and all the principals were on the scene, the back of the stage was practically deserted. The beautiful pearls, fresh from the hands of Mr. Kidd, were in Miss Morgan's dressing room, as she meant to wear them in the last act.

"Of course, since that memorable affair, many people have talked of the foolhardiness of leaving such valuable jewellery in the sole charge of a young girl—Miss Morgan's dresser—who acted with unpardonable folly and carelessness, but you must remember that this part of the theatre is only accessible through the stage door, where sits enthroned that uncorruptible dragon, the stage doorkeeper.

"No one can get at it from the front, and the dressing rooms for the supers and lesser members of the company are on the opposite side of the stage to that reserved for Miss Morgan and one or two of the principals.

"It was just a quarter-to-ten, and the curtain was about to be rung down, when George Finch, the stage doorkeeper, rushed excitedly into the wings; he was terribly upset and was wildly clutching his coat, beneath which he evidently held something concealed.

"In response to the rapidly whispered queries of the one or two stagehands that stood about, Finch only shook his head excitedly. He seemed scarcely able to control his impatience, during the close of the act, and the subsequent prolonged applause.

"When at last Miss Morgan, flushed with her triumph, came off the stage, Finch made a sudden rush for her.

"'Oh, Madam!' he gasped excitedly, 'it might have been such an awful misfortune! The rascal! I nearly got him though! but he escaped—fortunately it is safe—I have got it——!'

"It was some time before Miss Morgan understood what in the world the otherwise sober stage doorkeeper was driving at. Everyone who heard him certainly thought that he had been drinking. But the next moment from under his coat he pulled out, with another ejaculation of excitement, the magnificent pearl necklace which Miss Morgan had thought safely put away in her dressing room.

"'What in the world does all this mean?' asked Mr. Howard Dennis, who, as usual, was escorting his *fiancée*. 'Finch, what are you doing with Madam's necklace?'

"Miss Phyllis Morgan herself was too bewildered to question Finch; she gazed at him, then at her necklace, in speechless astonishment.

"'Well, you see, Madam, it was this way,' Finch managed to explain at last, as with awestruck reverence he finally deposited the precious necklace in the actress' hands. 'As you know, Madam, it is a very hot night. I had seen everyone into the theatre and counted in the supers; there was nothing much for me to do, and I got rather tired and very thirsty. I seed a man loafing close to the door and I ask him to fetch me a pint of beer from round the corner, and I give him some coppers; I had noticed him loafing round before, and it was so hot I didn't think I was doin' no harm.'

"'No, no,' said Miss Morgan impatiently. 'Well!'

"'Well,' continued Finch, 'the man, he brought me the beer, and I had some of it—and—and—afterwards, I don't quite know how it happened—it was the heat, perhaps—but—I was sitting in my box, and I suppose I must have dropped asleep. I just remember hearing the ring up for the second act, and the callboy calling you, Madam, then there's a sort of a blank in my mind. All of a sudden I seemed to wake with the feeling that there was something wrong somehow. In a moment I jumped up, and I tell you I was wide awake then, and I saw a man sneaking down the passage, past my box, towards the door. I challenged him, and he tried to dart past me, but I was too quick for him, and got him by the tails of his coat, for I saw at once that he was carrying something, and I had recognised the loafer who brought me the beer. I shouted for help, but there's never anybody about in this back street, and the loafer, he struggled like old Harry, and sure enough he managed to get free from me and away before I could stop him, but in his fright the rascal dropped his booty, for which Heaven be praised! and it was your pearls, Madam. Oh, my! but I did have a tussle,' concluded the worthy doorkeeper, mopping his forehead, 'and I do hope, Madam, the scoundrel didn't take nothing else.'

"That was the story," continued the man in the corner, "which George Finch had to tell and which he subsequently repeated without the slightest deviation. Miss Phyllis Morgan, with the lightheartedness peculiar to ladies of her profession, took the matter very quietly; all she said at the time was that she had nothing else of value in her dressing room, but that Miss Knight—the dresser—deserved a scolding for leaving the room unprotected.

"'All's well that ends well,' she said gaily, as she finally went into her dressing room, carrying the pearls in her hand.

"It appears that the moment she opened the door, she found Miss Knight sitting in the room, in a deluge of tears. The girl had overheard George Finch telling his story, and was terribly upset at her own carelessness.

"In answer to Miss Morgan's questions, she admitted that she had gone into the wings, and lingered there to watch the great actress' beautiful performance. She thought no one could possibly get to the dressing room, as nearly all hands were on the stage at the time, and of course George Finch was guarding the door.

"However, as there really had been no harm done, beyond a wholesome fright to everybody concerned, Miss Morgan readily forgave the girl and proceeded with her change of attire for the next act. Incidentally she noticed a bunch of roses, which were placed on her dressing table, and asked Knight who had put them there.

"'Mr. Dennis brought them,' replied the girl.

"Miss Morgan looked pleased, blushed, and dismissing the whole matter from her mind, she proceeded with her toilette for the next act, in which, the hapless heroine having come into her own again, she was able to wear her beautiful pearls around her neck.

"George Finch, however, took some time to recover himself; his indignation was only equalled by his volubility. When his excitement had somewhat subsided, he took the precaution of saving the few drops of beer which had remained at the bottom of the mug, brought to him by the loafer. This was subsequently shown to a chemist in the neighborhood, who, without a moment's hesitation, pronounced the beer to contain an appreciable quantity of chloral."

II

"The whole matter, as you may imagine, did not affect Miss Morgan's spirits that night," continued the man in the corner after a slight pause.

"'All's well that ends well,' she had said gaily, since almost by a miracle, her pearls were once more safely round her neck.

"But the next day brought the rude awakening. Something had indeed happened which made the affair at the Novelty Theatre, what it has ever since remained, a curious and unexplainable mystery.

"The following morning Miss Phyllis Morgan decided that it was foolhardy to leave valuable property about in her dressing room, when, for stage purposes, imitation jewellery did just as well. She therefore determined to place her pearls in the bank until the termination of her London season.

"The moment, however, that, in broad daylight, she once more handled the necklace, she instinctively felt that there was something wrong with it. She examined it eagerly and closely, and, hardly daring to face her sudden terrible suspicions, she rushed round to the nearest jeweller, and begged him to examine the pearls.

"The examination did not take many moments; the jeweller at once pronounced the pearls to be false. There could be no doubt about it; the necklace was a perfect imitation of the original, even the clasp was an exact copy. Half-hysterical with rage and anxiety, Miss Morgan at once drove to Bond Street, and asked to see Mr. Kidd.

"Well, you may easily imagine the stormy interview that took place. Miss Phyllis Morgan, in no measured language, boldly accused Mr. Thomas Kidd, late president of the London Chamber of Commerce, of having substituted false pearls for her own priceless ones.

"The worthy jeweller, at first completely taken by surprise, examined the necklace, and was horrified to see that Miss Morgan's statements were, alas! too true. Mr. Kidd was indeed in a terribly awkward position.

"The evening before, after business hours, be had taken the necklace home with him. Before starting for the theatre, he had examined it to see that it was quite in order. He had then, with his own hands, and in the presence of his wife, placed it in its case, and driven straight to the Novelty, where he finally gave it over to Miss Morgan herself.

"To all this he swore most positively; moreover, all his employees and workmen could swear that they had last seen the necklace just after closing time at the stop, when Mr. Kidd walked off towards Piccadilly, with the precious article in the inner pocket of his coat.

"One point certainly was curious, and undoubtedly helped to deepen the mystery which to this day clings to the affair at the Novelty Theatre.

"When Mr. Kidd handed the packet containing the necklace to Miss Morgan, she was too busy to open it at once. She only spoke to Mr. Kidd through her dressing-room door, and never opened the packet till nearly an hour later, after she was dressed ready for the second act; the packet at that time had been untouched, and was wrapped up just as she had had it from Mr. Kidd's own hands. She undid the packet, and handled the pearls; certainly, by the artificial light she could see nothing wrong with the necklace.

"Poor Mr. Kidd was nearly distracted with the horror of his position. Thirty years of an honest reputation suddenly tarnished with this awful suspicion—for he realised at once that Miss Morgan refused to believe his statements; in fact, she openly said that she would—unless immediate compensation was made to her—place the matter at once in the hands of the police.

"From the stormy interview in Bond Street, the irate actress drove at once to Scotland Yard; but the old-established firm of Kidd and Co. was not destined to remain under any cloud that threatened its integrity.

"Mr. Kidd at once called upon his solicitor, with the result that an offer was made to Miss Morgan, whereby the jeweller would deposit the full value of the original necklace, *i.e.,* £10,000, in the hands of Messrs. Bentley and Co., bankers, that sum to be held by them for a whole year, at the end of which time, if the perpetrator of the fraud had not been discovered, the money was to be handed over to Miss Morgan in its entirety.

"Nothing could have been more fair, more equitable, or more just, but at the same time nothing could have been more mysterious.

"As Mr. Kidd swore that he had placed the real pearls in Miss Morgan's hands, and was ready to back his oath by the sum of £10,000, no more suspicion could possibly attach to him. When the announcement of his generous offer appeared in the papers, the entire public approved and exonerated him, and then turned to wonder who the perpetrator of the daring fraud had been.

"How came a valueless necklace in exact imitation of the original one to be in Miss Morgan's dressing room? Where were the real pearls? Clearly the loafer who had drugged the stage doorkeeper, and sneaked into the theatre to steal a necklace, was not aware that he was risking several years' hard labour for the sake of a worthless trifle. He had been one of the many dupes of this extraordinary adventure.

"Macpherson, one of the most able men on the detective staff, had, indeed, his work cut out. The police were extremely reticent, but, in spite of this, one or two facts gradually found their way into the papers, and aroused public interest and curiosity to its highest pitch.

"What had transpired was this:

"Clara Knight, the dresser, had been very rigorously cross-questioned, and, from her many statements, the following seemed quite positive.

"After the curtain had rung up for the second act, and Miss Morgan had left her dressing room, Knight had waited about for some time, and had even, it appears, handled and admired the necklace. Then, unfortunately, she was seized with the burning desire of seeing the famous scene from the wings. She thought that the place was quite safe, and that George Finch was as usual at his post.

"'I was going along the short passage that leads to the wings,' she explained to the detectives, 'when I became aware of someone moving some distance behind me. I turned and saw a blue domino about to enter Miss Morgan's dressing room.

"'I thought nothing of that,' continued the girl, 'as we all know that Mr. Dennis is engaged to Miss Morgan. He is very fond of "walking on" in the ballroom scene, and he always wears a blue domino when he does; so I was not at all alarmed. He had his mask on as usual, and he was carrying a bunch of roses. When he saw me at the other end of the passage, he waved his hand to me and pointed to the flowers. I nodded to him, and then he went into the room.'

"These statements, as you may imagine, created a great deal of sensation; so much so, in fact, that Mr. Kidd, with his £10,000 and his reputation in mind, moved heaven and earth to bring about the prosecution of Mr. Dennis for theft and fraud.

"The papers were full of it, for Mr. Howard Dennis was well known in fashionable London society. His answer to these curious statements was looked forward to eagerly; when it came it satisfied no one and puzzled everybody.

"'Miss Knight was mistaken,' he said most emphatically, 'I did not bring any roses for Miss Morgan that night. It was not I that she saw in a blue domino by the door, as I was on the stage before the curtain was rung up for the second act, and never left it until the close.'

"This part of Howard Dennis' statement was a little difficult to substantiate. No one on the stage could swear positively whether he was 'on' early in the act or not, although, mind you, Macpherson had ascertained that in the whole crowd of supers on the stage, he was the only one who wore a blue domino.

"Mr. Kidd was very active in the matter, but Miss Morgan flatly refused to believe in her *fiancé's* guilt. The worthy jeweller maintained that Mr. Howard Dennis was the only person who knew the celebrated pearls and their quaint clasp well enough to have a facsimile made of them, and that when Miss Knight saw him enter the dressing room, he actually substituted the false necklace for the real one; whilst the loafer who drugged George Finch's beer was—as everyone supposed— only a dupe.

"Things had reached a very acute and painful stage, when one more detail found its way into the papers, which, whilst entirely clearing Mr. Howard Dennis' character, has helped to make the whole affair a hopeless mystery.

"Whilst questioning George Finch, Macpherson had ascertained that the stage doorkeeper had seen Mr. Dennis enter the theatre some time before the beginning of the celebrated second act. He stopped to speak to George Finch for a moment or two, and the latter could swear positively that Mr. Dennis was not carrying any roses then.

"On the other hand a flower girl, who was selling roses in the neighbourhood of the Novelty Theatre late that memorable night, remembers selling some roses to a shabbily dressed man, who looked like a labourer out of work. When Mr. Dennis was pointed out to her she swore positively that it was not he.

"'The man looked like a labourer,' she explained. 'I took particular note of him, as I remember thinking that he didn't look much as if he could afford to buy roses.'

"Now you see," concluded the man in the corner excitedly, "where the hitch lies. There is absolutely no doubt, judging from the evidence of George Finch and of the flower girl, that the loafer had provided himself with the roses, and had somehow or other managed to get hold of a blue domino, for the purpose of committing the theft. His giving drugged beer to Finch, moreover, proved his guilt beyond a doubt.

"But here the mystery becomes hopeless," he added with a chuckle, "for the loafer dropped the booty which he had stolen—that booty was the false necklace, and it has remained an impenetrable mystery to this day as to who made the substitution and when.

"A whole year has elapsed since then, but the real necklace has never been traced or found; so Mr. Kidd has paid, with absolute quixotic chivalry, the sum of £10,000 to Miss Morgan, and thus he has completely cleared the firm of Kidd and Co. of any suspicion as to its integrity."

III

"But then, what in the world is the explanation of it all?" I asked bewildered, as the funny creature paused in his narrative and seemed absorbed in the contemplation of a beautiful knot he had just completed in his bit of string.

"The explanation is so simple," he replied, "for it is obvious, is it not? that only four people could possibly have committed the fraud."

"Who are they?" I asked.

"Well," he said, whilst his bony fingers began to fidget with that eternal piece of string, "there is, of course, old Mr. Kidd; but as the worthy jeweller has paid £10,000 to prove that he did not steal the real necklace and substitute a false one in its stead, we must assume that he was guiltless. Then, secondly, there is Mr. Howard Dennis."

"Well, yes," I said, "what about him?"

"There were several points in his favour," he rejoined, marking each point with a fresh and most complicated knot; "it was not he who bought the roses, therefore it was not he who, clad in a blue domino, entered Miss Morgan's dressing room directly after Knight left it.

"And mark the force of this point," he added excitedly. "Just before the curtain rang up for the second act, Miss Morgan had been in her room, and had then undone the packet, which, in her own words, was just as she had received it from Mr. Kidd's hands.

"After that Miss Knight remained in charge, and a mere ten seconds after she left the room she saw the blue domino carrying the roses at the door.

"The flower girl's story and that of George Finch have proved that the blue domino could not have been Mr. Dennis, but it was the loafer who eventually stole the false necklace.

"If you bear all this in mind you will realise that there was no time in those ten seconds for Mr. Dennis to have made the substitution *before* the theft was committed. It stands to reason that he could not have done it afterwards.

"Then, again, many people suspected Miss Knight, the dresser; but this supposition we may easily dismiss. An uneducated, stupid girl, not three and twenty, could not possibly have planned so clever a substitution. An imitation necklace of that particular calibre and made to order would cost far more money than a poor theatrical dresser could ever afford; let alone the risks of ordering such an ornament to be made.

"No," said the funny creature with comic emphasis, "there is but one theory possible, which is my own."

"And that is?" I asked eagerly.

"The workman, Rumford, of course," he responded triumphantly. "Why! it jumps to the eyes, as our French friends would tell us. Who, other than he, could have the opportunity of making an exact copy of the necklace which had been intrusted to his firm?

"Being in the trade he could easily obtain the false stones without exciting any undue suspicion; being a skilled craftsman, he could easily make the clasp, and string the pearls in exact imitation of the original, he could do this secretly in his own home and without the slightest risk.

"Then the plan, though extremely simple, was very cleverly thought out. Disguised as the loafer——"

"The loafer!" I exclaimed.

"Why, yes! the loafer," he replied quietly, "disguised as the loafer, he hung round the stage door of the Novelty after business hours, until he had collected the bits of gossip and information he wanted; thus he learnt that Mr. Howard Dennis was Miss Morgan's accredited *fiancé;* that he, like everybody else who was available, "walked on" in the second act; and that during that time the back of the stage was practically deserted.

"No doubt he knew all along that Mr. Kidd meant to take the pearls down to the theatre himself that night, and it was quite easy to ascertain that Miss Morgan—as the hapless heroine—wore no jewellery in the second act, and that Mr. Howard Dennis invariably wore a blue domino.

"Some people might incline to the belief that Miss Knight was a paid accomplice, that she left the dressing room unprotected on purpose, and that her story of the blue domino and the roses was prearranged between herself and Rumford, but that is not my opinion.

"I think that the scoundrel was far too clever to need any accomplice, and too shrewd to put himself thereby at the mercy of a girl like Knight.

"Rumford, I find, is a married man, this to me explains the blue domino, which the police were never able to trace to any business place, where it might have been bought or hired. Like the necklace itself, it was 'homemade.'

"Having got his properties and his plans ready, Rumford then set to work. You must remember that a stage doorkeeper is never above accepting a glass of beer from a friendly acquaintance; and, no doubt, if George Finch had not asked the loafer to bring him a glass, the latter would have offered him one. To drug the beer was simple enough; then Rumford went to buy the roses, and, I should say, met his wife somewhere round the corner, who handed him the blue domino and the mask; all this was done in order to completely puzzle the police subsequently, and also in order to throw suspicion if possible upon young Dennis.

"As soon as the drug took effect upon George Finch, Rumford slipped into the theatre. To slip a mask and domino on and off is, as you know, a matter of a few seconds. Probably his intention had been—if he found Knight in the room—to knock her down if she attempted to raise an alarm; but here fortune favoured him. Knight saw him from a distance and mistook him easily for Mr. Dennis.

"After the theft of the real necklace, Rumford sneaked out of the theatre. And here you see how clever was the scoundrel's plan: if he had merely substituted one necklace for another there would have been no doubt whatever that the loafer—whoever he was—was the culprit—the drugged beer would have been quite sufficient proof for that. The hue and cry would have been after the loafer, and, who knows? there might have been someone or something which might have identified that loafer with himself.

"He must have bought the shabby clothes somewhere, he certainly bought the roses from a flower girl; anyhow, there were a hundred and one little risks and contingencies which might have brought the theft home to him.

"But mark what happens: he steals the real necklace, and keeps the false one in his hand, intending to drop it sooner or later, and thus send the police entirely on the wrong scent. As the loafer, he was supposed to have stolen the false necklace, then dropped it whilst struggling with George Finch. The result is that no one has troubled about the loafer; no one thought that he had anything to do with the substitution, which was the main point at issue, and no very great effort has ever been made to find that mysterious loafer.

"It never occurred to anyone that the fraud and the theft were committed by one and the same person, and that that person could be none other than James Rumford."

A CATALOGUE OF
SELECTED DOVER BOOKS
IN ALL FIELDS OF INTEREST

A CATALOGUE OF SELECTED DOVER
BOOKS IN ALL FIELDS OF INTEREST

CELESTIAL OBJECTS FOR COMMON TELESCOPES, T. W. Webb. The most used book in amateur astronomy: inestimable aid for locating and identifying nearly 4,000 celestial objects. Edited, updated by Margaret W. Mayall. 77 illustrations. Total of 645pp. 5⅜ x 8½.
20917-2, 20918-0 Pa., Two-vol. set $9.00

HISTORICAL STUDIES IN THE LANGUAGE OF CHEMISTRY, M. P. Crosland. The important part language has played in the development of chemistry from the symbolism of alchemy to the adoption of systematic nomenclature in 1892. ". . . wholeheartedly recommended,"—Science. 15 illustrations. 416pp. of text. 5⅝ x 8¼. 63702-6 Pa. $6.00

BURNHAM'S CELESTIAL HANDBOOK, Robert Burnham, Jr. Thorough, readable guide to the stars beyond our solar system. Exhaustive treatment, fully illustrated. Breakdown is alphabetical by constellation: Andromeda to Cetus in Vol. 1; Chamaeleon to Orion in Vol. 2; and Pavo to Vulpecula in Vol. 3. Hundreds of illustrations. Total of about 2000pp. 6⅛ x 9¼.
23567-X, 23568-8, 23673-0 Pa., Three-vol. set $26.85

THEORY OF WING SECTIONS: INCLUDING A SUMMARY OF AIR-FOIL DATA, Ira H. Abbott and A. E. von Doenhoff. Concise compilation of subatomic aerodynamic characteristics of modern NASA wing sections, plus description of theory. 350pp. of tables. 693pp. 5⅜ x 8½.
60586-8 Pa. $7.00

DE RE METALLICA, Georgius Agricola. Translated by Herbert C. Hoover and Lou H. Hoover. The famous Hoover translation of greatest treatise on technological chemistry, engineering, geology, mining of early modern times (1556). All 289 original woodcuts. 638pp. 6¾ x 11.
60006-8 Clothbd. $17.95

THE ORIGIN OF CONTINENTS AND OCEANS, Alfred Wegener. One of the most influential, most controversial books in science, the classic statement for continental drift. Full 1966 translation of Wegener's final (1929) version. 64 illustrations. 246pp. 5⅜ x 8½. 61708-4 Pa. $4.50

THE PRINCIPLES OF PSYCHOLOGY, William James. Famous long course complete, unabridged. Stream of thought, time perception, memory, experimental methods; great work decades ahead of its time. Still valid, useful; read in many classes. 94 figures. Total of 1391pp. 5⅜ x 8½.
20381-6, 20382-4 Pa., Two-vol. set $13.00

THE AMERICAN SENATOR, Anthony Trollope. Little known, long un-available Trollope novel on a grand scale. Here are humorous comment on American vs. English culture, and stunning portrayal of a heroine/villainess. Superb evocation of Victorian village life. 561pp. 5⅜ x 8½.
23801-6 Pa. $6.00

WAS IT MURDER? James Hilton. The author of *Lost Horizon* and *Good-bye, Mr. Chips* wrote one detective novel (under a pen-name) which was quickly forgotten and virtually lost, even at the height of Hilton's fame. This edition brings it back—a finely crafted public school puzzle resplendent with Hilton's stylish atmosphere. A thoroughly English thriller by the creator of Shangri-la. 252pp. 5⅜ x 8. (Available in U.S. only)
23774-5 Pa. $3.00

CENTRAL PARK: A PHOTOGRAPHIC GUIDE, Victor Laredo and Henry Hope Reed. 121 superb photographs show dramatic views of Central Park: Bethesda Fountain, Cleopatra's Needle, Sheep Meadow, the Blockhouse, plus people engaged in many park activities: ice skating, bike riding, etc. Captions by former Curator of Central Park, Henry Hope Reed, provide historical view, changes, etc. Also photos of N.Y. landmarks on park's periphery. 96pp. 8½ x 11. 23750-8 Pa. $4.50

NANTUCKET IN THE NINETEENTH CENTURY, Clay Lancaster. 180 rare photographs, stereographs, maps, drawings and floor plans recreate unique American island society. Authentic scenes of shipwreck, light-houses, streets, homes are arranged in geographic sequence to provide walking-tour guide to old Nantucket existing today. Introduction, captions. 160pp. 8⅞ x 11¾. 23747-8 Pa. $6.95

STONE AND MAN: A PHOTOGRAPHIC EXPLORATION, Andreas Feininger. 106 photographs by *Life* photographer Feininger portray man's deep passion for stone through the ages. Stonehenge-like megaliths, fortified towns, sculpted marble and crumbling tenements show textures, beauties, fascination. 128pp. 9¼ x 10¾. 23756-7 Pa. $5.95

CIRCLES, A MATHEMATICAL VIEW, D. Pedoe. Fundamental aspects of college geometry, non-Euclidean geometry, and other branches of mathematics: representing circle by point. Poincare model, isoperimetric property, etc. Stimulating recreational reading. 66 figures. 96pp. 5⅝ x 8¼.
63698-4 Pa. $2.75

THE DISCOVERY OF NEPTUNE, Morton Grosser. Dramatic scientific history of the investigations leading up to the actual discovery of the eighth planet of our solar system. Lucid, well-researched book by well-known historian of science. 172pp. 5⅜ x 8½. 23726-5 Pa. $3.00

THE DEVIL'S DICTIONARY. Ambrose Bierce. Barbed, bitter, brilliant witticisms in the form of a dictionary. Best, most ferocious satire America has produced. 145pp. 5⅜ x 8½. 20487-1 Pa. $2.00

THE ANATOMY OF THE HORSE, George Stubbs. Often considered the great masterpiece of animal anatomy. Full reproduction of 1766 edition, plus prospectus; original text and modernized text. 36 plates. Introduction by Eleanor Garvey. 121pp. 11 x 14¾.   23402-9 Pa. $6.00

BRIDGMAN'S LIFE DRAWING, George B. Bridgman. More than 500 illustrative drawings and text teach you to abstract the body into its major masses, use light and shade, proportion; as well as specific areas of anatomy, of which Bridgman is master. 192pp. 6½ x 9¼. (Available in U.S. only)
                                   22710-3 Pa. $3.00

ART NOUVEAU DESIGNS IN COLOR, Alphonse Mucha, Maurice Verneuil, Georges Auriol. Full-color reproduction of *Combinaisons ornementales* (c. 1900) by Art Nouveau masters. Floral, animal, geometric, interlacings, swashes—borders, frames, spots—all incredibly beautiful. 60 plates, hundreds of designs. 9⅜ x 8-1/16.   22885-1 Pa. $4.00

FULL-COLOR FLORAL DESIGNS IN THE ART NOUVEAU STYLE, E. A. Seguy. 166 motifs, on 40 plates, from *Les fleurs et leurs applications decoratives* (1902): borders, circular designs, repeats, allovers, "spots." All in authentic Art Nouveau colors. 48pp. 9⅜ x 12¼.
                                   23439-8 Pa. $5.00

A DIDEROT PICTORIAL ENCYCLOPEDIA OF TRADES AND IN-DUSTRY, edited by Charles C. Gillispie. 485 most interesting plates from the great French Encyclopedia of the 18th century show hundreds of working figures, artifacts, process, land and cityscapes; glassmaking, papermaking, metal extraction, construction, weaving, making furniture, clothing, wigs, dozens of other activities. Plates fully explained. 920pp. 9 x 12.
                         22284-5, 22285-3 Clothbd., Two-vol. set $40.00

HANDBOOK OF EARLY ADVERTISING ART, Clarence P. Hornung. Largest collection of copyright-free early and antique advertising art ever compiled. Over 6,000 illustrations, from Franklin's time to the 1890's for special effects, novelty. Valuable source, almost inexhaustible.
Pictorial Volume. Agriculture, the zodiac, animals, autos, birds, Christmas, fire engines, flowers, trees, musical instruments, ships, games and sports, much more. Arranged by subject matter and use. 237 plates. 288pp. 9 x 12.
                                   20122-8 Clothbd. $13.50

Typographical Volume. Roman and Gothic faces ranging from 10 point to 300 point, "Barnum," German and Old English faces, script, logotypes, scrolls and flourishes, 1115 ornamental initials, 67 complete alphabets, more. 310 plates. 320pp. 9 x 12.   20123-6 Clothbd. $15.00

CALLIGRAPHY (CALLIGRAPHIA LATINA), J. G. Schwandner. High point of 18th-century ornamental calligraphy. Very ornate initials, scrolls, borders, cherubs, birds, lettered examples. 172pp. 9 x 13.
                                   20475-8 Pa. $6.00

HISTORY OF BACTERIOLOGY, William Bulloch. The only comprehensive history of bacteriology from the beginnings through the 19th century. Special emphasis is given to biography-Leeuwenhoek, etc. Brief accounts of 350 bacteriologists form a separate section. No clearer, fuller study, suitable to scientists and general readers, has yet been written. 52 illustrations. 448pp. 5⅝ x 8¼.   23761-3 Pa. $6.50

THE COMPLETE NONSENSE OF EDWARD LEAR, Edward Lear. All nonsense limericks, zany alphabets, Owl and Pussycat, songs, nonsense botany, etc., illustrated by Lear. Total of 321pp. 5⅜ x 8½. (Available in U.S. only)   20167-8 Pa. $3.00

INGENIOUS MATHEMATICAL PROBLEMS AND METHODS, Louis A. Graham. Sophisticated material from Graham *Dial*, applied and pure; stresses solution methods. Logic, number theory, networks, inversions, etc. 237pp. 5⅜ x 8½.   20545-2 Pa. $3.50

BEST MATHEMATICAL PUZZLES OF SAM LOYD, edited by Martin Gardner. Bizarre, original, whimsical puzzles by America's greatest puzzler. From fabulously rare *Cyclopedia*, including famous 14-15 puzzles, the Horse of a Different Color, 115 more. Elementary math. 150 illustrations. 167pp. 5⅜ x 8½.   20498-7 Pa. $2.75

THE BASIS OF COMBINATION IN CHESS, J. du Mont. Easy-to-follow, instructive book on elements of combination play, with chapters on each piece and every powerful combination team—two knights, bishop and knight, rook and bishop, etc. 250 diagrams. 218pp. 5⅜ x 8½. (Available in U.S. only)   23644-7 Pa. $3.50

MODERN CHESS STRATEGY, Ludek Pachman. The use of the queen, the active king, exchanges, pawn play, the center, weak squares, etc. Section on rook alone worth price of the book. Stress on the moderns. Often considered the most important book on strategy. 314pp. 5⅜ x 8½.
                                                       20290-9 Pa. $4.50

LASKER'S MANUAL OF CHESS, Dr. Emanuel Lasker. Great world champion offers very thorough coverage of all aspects of chess. Combinations, position play, openings, end game, aesthetics of chess, philosophy of struggle, much more. Filled with analyzed games. 390pp. 5⅜ x 8½.
                                                       20640-8 Pa. $5.00

500 MASTER GAMES OF CHESS, S. Tartakower, J. du Mont. Vast collection of great chess games from 1798-1938, with much material nowhere else readily available. Fully annotated, arranged by opening for easier study. 664pp. 5⅜ x 8½.   23208-5 Pa. $7.50

A GUIDE TO CHESS ENDINGS, Dr. Max Euwe, David Hooper. One of the finest modern works on chess endings. Thorough analysis of the most frequently encountered endings by former world champion. 331 examples, each with diagram. 248pp. 5⅜ x 8½.   23332-4 Pa. $3.50

THE COMPLETE WOODCUTS OF ALBRECHT DURER, edited by Dr. W. Kurth. 346 in all: "Old Testament," "St. Jerome," "Passion," "Life of Virgin," Apocalypse," many others. Introduction by Campbell Dodgson. 285pp. 8½ x 12¼.   21097-9 Pa. $7.50

DRAWINGS OF ALBRECHT DURER, edited by Heinrich Wolfflin. 81 plates show development from youth to full style. Many favorites; many new. Introduction by Alfred Werner. 96pp. 8⅛ x 11. 22352-3 Pa. $5.00

THE HUMAN FIGURE, Albrecht Dürer. Experiments in various techniques—stereometric, progressive proportional, and others. Also life studies that rank among finest ever done. Complete reprinting of *Dresden Sketchbook*. 170 plates. 355pp. 8⅜ x 11¼.   21042-1 Pa. $7.95

OF THE JUST SHAPING OF LETTERS, Albrecht Dürer. Renaissance artist explains design of Roman majuscules by geometry, also Gothic lower and capitals. Grolier Club edition. 43pp. 7⅞ x 10¾   21306-4 Pa. $8.00

TEN BOOKS ON ARCHITECTURE, Vitruvius. The most important book ever written on architecture. Early Roman aesthetics, technology, classical orders, site selection, all other aspects. Stands behind everything since. Morgan translation. 331pp. 5⅜ x 8½.   20645-9 Pa. $4.00

THE FOUR BOOKS OF ARCHITECTURE, Andrea Palladio. 16th-century classic responsible for Palladian movement and style. Covers classical architectural remains, Renaissance revivals, classical orders, etc. 1738 Ware English edition. Introduction by A. Placzek. 216 plates. 110pp. of text. 9½ x 12¾.   21308-0 Pa. $8.95

HORIZONS, Norman Bel Geddes. Great industrialist stage designer, "father of streamlining," on application of aesthetics to transportation, amusement, architecture, etc. 1932 prophetic account; function, theory, specific projects. 222 illustrations. 312pp. 7⅞ x 10¾.   23514-9 Pa. $6.95

FRANK LLOYD WRIGHT'S FALLINGWATER, Donald Hoffmann. Full, illustrated story of conception and building of Wright's masterwork at Bear Run, Pa. 100 photographs of site, construction, and details of completed structure. 112pp. 9¼ x 10.   23671-4 Pa. $5.50

THE ELEMENTS OF DRAWING, John Ruskin. Timeless classic by great Viltorian; starts with basic ideas, works through more difficult. Many practical exercises. 48 illustrations. Introduction by Lawrence Campbell. 228pp. 5⅜ x 8½.   22730-8 Pa. $2.75

GIST OF ART, John Sloan. Greatest modern American teacher, Art Students League, offers innumerable hints, instructions, guided comments to help you in painting. Not a formal course. 46 illustrations. Introduction by Helen Sloan. 200pp. 5⅜ x 8½.   23435-5 Pa. $4.00

THE EARLY WORK OF AUBREY BEARDSLEY, Aubrey Beardsley. 157 plates, 2 in color: *Manon Lescaut, Madame Bovary, Morte Darthur, Salome,* other. Introduction by H. Marillier. 182pp. 8⅛ x 11. 21816-3 Pa. $4.50

THE LATER WORK OF AUBREY BEARDSLEY, Aubrey Beardsley. Exotic masterpieces of full maturity: *Venus and Tannhauser, Lysistrata, Rape of the Lock, Volpone,* Savoy material, etc. 174 plates, 2 in color. 186pp. 8⅛ x 11. 21817-1 Pa. $4.50

THOMAS NAST'S CHRISTMAS DRAWINGS, Thomas Nast. Almost all Christmas drawings by creator of image of Santa Claus as we know it, and one of America's foremost illustrators and political cartoonists. 66 illustrations. 3 illustrations in color on covers. 96pp. 8⅜ x 11¼. 23660-9 Pa. $3.50

THE DORÉ ILLUSTRATIONS FOR DANTE'S DIVINE COMEDY, Gustave Doré. All 135 plates from Inferno, Purgatory, Paradise; fantastic tortures, infernal landscapes, celestial wonders. Each plate with appropriate (translated) verses. 141pp. 9 x 12. 23231-X Pa. $4.50

DORÉ'S ILLUSTRATIONS FOR RABELAIS, Gustave Doré. 252 striking illustrations of *Gargantua and Pantagruel* books by foremost 19th-century illustrator. Including 60 plates, 192 delightful smaller illustrations. 153pp. 9 x 12. 23656-0 Pa. $5.00

LONDON: A PILGRIMAGE, Gustave Doré, Blanchard Jerrold. Squalor, riches, misery, beauty of mid-Victorian metropolis; 55 wonderful plates, 125 other illustrations, full social, cultural text by Jerrold. 191pp. of text. 9⅜ x 12¼. 22306-X Pa. $6.00

THE RIME OF THE ANCIENT MARINER, Gustave Doré, S. T. Coleridge. Dore's finest work, 34 plates capture moods, subtleties of poem. Full text. Introduction by Millicent Rose. 77pp. 9¼ x 12. 22305-1 Pa. $3.50

THE DORE BIBLE ILLUSTRATIONS, Gustave Doré. All wonderful, detailed plates: Adam and Eve, Flood, Babylon, Life of Jesus, etc. Brief King James text with each plate. Introduction by Millicent Rose. 241 plates. 241pp. 9 x 12. 23004-X Pa. $6.00

THE COMPLETE ENGRAVINGS, ETCHINGS AND DRYPOINTS OF ALBRECHT DURER. "Knight, Death and Devil"; "Melencolia," and more—all Dürer's known works in all three media, including 6 works formerly attributed to him. 120 plates. 235pp. 8⅜ x 11¼. 22851-7 Pa. $6.50

MAXIMILIAN'S TRIUMPHAL ARCH, Albrecht Dürer and others. Incredible monument of woodcut art: 8 foot high elaborate arch—heraldic figures, humans, battle scenes, fantastic elements—that you can assemble yourself. Printed on one side, layout for assembly. 143pp. 11 x 16. 21451-6 Pa. $5.00

UNCLE SILAS, J. Sheridan LeFanu. Victorian Gothic mystery novel, considered by many best of period, even better than Collins or Dickens. Wonderful psychological terror. Introduction by Frederick Shroyer. 436pp. 5⅜ x 8½.   21715-9 Pa. $6.00

JURGEN, James Branch Cabell. The great erotic fantasy of the 1920's that delighted thousands, shocked thousands more. Full final text, Lane edition with 13 plates by Frank Pape. 346pp. 5⅜ x 8½.
                                                            23507-6 Pa. $4.50

THE CLAVERINGS, Anthony Trollope. Major novel, chronicling aspects of British Victorian society, personalities. Reprint of Cornhill serialization, 16 plates by M. Edwards; first reprint of full text. Introduction by Norman Donaldson. 412pp. 5⅜ x 8½.   23464-9 Pa. $5.00

KEPT IN THE DARK, Anthony Trollope. Unusual short novel about Victorian morality and abnormal psychology by the great English author. Probably the first American publication. Frontispiece by Sir John Millais. 92pp. 6½ x 9¼.   23609-9 Pa. $2.50

RALPH THE HEIR, Anthony Trollope. Forgotten tale of illegitimacy, inheritance. Master novel of Trollope's later years. Victorian country estates, clubs, Parliament, fox hunting, world of fully realized characters. Reprint of 1871 edition. 12 illustrations by F. A. Faser. 434pp. of text. 5⅜ x 8½.   23642-0 Pa. $5.00

YEKL and THE IMPORTED BRIDEGROOM AND OTHER STORIES OF THE NEW YORK GHETTO, Abraham Cahan. Film *Hester Street* based on *Yekl* (1896). Novel, other stories among first about Jewish immigrants of N.Y.'s East Side. Highly praised by W. D. Howells—Cahan "a new star of realism." New introduction by Bernard G. Richards. 240pp. 5⅜ x 8½.   22427-9 Pa. $3.50

THE HIGH PLACE, James Branch Cabell. Great fantasy writer's enchanting comedy of disenchantment set in 18th-century France. Considered by some critics to be even better than his famous *Jurgen*. 10 illustrations and numerous vignettes by noted fantasy artist Frank C. Pape. 320pp. 5⅜ x 8½.   23670-6 Pa. $4.00

ALICE'S ADVENTURES UNDER GROUND, Lewis Carroll. Facsimile of ms. Carroll gave Alice Liddell in 1864. Different in many ways from final Alice. Handlettered, illustrated by Carroll. Introduction by Martin Gardner. 128pp. 5⅜ x 8½.   21482-6 Pa. $2.00

FAVORITE ANDREW LANG FAIRY TALE BOOKS IN MANY COLORS, Andrew Lang. The four Lang favorites in a boxed set—the complete *Red, Green, Yellow* and *Blue* Fairy Books. 164 stories; 439 illustrations by Lancelot Speed, Henry Ford and G. P. Jacomb Hood. Total of about 1500pp. 5⅜ x 8½.   23407-X Boxed set, Pa. $14.95

DRAWINGS OF WILLIAM BLAKE, William Blake. 92 plates from Book of Job, *Divine Comedy, Paradise Lost,* visionary heads, mythological figures, Laocoon, etc. Selection, introduction, commentary by Sir Geoffrey Keynes. 178pp. 8⅛ x 11. 22303-5 Pa. $4.00

ENGRAVINGS OF HOGARTH, William Hogarth. 101 of Hogarth's greatest works: *Rake's Progress, Harlot's Progress, Illustrations for Hudibras, Before and After, Beer Street and Gin Lane,* many more. Full commentary. 256pp. 11 x 13¾. 22479-1 Pa. $7.95

DAUMIER: 120 GREAT LITHOGRAPHS, Honore Daumier. Wide-ranging collection of lithographs by the greatest caricaturist of the 19th century. Concentrates on eternally popular series on lawyers, on married life, on liberated women, etc. Selection, introduction, and notes on plates by Charles F. Ramus. Total of 158pp. 9⅜ x 12¼. 23512-2 Pa. $5.50

DRAWINGS OF MUCHA, Alphonse Maria Mucha. Work reveals drafts-man of highest caliber: studies for famous posters and paintings, render-ings for book illustrations and ads, etc. 70 works, 9 in color; including 6 items not drawings. Introduction. List of illustrations. 72pp. 9⅜ x 12¼. (Available in U.S. only) 23672-2 Pa. $4.00

GIOVANNI BATTISTA PIRANESI: DRAWINGS IN THE PIERPONT MORGAN LIBRARY, Giovanni Battista Piranesi. For first time ever all of Morgan Library's collection, world's largest. 167 illustrations of rare Piranesi drawings—archeological, architectural, decorative and visionary. Essay, detailed list of drawings, chronology, captions. Edited by Felice Stampfle. 144pp. 9⅜ x 12¼. 23714-1 Pa. $7.50

NEW YORK ETCHINGS (1905-1949), John Sloan. All of important American artist's N.Y. life etchings. 67 works include some of his best art; also lively historical record—Greenwich Village, tenement scenes. Edited by Sloan's widow. Introduction and captions. 79pp. 8⅜ x 11¼. 23651-X Pa. $4.00

CHINESE PAINTING AND CALLIGRAPHY: A PICTORIAL SURVEY, Wan-go Weng. 69 fine examples from John M. Crawford's matchless private collection: landscapes, birds, flowers, human figures, etc., plus calligraphy. Every basic form included: hanging scrolls, handscrolls, album leaves, fans, etc. 109 illustrations. Introduction. Captions. 192pp. 8⅞ x 11¾. 23707-9 Pa. $7.95

DRAWINGS OF REMBRANDT, edited by Seymour Slive. Updated Lipp-mann, Hofstede de Groot edition, with definitive scholarly apparatus. All portraits, biblical sketches, landscapes, nudes, Oriental figures, classical studies, together with selection of work by followers. 550 illustrations. Total of 630pp. 9⅛ x 12¼. 21485-0, 21486-9 Pa., Two-vol. set $15.00

THE DISASTERS OF WAR, Francisco Goya. 83 etchings record horrors of Napoleonic wars in Spain and war in general. Reprint of 1st edition, plus 3 additional plates. Introduction by Philip Hofer. 97pp. 9⅜ x 8¼. 21872-4 Pa. $3.75

THE COMPLETE BOOK OF DOLL MAKING AND COLLECTING, Catherine Christopher. Instructions, patterns for dozens of dolls, from rag doll on up to elaborate, historically accurate figures. Mould faces, sew clothing, make doll houses, etc. Also collecting information. Many illustrations. 288pp. 6 x 9.   22066-4 Pa. $4.50

THE DAGUERREOTYPE IN AMERICA, Beaumont Newhall. Wonderful portraits, 1850's townscapes, landscapes; full text plus 104 photographs. The basic book. Enlarged 1976 edition. 272pp. 8¼ x 11¼.
23322-7 Pa. $7.95

CRAFTSMAN HOMES, Gustav Stickley. 296 architectural drawings, floor plans, and photographs illustrate 40 different kinds of "Mission-style" homes from *The Craftsman* (1901-16), voice of American style of simplicity and organic harmony. Thorough coverage of Craftsman idea in text and picture, now collector's item. 224pp. 8⅛ x 11.   23791-5 Pa. $6.00

PEWTER-WORKING: INSTRUCTIONS AND PROJECTS, Burl N. Osborn. & Gordon O. Wilber. Introduction to pewter-working for amateur craftsman. History and characteristics of pewter; tools, materials, step-by-step instructions. Photos, line drawings, diagrams. Total of 160pp. 7⅞ x 10¾.   23786-9 Pa. $3.50

THE GREAT CHICAGO FIRE, edited by David Lowe. 10 dramatic, eyewitness accounts of the 1871 disaster, including one of the aftermath and rebuilding, plus 70 contemporary photographs and illustrations of the ruins—courthouse, Palmer House, Great Central Depot, etc. Introduction by David Lowe. 87pp. 8¼ x 11.   23771-0 Pa. $4.00

SILHOUETTES: A PICTORIAL ARCHIVE OF VARIED ILLUSTRATIONS, edited by Carol Belanger Grafton. Over 600 silhouettes from the 18th to 20th centuries include profiles and full figures of men and women, children, birds and animals, groups and scenes, nature, ships, an alphabet. Dozens of uses for commercial artists and craftspeople. 144pp. 8⅜ x 11¼.
23781-8 Pa. $4.00

ANIMALS: 1,419 COPYRIGHT-FREE ILLUSTRATIONS OF MAMMALS, BIRDS, FISH, INSECTS, ETC., edited by Jim Harter. Clear wood engravings present, in extremely lifelike poses, over 1,000 species of animals. One of the most extensive copyright-free pictorial sourcebooks of its kind. Captions. Index. 284pp. 9 x 12.   23766-4 Pa. $7.95

INDIAN DESIGNS FROM ANCIENT ECUADOR, Frederick W. Shaffer. 282 original designs by pre-Columbian Indians of Ecuador (500-1500 A.D.). Designs include people, mammals, birds, reptiles, fish, plants, heads, geometric designs. Use as is or alter for advertising, textiles, leathercraft, etc. Introduction. 95pp. 8¾ x 11¼.   23764-8 Pa. $3.50

SZIGETI ON THE VIOLIN, Joseph Szigeti. Genial, loosely structured tour by premier violinist, featuring a pleasant mixture of reminiscenes, insights into great music and musicians, innumerable tips for practicing violinists. 385 musical passages. 256pp. 5⅜ x 8¼.   23763-X Pa. $3.50